P9-CMK-418

SILENCED

Center Point
Large Print

Also by Dani Pettrey and available from
Center Point Large Print:

Submerged
Shattered
Stranded

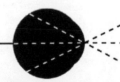

Alaskan Courage
• Book Four •

SILENCED

Dani
Pettrey

CENTER POINT LARGE PRINT
THORNDIKE, MAINE

ISBN: 978-1-62899-141-3

Library of Congress Cataloging-in-Publication Data

Pettrey, Dani.
  Silenced / Dani Pettrey. — Center Point Large Print edition.
    pages ; cm
  Summary: "After Kayden McKenna discovers the body of a fellow climber, she and Jake Westin team up to investigate the death—provoking threats on her entire family"—Provided by publisher.
  ISBN 978-1-62899-141-3 (library binding : alk. paper)
  1. Mountaineers—Fiction. 2. Murder—Investigation—Fiction. 3. Alaska—Fiction. 4. Large type books. I. Title.
PS3616.E89S55 2014b
813'.6—dc23
                                                        2014011820

To Calvin Michael Miner
Your Grammie loves you silly!

— 1 —

Kayden scaled the rock face, the addictive burn spreading through her arms, her body. Man, she loved this—hanging on the edge of a seven-hundred-fifty-foot sheer cliff face, knowing one wrong grab meant death.

"You're not going to beat me this time," her younger sister, Piper, hollered, her voice echoing across the twenty-foot-wide crevice separating them. She'd been trying to distract Kayden all morning, but Kayden knew how to ignore her sister. The person who wasn't as easy to ignore was Jake. He was watching from the base nearly seven hundred feet below with her older brother Gage. The men had come along to "enjoy the show," as they put it.

Unfortunately, putting Jake's presence out of her mind was proving to be a lot harder than dismissing Piper's taunts. Knowing his gaze was fastened to her was exhilarating.

Pushing off with her right foot, she lunged the eighteen inches to the next handhold, knowing the move had Jake holding his breath. She held hers until her fingers grasped the hold, heat searing through her.

Jake Westin—Check that . . . Jake Westin *Cavanagh* was so much more than she'd realized, and quite frankly, over the past month her deepening feelings for the man had frightened her a whole lot more than the vast leap ahead.

She reached the last overhang—a granite ledge butting out eight feet from the rock face. She'd have to boulder her way along the edge and then make the final leap of faith, praying she'd timed it right and used enough force to land on its leveled surface.

It was the deadliest point of the route—the one that separated the experts from the average.

Granite crunched beneath her nails as she clawed her way across the jagged rock.

The wind, growing in force, howled through the canyon below, echoing through the crevice in a high-pitched whir.

Kayden closed her eyes and stilled her mind. *I can do this.* She'd mastered it before. She could do it again. Her breath caught in her throat as she pushed off and lunged through the air, stretching her fingers until they burned—reaching, grasping for a safe hold. Her fingers made contact, and she wedged herself along the rock, her hands locked on the overhang's lip.

Her feet found a stable notch. Pushing up with her legs and arms at the same time, with sheer will and determination, she lifted herself up.

Relief swarmed inside as she crested the ledge, her arms shaking . . . and then horror struck.

A man, his skull bashed in, faced her—his

visible eye open and staring directly at her.

She swallowed the vibration churning in her throat, the scream fighting to tear from her lips. Every fiber of her being said *Let go, push back, get away,* but wrestling instinct, she maintained her hold as she balanced on the edge of the overhang.

Glancing over her shoulder, she assessed her options. Moving back down the way she'd come at this point in the strenuous climb was suicide. Her arms were burning limbs of Jell-O, and if she didn't make a decision within seconds, they'd give out. She needed to climb onto the ledge with the man, needed to make sure he didn't require help, verify that he was already . . .

She squeezed her eyes shut for the briefest of seconds, trying to drown out everything else and focus. Mustering what strength remained, she hefted herself fully onto the outcrop, her body brushing against the man's. Swallowing the bile creeping up her throat, she edged around him, scooted toward the rear of the ledge, and took a quick moment to catch her breath before shifting into search-and-rescue mode. She needed to check his vitals, make certain he was beyond help. She prayed she would detect a heartbeat, but her gut said the organ had stopped long ago.

"Woo-hoo!" Piper shouted from overhead. "Beat you."

Fighting the wave of nausea roiling through

her, Kayden stretched out her index and middle finger, feeling for a pulse.

Just as she'd suspected. *Nothing.*

"Kayden?" Piper's voice grew closer, nearly directly overhead.

Kayden glanced up, shielding her eyes from the sun, as Piper leaned over the top of the face, more than fifty feet above. Her infectious smile faded as her big brown eyes fixed on the crumpled form beside Kayden.

Kayden cleared her throat. "We've got a downed climber on the ledge."

"Downed or—"

She swallowed. "Dead."

"I'll tell the guys." Piper pulled the radio from her harness.

Kayden nodded. "I'm coming up. Have Jake call it in."

— 2 —

Kayden had found a dead climber on the ledge. Piper's shaky voice echoed through Jake's ears as he pulled his satellite phone from his pocket. His fingers wrapped around the metal casing, and the phone vibrated in his palm, ringing out at the same time.

"Westin . . ." He blinked. "Cavanagh." How long would it take him to go back to his full name? He'd been Jake Westin for so long, switching back to Jake Westin *Cavanagh* was proving a lot harder than he'd expected.

"It's Landon."

"Perfect timing, Sheriff."

"Huh?"

With Sheriff Bill Slidell's sudden departure from law enforcement and Yancey, the town council had voted then-deputy Sheriff Landon Grainger into the leadership role until the fall elections would no doubt make it his permanent position.

"Kayden found a dead climber up on the last ledge of Stoneface's route."

"Dead?"

"I'm afraid so."

"His climbing buddy just called from Ranger Station Four." The closest to them.

"Did he say what happened?"

"The guy missed a handhold and slipped."

That's all it took, one missed handhold. No wonder his heart lodged in his throat every time Kayden climbed. He'd even taken to climbing with her, feeling he'd at least be in a better position to help if something went awry. But he was kidding himself. She was so far above his level of experience, all his being present would accomplish was to give him a front-row view of her fall.

He blocked off the horrific thought. "You heading out here?"

"Yeah, already called Cole and Booth. We'll be there as soon as we can."

"We're going to need to bring retrieval gear up the back side." The vehicles would only be able to make it so far, and then the rest of the rescue team would have to hike in and, when they were finished retrieving, hike the body back out.

"How are the girls?" Landon asked.

"We're headed up to them now."

"Let Piper know I'm on my way," he said, clearly worried about his fiancée.

"Will do." Jake shut the phone and relayed the conversation to Gage as they worked their way around the back face of the mountain. The path—what there was of one—was narrow and winding, overgrown with tree roots and moss still damp from last night's rain.

Maybe that was why the man had slipped. Maybe he'd started climbing too early, before the sun had a chance to completely dry the rock face.

Sweat beaded on Jake's skin as he mounted the last rise, having gone up seven hundred feet in elevation. The air was thinner, but fresh and brisk in his lungs. Piper caught sight of them first, her eyes filled with tears. Kayden stood with her back to them, and he moved for her, yearning to comfort her but knowing she'd never let him.

"Jake," Piper greeted him.

Kayden turned. Just as he suspected, her eyes

were dry, but her face was tinged red—she was upset. How could she not be?

"Gage." Piper ran into her brother's arms.

He patted her back. "How ya holding up, kid?"

"I'm okay, but Kayden's—"

"Fine." Her gaze met Jake's, answering his unvoiced question. "I'm fine."

He nodded, knowing it was a lie.

"Landon's on his way," Gage said, and Piper's tension visibly eased.

"Booth coming with him?"

Why was Kayden asking about the ME? "Yeah."

"Good." She rubbed her arms. "Because something doesn't feel right."

Jake sidled up beside her, and she tried to ignore how good his presence felt. How she longed to run into his arms as Piper had into Gage's.

"You said something doesn't feel right?" Concern marred his handsome brow.

"I just have this feeling. Great . . ." She shook her head on a laugh. "Now I sound like Piper." Her sister had great instincts. *Kayden's . . . ?*

He nudged her arm with his, and peace lingered the moment his skin touched hers. "Don't discount instinct. It can be a great help."

She shrugged. She couldn't put her finger on it, but something was nagging at her.

"They're here," Piper said, jumping up and

running for her fiancé's arms. Booth appeared, with Cole close behind.

"Booth." Kayden lifted her chin to greet Yancey's medical examiner.

Cole stepped around Booth, moving straight for her. If she'd let anyone comfort her, it would be her big brother, the oldest McKenna sibling and head of the clan since their parents' passing.

"How you holding up?" he asked, clamping a reassuring hand on her shoulder, gently forcing her to look him in the eye.

She glanced across at her sister, still a bit green in the gills. "Better than Piper."

A hint of a resigned smile tugged at the corner of Cole's lips. "It's not a competition, Kayden."

She stiffened her shoulders and forced a slight smile in return. "Everything's a competition."

Cole shook his head. "You're impossible." He bent, looking her in the eye. "You know, there's nothing wrong with admitting something is upsetting."

"Not everyone has to tear up to move past something."

"I know." His green eyes softened. "But I also know when you're shaken."

She exhaled at the deep sincerity reflecting in her brother's eyes. He was just trying to be helpful. "I know, and I appreciate it."

Now she needed to prepare for what lay ahead. Finding the victim had been bad enough, but the grislier task of the day approached—retrieving the body.

It had been hard to tell with the extent of his injuries—and she hadn't been able to get herself to look too closely at his face—but if the man was local, or even regional, chances were she knew him, at least by name. The climbing community along the Alaskan Peninsula was tight. The Alaskan climbing community *period* was tight.

"Our victim's name is Conrad Humphries," Landon said as Kayden's brothers readied the retrieval gear.

"Conrad?" Piper swallowed.

"You knew him?"

"We both did," Kayden said. "Not well, but he visited Yancey's climbing gym a couple times last winter. I think he lives over on Imnek. How'd you know his name?"

"His climbing buddy provided it."

"He was climbing with someone?" she asked, surprised his buddy had left him.

Landon nodded.

She stepped closer. "What did the buddy report?"

"He said everything was going smoothly. Conrad made it past the overhang and the buddy lost visual. Not long after, he heard Conrad holler and then . . ."

"Then?" she pressed.

Landon grimaced. "A thud."

She tried not to wince. She'd seen the result of that thud up close and personal. Her stomach twinged. "Where'd the buddy call from?"

"Ranger Station Four. Apparently he had no cell reception and knew Conrad needed help, so he climbed down and hiked back out to his rental car. Drove to the ranger station that he and Conrad had passed on the way in. Said it was the quickest way he knew to get help."

"Did he check to see if Conrad was conscious before he left?"

"I don't know, but he seemed to be under the impression this was a rescue mission, not a retrieval."

"So he thinks Conrad is still alive?" Jake asked.

Landon nodded. "That's the impression I got."

"Even with the sound of the impact?"

"Our minds go where we want them to in times of tragedy."

"Where's the buddy now?" she asked.

"Still at the ranger station. I asked him to stay put. I didn't want him coming back out here while we're trying to work. I told Ranger Aikens I'd be by to talk with him when we're finished here."

"What's his name?"

Landon checked his notebook. "Stuart Anderson."

Stuart Anderson? The name wasn't familiar. Where had he come from?

"Okay," she said, her mind racing. "I definitely

16

think you're going to want to question him."

Landon cocked his head. "I was already planning on it. It's standard procedure in any climbing accident. Do you have a specific concern?"

She shrugged her hands into her fleece pockets. "I don't think this is your standard accident."

Landon's eyes narrowed. "Why?"

"Something feels off, but I can't piece it together until I get a better look."

"Okay. Everyone, round up." Landon grouped everyone together at the edge of the overlook. "According to protocol, this is a crime scene until determined otherwise. I'll perform the analysis with Booth, and we'll need two with us on the ledge."

"I'll go," Kayden and Jake volunteered in near unison.

Jake glanced over at her, but she kept her gaze fixed on Landon. She was going.

"I found him. I want to bring him home."

Landon nodded.

Cole scooped up the top rope. "Gage and I will run the line. Do the heavy hoisting."

"All right." Landon lifted his chin in Kayden and Jake's direction. "Let's go."

The quickest, safest, and easiest route to the outcrop from their vantage point was to rappel down. Jake strapped in beside Booth, Landon,

17

and Kayden, and then they took turns double-checking each other's equipment.

Once all four were confirmed secure, Landon lowered first, followed by Booth, and then Kayden. Jake loved the skill and dexterity with which she moved, or rather glided. Her sculpted arms, though still extremely feminine, were evidence of the strength she possessed—a strength that ran much deeper than mere athleticism. He admired her physical strength, but it was the rare glimpses of her heart that had him enthralled.

As hard as he'd tried fighting his feelings, he'd fallen madly in love with Kayden long ago, and he feared the love was rooted in his heart for good. Question was—now that the truth of his past was out in the open, now that she was no longer skeptical about his character—could she move beyond all that and ever love him for the man he was?

"Jake?" Landon called from below.

"On my way." Jake planted the soles of his boots against the gray granite, lowering his body until he was sitting into it and nearly horizontal with the overhang below.

Feeding the rope through his belay device, he slowly walked himself down as the top rope overhead kept him secure.

Reaching the overhang with both feet planted securely on the solid surface, he unclipped and turned to—

His gut clenched at the sight of the battered victim, and his gaze shifted to Kayden. No wonder she'd been shaken.

Landon retrieved his camera from his pack. "I need to take photos before we move anything."

Booth squatted on his haunches beside the body, beginning his cursory examination.

Jake leaned against the rock face beside Kayden, both trying to stay out of Landon and Booth's way until either required their assistance. She kept her gaze fixed on the darkening horizon. Rain was on the way. The wind tossed her hair about her face. The summer sun had lightened her typically dark-brown hair with natural sandy highlights. Man, he could watch her for hours.

Not wanting her to catch him staring yet again, he took a deep breath and shifted his attention to the victim.

The man lay facedown. Only a small portion of the right side of his face was visible, his right eye open and protruding from the impact.

"That's what it was. See the chalk." Kayden pointed as Landon's lens fastened on the white chalk streaks tracking down the victim's arms. "Chalk should never run like that."

"Maybe he was out here too early and the rocks were still wet. Maybe he grasped a handhold with standing water," Jake said, playing devil's advocate.

She shook her head. "No. Water would wash

the chalk away, not track it down his arms."

"So, what are you thinking?" Landon asked.

She strode forward, kneeling beside the body. "I'd say he was sweating profusely, except sweat doesn't normally streak chalk."

"Sweating profusely? You think he had a heart attack or something like that?"

"No, if he was sweating, the chalk would absorb any liquid on his hands—cake to them, not run down his arms."

"So you're saying . . . ?"

"Maybe something was off with his chalk. That's a huge factor when we're looking at a climbing fall."

"Maybe he used cheap chalk," Jake said as Landon's camera flashed over the streaks.

"It's possible." Kayden stood. "Booth will determine that at the lab. . . ."

"But?" he pressed.

She sighed. "I don't know . . ."

Jake could tell she was hesitant about pressing her observation, but she was the most skilled climber in the area. "Trust your instinct, Kayden. It's often what cracks a case wide open."

"All right," Landon said, standing. "Huddle up."

"What do you think?" Jake asked him.

Landon pulled his baseball cap from his back pocket and slipped it on as the first drops of rain fell. "I think we need to move fast."

The storm was rolling in. What was now a soft

drizzle would soon be a torrential downpour if the dark clouds were any indication.

On Landon's signal, Cole and Gage lowered the gurney down. Landon and Jake grabbed hold, resting it parallel to the victim's body, while Booth observed the scene.

Kayden moved to assist.

Landon shook his head. "Let me and Jake lift."

She blew a wisp of hair from her eye. "I'm fine. Let me help."

Landon sighed as he knelt beside the man. "It could get a whole lot uglier when we roll him over. Besides, I need you to put on a pair of gloves and seal up his chalk bag in this." He tossed her an evidence bag from his kit. "As soon as we can reach his chalk bag, I'll slide it off his belt and hand it to you. We need to keep it dry."

She nodded, standing a few feet behind Landon, her latex gloves now in place.

Landon crouched, looking across the victim's body at Jake. "You ready?"

Jake took a deep breath, holding it, and nodded.

"On three," Landon said. "One, two, three."

They lifted and rolled the man faceup onto the gurney.

Kayden stifled her intake of breath, but Jake heard it all the same.

Landon removed the chalk bag from the man's belt and handed it off to her.

"We've still got some chalk to work with," she said.

Landon took another quick round of photographs while Booth assessed the victim from the new vantage point, and then they covered the man's body and harnessed him in. Cole and Gage hoisted him up, careful to keep a safe distance between the gurney and the jagged rocks, not wanting to batter the victim's body any more than it already had been.

— 3 —

"You know . . ." Booth offered Jake a stick of gum after they'd finished loading Conrad Humphries' body into the rescue vehicle. "When I moved up here twenty some years ago, I thought I was in for a quieter life, but this past year is proving me wrong."

"You and me both," Jake said, folding the gum into his mouth. When he'd first arrived, Yancey had seemed like the perfect small town to hide away in for a while before he moved on again. But now . . . He looked over at Kayden, the rain dripping off her hood. He couldn't leave if he wanted to. His heart belonged to her.

As Landon approached, Booth said, "If Kayden's right about the chalk being off, looks like you could have your first murder case as sheriff."

"Let's not go tossing around that word just yet—not until the tests on the chalk come back."

Booth looked over at Kayden. "If I were a gambler, I wouldn't bet against the lady."

Neither would Jake.

"She knows her stuff," Booth said.

"That she does." He smiled in her direction.

"How long until you have the results?" Landon asked.

"Hopefully tomorrow morning," Booth said.

"Great. I have yet another meeting with Mayor Cox and the town council that will probably last well into the afternoon, so I'll have to send a deputy over as soon as you get your results." Landon's gaze rested on Jake.

"Oh no," Jake said. He knew that look. Ever since Landon had discovered the truth of his investigative background, he'd been trying to get him to join the force. With Slidell's departure and Deputy Tom Wilkinson following suit, Landon was short two men.

Jake understood why Landon wanted his help. It was a rough spot to be in. He couldn't deny he'd been invigorated by the *Bering*-cruise-ship case they'd recently solved, but he needed to stifle those urges, to get the thought of returning to the job he loved out of his mindset, because it couldn't happen. He'd thought he was born to be a detective until his pride and singular focus on the job had cost Becca her life—along with that of their unborn child. Clearly his priorities had been wrong. Clearly God hadn't intended for him to be a cop.

Landon broke the silence. "Jake, I know we talked about this when I got appointed, and you—"

"I told you, I'm out of the game." He had to be.

"I understand, but I could really use your expertise. Especially with Mayor Cox bogging me down in paperwork and meetings. What if it was just a temporary assignment? Just until this gets sorted out?" Landon exhaled. "I could really use your help, man."

Jake's shoulders dropped. How could he say no? Landon was like family, and he needed him. He'd helped with the *Bering* case, and nothing had gone horribly wrong. . . . Maybe enough time had passed. Maybe he could help on just one more case. He wavered, fearing he was going to regret it, but he couldn't let his family down when they needed him. "All right, but just until this gets sorted out."

"That's a yes?"

Jake nodded and watched some of the weight lift from Landon's countenance.

"Thank you, Jake."

"Just this case," he reiterated, knowing Landon hoped he'd get hooked and stay on.

Landon smiled. "Fine. You can start by going with Kayden to interview Stuart Anderson. She's got the climbing expertise and will know if he's lying about anything related to the climb."

She stepped beside him. "Sounds good."

Jake looked over at her. She seemed to be pleased. *Interesting.* Was she happy he was going to work the case?

"Before you go, I need to swear you in," Landon said.

"Is that really necessary?" Jake asked, his mind flashing back to his first swearing-in ceremony. He'd been so young and cocky. Life had kicked that out of him—or at least a good portion of it.

"Gotta make it official." Landon proceeded with deputizing Jake as Kayden and her siblings watched.

When they wrapped up, Landon grabbed a gun and badge from his truck's glove box, handing them to Jake.

Jake cocked his head. "Were you that confident I'd say yes?"

"I knew if I ever really needed your help, I could count on you." Landon clapped him on the back.

Jake prayed that was true, but Becca had believed she could count on him, too, and he'd let her down terribly.

25

Jake held the door for Kayden as she stepped into Tariuk's Ranger Station Four. Having worked search and rescue for years, Kayden and all of her siblings were well acquainted with the various stations and the rangers who staffed them. Ryan Aikens stood at the communications station, relaying the incoming weather report to the rangers out in the field. "Weather service says a stronger front is moving in. High winds and heavy downpours."

"Roger that," the men replied, almost as one voice.

Ryan set the radio back on the clip and turned to face them. "Hey there."

"Hey, yourself," Kayden said.

"Landon said you found the downed climber?" She nodded.

"Anderson's pretty upset, but I didn't tell him his friend is dead."

She nodded. "Probably for the best."

"Where is he?" Jake asked.

"Back in the break room. Wasn't the least bit happy about being told to stay put."

She sighed. "That should make this go a whole lot smoother."

"Landon coming?" Ryan looked past Jake.

"Nope. Just me and Deputy Jake," Kayden said with a smile.

Ryan crossed his arms with a grin. "So Landon finally talked you into signing up?"

"Just until this gets sorted out."

"Uh-huh." Ryan chuckled.

"You got anything warm to drink?" She asked, a chill nipping at her.

"Coffee's in the kitchen, and there's hot water if you wanna make tea or cocoa. Matt brought some of his herbal junk in yesterday."

She moved toward the kitchen. "Ignoring the insult in that. Herbal tea's a whole lot better for you than coffee."

"Knew that'd push a button." Ryan chuckled to Jake, and she slowed her step to hear if he responded. If he did, it wasn't verbally, and his footsteps came quickly behind her.

"How do you want to approach this?" she asked, her gaze pinned on the break-room door.

"You start with the climbing questions. Approach him as you see best, and I'll jump in if necessary."

"All right." Never in a million years did she think she'd be paired with Jake on an inquiry.

She pushed open the door to find a man pacing. "Mr. Anderson?"

He looked up. "Finally." He rushed forward. "How's Conrad?"

"Mr. Anderson, I suggest you take a seat." She

27

gestured to the round wooden table and the four mismatched chairs encircling it.

"No." He shook his head. "Not until I get answers. I've been waiting for hours."

Kayden looked at Jake, and he nodded. She exhaled. She hated this part. "Mr. Anderson, I'm very sorry to inform you that Conrad Humphries is dead."

"Dead?" His face paled. "I knew it was a hard fall, but . . ."

Kayden pulled out a chair. "Why don't you sit."

He looked at her, confused. "Who are you?"

She extended her hand. "Kayden McKenna."

He was older. Upper forties, perhaps early fifties. Tall, lean, slightly balding. He shook her hand, but instead of meeting her eyes, he stared straight past her at Jake. "And you're the sheriff?"

"No, I'm a deputy."

She'd witnessed a glimpse of Jake as investigator during the cruise ship case. He was highly enticing in his natural element, even more than usual. And now she had been given the pleasure of investigating with him. A tingle of anticipation shot through her.

Stuart shook his head. "I can't believe . . ." He swallowed. "Vivienne. Have you told Vivienne yet?"

Kayden arched her brows. "Vivienne?"

"Conrad's wife. She's going to be devastated. I should go to her." He started for the door.

Jake intercepted his path. "I'm afraid we need to ask you some questions first."

Stuart stilled. "Questions? About what?"

Kayden moved to face him. "What happened on today's climb?"

"What about it? I already told the ranger and the sheriff over the phone."

"I'm going to need you to tell *us,*" she insisted.

"You just told me my friend is *dead,* and you want me to answer *questions?*"

"I'm afraid it's necessary."

He once again looked past her at Jake. "Seriously?"

"It's important, Mr. Anderson," she said, holding her ground.

After a moment's hesitation, with a stiff exhale, he dropped into the chair Kayden had pulled out for him. "All right, but let's make it quick. I need to get to Vivienne."

"We'll go as quickly as we can. Now, would you please tell me how your day started?"

"Conrad and I went for a climb. Things were going fine. Conrad made it over the outcrop, and I lost visual. A minute or so later, I heard him scream and then . . ." Stuart's eyes flicked wide.

"And then?" she pressed.

Stuart squeezed his eyes shut. "A horrible thump."

She paused a moment, letting him absorb the trauma. "And after that?"

He looked up at her. "You really expect me to go back through that?"

"I'm sorry, but I'm going to need you to go through it step by step for me."

Stuart's eyes narrowed. "Who, exactly, are you?"

"Kayden Mc—"

He waved his hand. "I got that part. What I mean is why are *you* questioning me? Are you a deputy too?"

"No. I'm the one who found Conrad."

"Oh." Stuart swallowed. "Was he . . . ?"

Jake nodded. "I'm afraid your friend was already gone by the time Kayden reached him."

"Look . . ." Stuart clasped his hands together. "I need to get to Vivienne. I don't want her facing this alone."

"I understand, but we have a few more questions."

"Conrad had a tragic accident. What more do you need to know?"

"We need to be thorough, Mr. Anderson, and we'd appreciate your cooperation. It won't take long."

Rain pelted the glass on the front windows, the storm finally hitting its full fury.

"I'll give you five more minutes, and that's being generous under the circumstance," Stuart said.

"Take all the time you need," Jake whispered in Kayden's ear as he pulled out a chair for her.

The warmth of his breath on her neck sent shivers up her spine—the good kind—making it extremely difficult to focus on the task at hand. She scooted her chair in, the metal legs scuffing along the wooden planks, directing her attention on Stuart Anderson.

"How did you know Conrad?"

He gaped at Kayden. "You've got to be kidding."

Jake crossed his arms over his chest. "Just answer the lady's questions."

Stuart exhaled. "We went to college together. Been friends for twenty-nine years."

"Do you live on Imnek as well?" She didn't know everyone on the island, but she did know most of the climbers, at least by sight, and she'd never seen or heard of him.

"No. I'm up in Anchorage. What does any of this have to do with Conrad's accident?"

"I'm just trying to establish the events that led up to the climb, your relationship with the deceased, both of your climbing experience . . ."

"I had business in Spruce Harbor and figured I'd spend some time with Conrad while I was down here."

"When did you plan the climb?"

"We first talked about it a couple months back, when I learned I'd be in town."

"What kind of business are you in?"

"Real estate."

"So you were in town for business, and . . ."

"I stayed through the weekend so we could do some climbing."

"And the trip had been planned for two months?"

"More or less."

So there'd been plenty of time for someone to compromise or tamper with Conrad's chalk. "Who knew you two were planning the climb?"

"Well . . . Vivienne, and my wife, Gail."

Surely more people knew than that. Climbers liked to discuss their upcoming climbs, to get feedback and generate excitement—it pumped them up for the climb ahead. "How long have you and Conrad been climbing?"

A chill whisked through the break room, the wind gusts rattling the window frame.

Stuart looked at Kayden.

"Please continue," she said, wishing she'd taken the time to make that cup of warm tea.

"I've been climbing for seven years and Conrad for three."

Only three years? "Was he proficient enough to be out on Stoneface?"

"It's a tough climb, but yeah, we were both up for it."

"Was it his first time out there?"

"Yes."

"And yours?"

"No. I climbed it last summer. Told Conrad about it and he'd been raring to go ever since."

"Did he train for it?"

"Sure. Conrad was at that gym of his nearly every day. Went right after work."

"That's great, but we both know climbing indoors is nowhere near the same as out." Outdoors you had to take into account the weather, natural erosion, shifting rocks . . .

"Conrad said he was ready for it."

"Any physical signs to indicate differently?"

"Like what?"

"Pacing before the climb, perspiring . . . ?"

"He was going through his chalk pretty good, but I figured he just wanted the extra grip."

"Was he perspiring excessively?"

"Not that I noticed."

"But you did notice him using his chalk quite a bit?"

"Yes, I'd glance up from time to time and the farther up he got, the more he dipped his hand in the chalk bag."

"How were his handholds?"

"Handholds? Are you actually asking me to critique my buddy's final climb?"

"I'm asking if he was having trouble gaining grip."

"I don't know. We weren't side by side."

"Was he complaining about anything?"

"I don't know about women, but men don't chitchat while climbing."

She pushed past the insult, knowing she could outclimb him any day. "Do you know where Conrad bought his chalk?"

The light dimmed as the sky darkened a deeper shade of charcoal gray. Jake moved to the light switch situated by the door and flipped it. An older yellow droplight flicked to life overhead, bathing the room in a golden glow.

"I'm guessing the gym he always climbs at. They have a shop in the front."

"Which gym?" Imnek only had one, so chances were . . .

"Rocktrex."

That's what she was afraid of. *Brody's gym.*

"What about you?" Jake asked. "Did you use the same chalk as Conrad?"

"I always bring my own gear—shoes, chalk bag, chalk." He glanced at his watch. "Are we done here? I really should be with Vivienne."

"We're done for now. How can we get in touch with you?"

"I'm staying at Vivienne and Conrad's." He fished something from his pocket. "Here's my business card." He scribbled a number on the back. "That's my cell."

"Thank you, Mr. Anderson. We appreciate your help."

He gave a curt nod.

Kayden glanced over at Jake as Stuart exited the room. "What do you think?"

"Sounds like Conrad Humphries should never have been making that climb in the first place."

— 5 —

Kayden followed the winding dirt road that led to Nanook Haven, a shelter for abused, neglected, and retired sled dogs; the Yancey Veterinary Clinic; and the private residence of the woman who ran both, Kirra Jacobs.

Kirra's family had moved to Yancey when she was a kindergartner, in the same class as Kayden's youngest brother, Reef. They'd grown up together, in a sense—the school only large enough to have one class per grade—but there had been no love lost between Kirra and Reef. The do-gooder and the town scamp.

None of that had any bearing on Kayden's relationship with Kirra, however. Kirra had helped her father run Yancey's search-and-rescue canine unit, while Kayden worked primarily with aerial SAR operations, but they had worked together often over the years, and Kayden liked and admired the dedicated woman.

After high school, with her parents' assistance while she was away at college, Kirra had started taking in sled dogs that had been abandoned or were destined to be put down. Conventional wisdom declared the older sled dogs were past their prime, but she trained them as search-and-rescue dogs, with great success. The dogs still had more to give, even after their days of running the Iditarod were over. It hadn't taken long for Kayden to become fascinated with Kirra's canine-rescue work, and she'd been volunteering on a regular basis at Nanook Haven for years.

The predawn air wafting in Kayden's windows was cool as she rounded the last bend. The fresh scent of Kirra's sweet alyssum blossoms lining the drive drifted in—always such a welcoming aroma.

She pulled to a stop in front of the barn, knowing that was where Kirra would be at such an early hour, finishing up the dogs' morning feeding before her veterinary practice hours began at eight.

Kayden's responsibility was running the dogs to keep them in shape. A sled dog was no different from any other athlete—with age, they slowed some, but they never lost the urge to run.

Kirra stepped from the barn as Kayden stepped from her 4Runner—her metallic aqua '97 SUV that everyone teased her for hanging on to. But it had been a sixteenth-birthday present from her dad, not long before he died, and it still ran great. As long as it ran, she'd drive it. It was foolish to get rid of something just because it was no longer deemed in style.

Kirra lifted her chin in greeting. She was average height and build, with shoulder-length blond hair she typically wore in a braid and vibrant blue eyes—the only remnant of her once-vibrant countenance.

When Kirra had returned after graduation a little over a year ago, she had been different. Maybe it was a result of her parents moving away to deal with her mother's health issues and her taking over the vet practice from her father rather than partnering with him, as they had planned, but Kayden didn't know that for sure. She only knew that something had moved Kirra from vibrant to guarded.

"You're here earlier than usual," Kirra said, slipping her hands into the pockets of her white vet coat.

Kayden glanced at her watch. Only by twenty minutes. "I have a feeling today's going to be a busy one." She planned on finishing up at Kirra's, heading home for a quick shower, and then going straight to the ME's office, praying the results were in by then and she could feel a sample of the chalk for herself. Simply holding the chalk would tell her so much—texture, consistency, etc.

She had no doubt Booth's lab results would show discrepancies in the chalk, whether because of poor quality or something more sinister—either way, something wasn't right.

"Thanks for still taking time to stop by," Kirra said.

"Absolutely, and I can come back by tonight too."

"No need to come twice. Carol will be here from eight to four."

Carol Jones was such a blessing. After Kirra's parents had left for Juneau, the canine shelter had been staffed by Kirra, herself, Jill from Cole's youth group in the evenings, and the occasional volunteer or service group. Having Carol now volunteering on a regular basis during the day made covering the basics so much easier.

"I don't mind coming back." Kayden watched the dogs eating voraciously around her. "They need the exercise." She bent down and signaled Rex, her favorite, to come. The husky jaunted over, excitement dancing in his ten-year-old eyes. She rubbed him behind the ear. "Plus it gives me an excuse to exercise."

"Like you need an excuse." Kirra laughed. "You're a workout machine. Just like Rex here. Maybe that's why you two get along so well."

Apparently Rex didn't play so well with the other volunteers, but she and Rex, they understood one another.

"Ready, boy?" She crouched.

He pawed the ground.

"Set." She smiled.

He howled.

"Go." She burst into a run, Rex flying beside her, the sun just peeking over the horizon. Life didn't get much better than this.

Jake rapped on the morgue's glass outer doors, his breath faintly visible in the early dawn air. Hard to believe they were going to reach a high near sixty-five today, but that's what the weather forecast claimed. He'd be glad for it.

Last summer they'd had an exceptionally warm streak by Yancey standards. Unfortunately, this one seemed to be following the norm—average daily highs in the low sixties.

Booth Powell waved from the end of the hall—his lanky physique silhouetted by the dim fluorescent lighting overhead.

With a rare smile, he sauntered to the doors, unlocked them, and welcomed Jake in.

"I hear it's official," Booth said.

"What's that?' Jake asked, stepping inside. The long tile hall still held the chill of night and death.

"Deputy Cavanagh." Booth turned, heading back for the exam room.

Jake halted at the name. Until recently, it had been more than four years since he'd gone by Cavanagh. After Becca's and his baby's deaths, after Joel Markum's death and his wife's imprisonment, after leaving his job and Boston behind, he'd left his surname behind, too, going instead by his middle name—his mother's maiden name. He'd hoped to leave as much of his old self as possible dead and buried in Boston, just as Becca and their baby were.

And now he was Jake Cavanagh again. The McKennas, and all of Yancey by now, knew the truth of his fractured past.

Reining in his thoughts, he followed Booth into the exam room. Conrad Humphries lay on the cold steel table, covered with a sheet from the neck down.

"Come on back to my office. I heard the fax machine start up when you knocked."

"Think the results are in?"

"Here's hoping." Booth moved for the printer tray.

Fresh coffee dripped into the pot of a coffee maker on the counter.

"Mind if I grab a cup?"

"Help yourself." Booth took a seat behind his desk, his eyes scanning the information.

"Thanks." Jake grabbed a Styrofoam cup and pulled the pot out. "So is that it?"

"Uh-huh."

"And?"

"And looks like you've got your first murder case as deputy."

Jake shut his eyes as he poured the coffee—the cup warming in his hand—and opened them just before the liquid spilled over. As much as his instincts clamored to be part of an investigation again—fully part of one—he couldn't help but fear the past would repeat itself. He wasn't meant to be a cop, no matter how deeply he longed for it. It wasn't safe—not for those he loved.

But he was *helping* those he loved this time, wasn't he? Landon was short staffed. Kayden needed someone with her when Landon inevitably sent her to question people at the gym where Conrad purchased his chalk. *Time alone with Kayden.* It was like a dream come true. Who would have thought it would have come through a murder case?

"You with me, Jake?" Booth asked.

"Yeah." Jake returned the coffeepot to its warmer. "You going to call Landon?"

"Figured you could let him know, since you're the deputy in charge."

He nodded. It was strange how easily Booth and the McKennas accepted his past, accepted the job he'd done for so long.

"I know someone else you'd better tell."

Kayden. She'd been right. It didn't surprise him, though. She knew climbing, and everything related to it.

"Speaking of the lady." Booth nodded toward the glass front doors and grinned over the edge of the paper. He, more than anybody, seemed to enjoy the idea of pairing Jake and Kayden.

"Morning, boys," she said, sauntering in.

She leaned against the doorjamb. "Any news?"

"Booth was just getting ready to explain," Jake said, giving the ME the floor.

"Conrad Humphries' chalk—" Booth began.

"Is there a sample left?" she cut in. "Can I take a look?"

Booth smiled. "Absolutely."

"Don't you want to know what the report says first?" Jake asked.

"Actually, I'd like to see if I can feel anything that's off before you tell me," she said, looking back to Booth.

He nodded. "As the lady wishes." He led her back into the examination room and lifted a small evidence bag of chalk off the table. "I kept a sample for you."

"Thanks." She washed and dried her hands thoroughly and then dumped a portion of the chalk into her palm, rubbing it between her fingers. "Interesting."

Jake leaned against the counter. "What?"

"It feels normal. Typical texture. Basically the same consistency."

"Basically?" Jake asked, enjoying watching her work.

"It has a slightly different consistency than the chalk I use, but it could just be the brand." She lifted her hand to her nose. "Smells the same. . . . Huh." She turned to Booth, frowning, clearly disappointed. "I give up. What did the report say?"

"There was a small amount of Dodecanol mixed in with the chalk."

"Dodecanol?"

"It's a dry moisturizer used in homemade soaps."

"Moisturizer?" Kayden said.

Booth nodded.

"So what's moisturizer doing in Conrad's climbing chalk?" Jake asked.

"Can't tell you that, but he would have had no reason to put it there himself. And at this concentration, the Dodecanol would have totally negated the chalk's effects, making Conrad's hands slipperier than a seal in water."

"Which would explain why he was going through his chalk so fast." Kayden brushed off her hands.

Jake shook his head. "So why didn't the fool stop climbing?"

"By the time it really became a problem, he was probably too far up and didn't understand the issue. He kept putting on more chalk, thinking that would help the problem, and all the while . . ."

"He was making it worse," Jake said.

She nodded, then looked at Booth. "So someone definitely compromised Conrad's chalk?"

"Yes."

"So we're looking at murder?"

"Most definitely."

"We need to go see Landon," Kayden said.

Jake lifted his chin. "You head over. I'll be right behind you."

She nodded, took a moment to wash her hands, and then left.

"So you two are paired up on this one?" Booth said, doing a poor job of smothering a smile.

"She's the climbing expert," Jake responded, just grateful to get some one-on-one time with her.

"That she is," Booth said, no longer bothering to hide his grin. "You two have fun, and try not to kill each other." He winked.

Jake turned, leaving the morgue and Booth's wide grin behind, wondering just how painfully obvious his feelings for Kayden were.

— 6 —

Kayden and Jake sat silent while Landon read the report Booth had sent over with Jake. Well, Kayden sat; Jake stood. He always felt better standing. A by-product no doubt of his profession—always ready to move if a call came in or danger threatened.

Landon finished the report and set it to the side. "Kayden, you were right. We're dealing with murder."

"I wish I was wrong. Hard to believe someone

in the climbing community would do something like this."

"How do you know it was someone in the climbing community?"

"Only someone with climbing expertise would know how Dodecanol's interaction with chalk would affect a climb."

"So either a climber or someone with a climber to help them out?" Landon said.

Jake nodded.

"Kayden, are you available to head over to Spruce Harbor with Jake today? We could really use your expertise on this one, not to mention your ties to the climbing community."

Jake moved instinctively closer to her. Killing a fellow climber was cold, unforgivable, but Imnek Island's climbers wouldn't appreciate her coming after one of their own. He wanted her to know he'd be there to run interference.

"No problem," she said. "I'll do everything I can to see whoever did this behind bars."

"Start with the widow," Landon said, "and then move on to the climbing gym. See if that's where Conrad purchased his chalk."

Jake followed Kayden back to the home she shared with her sister, Piper. It'd been their family home, and after their mother died, the siblings stayed. Gradually the brothers moved out, and now the girls shared it, but soon it would just be

Kayden's. Piper would be moving in with Landon after their August wedding.

Hard to believe all the changes that had occurred in the last year—Cole and Bailey getting engaged and in a couple days married, Piper and Landon soon to follow, Gage meeting Darcy and the two now dating. It left only Kayden and Reef single. That number would drop in half if he had any say about it, but sadly he didn't. Kayden might be intrigued by him, but she clearly didn't love him.

Rori, the girls' husky, bounded down the porch steps the minute Kayden stepped from her vehicle.

"Hey, girl." Kayden bent, patting her up.

"I think she's ready for another plane ride," Jake said, laughing at Rori's exuberance.

"Maybe next time, when we don't have suspects to question."

Piper stepped from the door, a picnic basket in hand. "Hey, Jake."

"Hey, kid." As the youngest McKenna, all her siblings referred to her as *kid,* and during his time in Yancey, he'd taken on the habit. The fact that she was going to be Landon's wife in less than two months signaled yet another change needed to be made. She was clearly no longer a kid.

"Landon said you're heading over to Spruce Harbor."

"Yeah. We need to speak with Conrad

Humphries' widow and the climbing-gym owner," Jake said.

A look passed between Piper and Kayden, but neither said a word. *Curious.*

"I figured you could use some munchies." She handed the basket to Jake.

"Thanks. That was thoughtful of you." And so very Piper—always looking out for others. Kayden did, too, just in a very different way.

"See you two later."

"See ya." Kayden pulled her hair back into a lopsided bun and looked at Jake. "Ready?"

He nodded and followed her down to the Cessna floatplane. She wore her typical T-shirt, casual cotton capris, and tennis shoes. He couldn't wait to see her in a dress for the wedding. It would be a first. She'd apparently worn them on dates, but he'd always been careful never to be present when she was going on one—it was simply too painful.

They climbed on board, set the picnic basket on one of the backseats, and strapped in side by side. Jake loved watching Kayden fly. Flying and climbing were the only times he got to see the unreserved her—in her element and full of joy. It was addictive. If only being in his presence had the same effect.

Reef approached the house as the Cessna lifted off the water around back. He clasped Anna's hand. "Guess you'll have to meet my older sister later."

Anna's eyes darted up to the floatplane. He couldn't wait to introduce her to all his siblings. Couldn't wait to see their happiness that he'd finally brought home a good girl—a stellar one. She was a pastor's daughter, sweet, thoughtful . . . and most importantly, serious about her faith. He'd met her his first day at Calvary Chapel. She'd greeted him with a warm, welcoming smile when he hadn't believed he belonged, hadn't believed he'd ever belong.

Last winter had been a stark wake-up call, and while he would have been glad to avoid the death of a friend and all it led to, perhaps it had been the kick in the pants he needed to make some serious life changes.

He looked over at Anna, sweetly standing by his side. "Ready?" he asked, gesturing to the front door of his sisters' home.

"Ready."

She was brave to come all the way to Alaska to meet his family—all of them at once and all at his brother's wedding. The first of the McKenna siblings to tie the knot, though Piper's wedding was only a couple months away. He'd be back in August for it. He'd given Piper his word, and that was something he actually kept now.

Piper caught sight of him in the doorway and broke into a full-out run. She yanked open the door with a ginormous smile—"Reef, you're finally here!"—and engulfed him in a hug. For such a petite thing, her hugs were somehow all encompassing, and he loved them. "You're home."

"I told you I'd be here." He smiled. "How you doing, kid?"

"Kid?" She pulled back. "Please, you're only a year older than me." Her friendly gaze shifted to Anna. "Hi, I'm Piper."

"Anna." She extended her slender hand.

"My girlfriend," Reef said proudly, wrapping his arm snugly around Anna's slender shoulders.

Piper's smile didn't waver, but she had to be curious. Piper was *always* curious. "It's so nice to meet you. Please, come in." She ushered them inside.

Reef stepped into his childhood home, a wealth of memories flooding back—good memories of laughter and spending time together as a family, bad memories of his father's sudden heart attack and his mom's passing a couple years later. It was all wrapped up in this house. The memories made him long to stay and yet, at times, made it difficult. It was easier to forget painful memories when you were far removed from where they occurred or the loved ones they involved. Up close and personal made them flare to life.

Yet home was so much more than the memories. It was the people—his siblings. He loved them fiercely, and it was time he started acting like it. "Where's Kayden off to?"

The scent of apples and cinnamon wafted from

the kitchen, shifting his thoughts. "Do I smell . . ." He inched toward it. "Did you . . . ?"

Piper smiled. "Apple pie's in the oven." She glanced at her watch. "Should be ready in about five minutes."

His favorite. "Thanks, kid." He hugged her.

"You can thank me by stopping calling me *kid*. I'm about to be a married woman, you know."

"I know, and I'm still trying to wrap my head around it."

"If it makes you feel any better, so is Landon, I think." She laughed.

"I can only imagine." Piper and Landon were perfect, but entertaining as all get-out. "So where'd you say Kayden was off to?"

"I didn't. You got sidetracked." Piper led the way into the kitchen, the scents of nutmeg and cloves joining the amazing aroma. "She and Jake are headed over to Imnek. She discovered a murdered climber out at Stoneface yesterday."

Anna gasped. "How awful."

"Another murder?" Reef asked as the horrors of last winter came crashing back.

"I'm afraid so. Landon deputized Jake, and he and Kayden are heading out to question the deceased's wife and visit the climbing gym where he climbed."

Reef held a chair out for Anna. "Wait . . . Landon deputized Jake?" He scooted Anna in and took the seat beside her at the kitchen table. Piper already had plates waiting.

"This is why you need to stay in better touch," she said, setting down a fresh pitcher of ice tea. "You have no idea what all you've missed."

Neither did she. He was a new man, or at least was working his way there.

Piper went on to explain that with Slidell's sudden resignation and departure from Yancey, the town council had voted Landon in as temporary acting sheriff until the fall elections could be held.

"But why Jake?" Reef asked. "Kind of a random choice, isn't it? What made him decide to be a cop?"

"Actually," Piper said, pulling the pie from the oven and setting it on a trivet on the table between them, "he was . . . is . . ." She explained the revelation of Jake's past—that he'd been an up-and-coming homicide detective with the Boston PD who'd lost his wife and unborn child to a hit-and-run driver after receiving threats to back off a high-profile case. Threats Jake had refused to give in to.

"Dude." Reef raked a hand through his hair. "I had no idea."

"The poor man." Anna's eyes filled with compassion. "He must feel so lost."

"I pray he doesn't," Piper said, her eyes equally full of compassion, "but I'm afraid you're right."

Reef poured Anna and Piper a glass of ice tea before filling his. "How did Kayden respond?"

"To the murdered climber or Jake's past?"

"Both."

"She's been great with Jake's past. I think the truth helped her to finally see what a great guy he is, erased all the doubts she had about him."

Piper waited a few minutes before slicing the pie and serving them all a slice. "Would you like whipped cream or ice cream?" she asked Anna.

"It's homemade whipped cream," Reef said, loving that Piper always made the homemade stuff.

"You just assume it's homemade?" Piper said with a smirk.

"I know *you.*"

She moved for the fridge. "I suppose you do." She pulled the bowl out and brought it to the table.

"Fresh whipped cream sounds amazing," Anna said as Piper scooped some on her pie. The cool cream melted as it made contact with the warm apples, making that gooey puddle Reef loved. "And how did Kayden deal with the murdered climber?" he asked.

"It was rough, but you know Kayden."

"She's fine."

"You got it."

"But how is she *really?*"

"She was strong as usual, but I know it bothered her. A climber killing a climber is horrible."

"You already know who did it?"

"No, but Kayden said it had to be someone with climbing expertise."

"The climbing community isn't going to like her going after one of their own."

"I know, but she's got Jake with her."

"She's tough. She could handle it on her own."

"She could, but I think she likes having Jake along."

"Oh no, do I hear Miss Matchmaker at play?" He took a bite of pie. *Scrumptious.* "Piper, you've really outdone yourself. This pie is kicking."

"Mm-hmm." Anna smiled between bites. "It's delicious."

"Glad you're enjoying it."

"So are you playing matchmaker?"

"Nope. I believe those two are already on their way."

"Seriously? Kayden and Jake?"

"I think so. I see the way they look at each other."

"Kayden's making googly eyes for Jake?" Not Kayden. She didn't make googly eyes for anyone. Not since Brody Patterson back in high school. At least not that he'd seen or Piper had reported to him.

"It's rare. I've only caught her once or twice, but believe me, she's looking at him a lot differently these days. You tell her I said that and I'll punch you."

"I think you mean *she'll* punch *you*." He smirked. Kayden prized her privacy above all. If she had any idea they were sitting around the table discussing her love life . . . All he could say was he was glad she was halfway to Imnek by then, though he worried what kind of reception she'd get.

— 7 —

Kayden let Jake take the lead to the widow's door. They'd called ahead to let Mrs. Humphries know they'd be coming, but Jake insisted they arrive half an hour early. He said a lot could happen in a half hour.

Kayden was curious to know if that'd prove to be true. The Humphries place was a white two-story home with black shutters and a two-story porch, looking more *Gone with the Wind* than Alaskan Peninsula.

Jake rapped on the door and a young woman answered—early-to-mid twenties, petite and slender, with long dark hair pulled back in a braid.

"Deputy Wes—" Jake cleared his throat. "Deputy Cavanagh to see Mrs. Humphries. She's expecting us."

The woman dipped her head. "Come in. I'll let Mrs. know you are here."

They stepped inside the large foyer—black-

and-white marble decorated the floor while white marble stairs commanded the center of the space, winding up to a secondary foyer.

"Was that the d—" A faux-blonde in her upper forties hitched at the sight of them.

Stuart Anderson followed immediately behind Mrs. Humphries, also stopping short at their presence.

"Mr. Anderson." Jake smiled. "Nice to see you again."

"I'm here for Vivienne, of course. To be a comfort during this tragic time."

Jake linked his hands behind his back and nodded. "Of course." He glanced between Stuart and Humphries' widow. Even Kayden didn't miss the casual affection of Stuart's hand resting protectively against the small of Vivienne Humphries' back. *Interesting.*

Vivienne smoothed her silk blouse. "Why don't we sit in the parlor." She gestured to the front room on their left, her two-inch heels clacking along the tiles as she led them in. The room was appointed with burgundy and gold furnishings. Kayden would have found the decor overbearing if it weren't for the openness of the space. The south-facing wall was floor-to-ceiling windows, and strategically placed mirrors on the opposite wall magnified the effect, resulting in the appearance of a much larger space than what actually existed.

Stuart moved to sit beside Vivienne on the large burgundy sofa.

Jake leaned forward. "We need to speak with Mrs. Humphries alone."

Vivienne glanced nervously at Stuart.

He squeezed her hand. "I'll be in the next room if you need me."

She nodded.

"It's kind of Mr. Anderson to be here for you," Kayden said as Stuart excused himself from the room.

"The three of us go way back."

"Mr. Anderson mentioned that. College, I believe?" Jake said.

"Stuart and Conrad were roommates."

"And you?"

"And me, what?" Her nose crinkled.

"Were you friends with both?"

"I met Stuart when Conrad and I started dating."

"Did you and Stuart ever date?"

She laughed. "No. Conrad and I have been together since freshman year of college. Only other boy I dated was Rob Williams in high school."

"I'm very sorry for your loss, Mrs. Humphries," Jake said, taking a seat opposite her. "It must have come as quite a shock."

Vivienne swallowed with a nod, sadness draping over her. "I still can't believe it."

Jake handed her a tissue, though no tears had

been shed yet. "I was told you and Mr. Humphries have children?"

"Yes." She dabbed at her dry eyes. "Two boys. Derek is fifteen, and Phillip is twelve."

"I'm very sorry." Kayden knew the overwhelming sorrow of losing a parent at such a tender age. She'd been sixteen when her dad had died suddenly of a heart attack, her mom from illness only two years later. Neither were murder, but the loss of a parent was the same—leaving the children feeling lost, alone, and bewildered.

"Would either of you care for a drink? Tea, water?" Vivienne asked, glancing at the young woman waiting in the doorway.

"I'm fine, thanks," Kayden said.

"Nothing for me." Jake shook his head.

"I'll have a water with lemon, Amelia," Vivienne said.

The young woman nodded as she backed from the room, disappearing down the hall with nearly silent footsteps.

"Thank you for speaking with us during this difficult time," Jake said in a soothing tone as he leaned closer.

Vivienne responded, leaning forward too. "Of course."

Jake glanced about the room. "You have a beautiful home."

Vivienne smiled. "Thank you."

"You have quite an eye for decorating."

Color imbued her cheeks. "I try."

"Well, you've done a lovely job."

Lovely job? Had Jake—mountain man, tracker —just said *lovely job?* Landon had mentioned Jake's parents were members of Boston high society, but somehow the knowledge was incongruent with the rugged outdoorsman she knew.

Amelia returned with Mrs. Humphries' water.

"Thank you, Amelia." She took a sip, and then waved her hand. "That will be all."

Amelia disappeared as quickly and quietly as she'd come.

"Are you certain I can't offer you anything?" Vivienne smiled at Jake.

"No, ma'am. I'm fine, thank you."

"Ma'am?" She chuckled. "People call my mother *ma'am*."

Kayden narrowed her eyes. Was the woman actually *flirting* with Jake?

Jake smiled slowly. "I only meant it as a sign of respect."

Mrs. Humphries shifted, the sleeve of her sheer peach silk blouse draping over the burgundy sofa arm. "*Vivienne* will be just fine."

Jake dipped his head. "*Vivienne* it is, then. Could we begin with you sharing the events that led up to Conrad's climb?"

Something shifted in Vivienne's demeanor, as if she suddenly recalled the circumstances surrounding their meeting. "I suppose." She sat back, folding her hands in her lap, the water resting on a coaster beside her.

"Wonderful." Jake pulled a small notebook and pen from his shirt pocket and flipped to an empty page. "When did you first learn of Conrad's plans for the climb?"

"He informed me of his intentions on Thursday morning."

"His intentions?" Jake asked.

"Said he and Stuart were heading to Tariuk on Saturday. They were going to spend the day climbing some . . . face."

"Stoneface," Kayden said.

Vivienne waved her perfectly manicured hand. "Whatever, dear."

"Did it come as a surprise?" Jake asked.

"That he was going climbing or that he dumped something on me last minute?"

"Either."

"No, on both accounts." She lifted her water glass. "Conrad had a nasty habit of informing me of his plans with very little notice. Never mind that he'd promised our son he'd be at his soccer game. Never mind that I had a luncheon that had been planned for two months. No, he decided to go climbing, and I had to take a disappointed Phillip to his game. No consideration for anyone other than . . ." She shook her head, as if remembering who she was talking to "Forgive me. Where are my manners? It's wrong to speak ill of the dead."

"It's fine to speak the truth," Jake reassured her. "Do you think it was a last-minute decision to climb or that Conrad simply waited until the last minute to tell you?"

"Stuart said they'd had it planned for some time."

"When did he tell you that?"

"When he came here last night." With a slight catch in her throat, she added, "After the accident."

Jake cleared his throat. "I'm sorry to inform you that Conrad's death wasn't an accident."

Vivienne blanched. "I beg your pardon?"

"Forensics confirmed our hunch this morning. Conrad's equipment was compromised."

"Equipment. What equipment? Conrad went on and on about being one with the rock. The power of bare human hands."

"Not completely bare," Kayden said.

Vivienne's gaze shifted to her. "Excuse me?"

"All climbers, whether free climbers or boulderers, such as your husband, use chalk."

"Chalk?"

"Yes, ma'am. It helps you grip."

"I was a gymnast. I understand the concept." Interestingly, she didn't mind Kayden addressing her as *ma'am*.

"Then you understand its importance. Its necessity."

Her gaze swung back to Jake. "What does any of this have to do with Conrad?"

"His chalk was compromised."

"Compromised? How?"

"I'm afraid we cannot divulge the details, but rather than being a help, your husband's chalk became his murder weapon."

"Murder?" She swallowed. "Are you saying . . . ?"

"Your husband was murdered, Vivienne."

She blinked, then stared at the water glass in her hand. "On second thought, I believe I'm going to require something a bit stronger. If you will excuse me." She stood and swiftly exited the room, her heels clicking along the marble floor.

Kayden scooted to sit beside Jake. "That didn't seem like a typical widow reaction."

"There's no *typical* when it comes to death. Though Stuart's presence is intriguing."

She glanced toward the hall. "Doesn't sound like Conrad and Vivienne had an ideal marriage." Rather far from it, if Vivienne's behavior was any indication.

"No." Jake shook his head. "It certainly doesn't."

"You think their shaky marriage could be motive for murder?" She couldn't help wondering what his and Becca's marriage had been like, brief as it was.

"I've seen murders committed for far less."

"Do you think she's telling Stuart what we said?"

"Most definitely."

"And that's okay? I mean, letting the two chat?"

"Vivienne's demeanor after speaking with Stuart will tell me a lot."

"Such as?"

"What do you mean Conrad's death was murder?" Stuart asked, surging into the room, followed by a very agitated Vivienne.

Jake stood to meet Stuart eye to eye. "Exactly that. Conrad was murdered."

"Are you forgetting I was there? No one was holding a gun to his head."

Jake crossed his arms. "I never suggested there was."

"Then what exactly are you suggesting? You aren't implying *I* had anything to do with Conrad's death?"

"I'm simply stating the fact that Conrad Humphries' death was murder."

"He fell. How on earth is that murder?"

"His chalk was compromised."

"What?" Stuart paled. "When, how?"

"That's what we're trying to determine. You said you didn't use the same chalk as Conrad?"

"No, I told you—" He stopped. "I see what you're doing. You're twisting Conrad's fall to call it murder and trying to pin it on me. What? Do you not get enough crime out here? You need to invent some so you can look like real cops?"

"Mr. Anderson, I suggest you settle down."

"And I suggest you speak with my lawyer if you have any further questions."

"No one is suggesting you had anything to do with Mr. Humphries' death. We weren't even questioning you. We're simply trying to determine who had access to Conrad's chalk before his climb."

"Which would be me or Vivienne."

"Or whoever worked at the shop where he bought it," Vivienne added, placing a calming hand on Stuart's back.

Jake followed Vivienne to the utility room, where Conrad kept his climbing gear, but as he suspected, no chalk remained. Conrad must have filled his bag, leaving none left over.

"Where did Mr. Humphries purchase his chalk?"

"I already told you that," Stuart said, impatiently. "Vivienne, this is highly irregular. You shouldn't allow them to search your home. They need a warrant."

"Mr. Anderson, I asked you to wait in the front room."

"I don't want Vivienne alone after hearing such shocking news."

"She's not alone. Miss McKenna and I are right here."

"She needs a friend with her. Not a cop and his assistant."

"Kayden's not my assistant. She's a renowned climbing expert."

"McKenna." Stuart snapped. "That's where I knew you from. You're the gal that holds the free-climbing record for Stoneface."

Kayden nodded.

"I find climbing to be such a masculine pastime," Vivienne said.

Kayden ignored the insult.

"Mr. Anderson," Jake said, stepping between him and Conrad's utility room. "I appreciate you wanting to be here for Mrs. Humphries, but I assure you, she's in good hands, and we won't be long."

"It's all right, Stuart." Vivienne rubbed her arms as if she'd caught a sudden chill. "Go on and wait in the parlor. I'll be fine."

He inclined his head. "You're sure? You can say no."

"I'm positive."

He glared at Jake before leaving.

"He's very protective of you," Kayden said.

"Like I said, the three of us go way back."

"Do you know where Conrad bought his chalk?"

"I assume at the climbing gym, but I don't pay attention to that sort of thing."

"Do you know when he purchased it?"

"Couldn't tell you that either, but I know he went climbing at the gym the day before he went to Stoneface. Actually left work early to do it and then had to go back in after dinner to finish his work. It was ridiculous. Who does that?"

"So to your knowledge, Conrad left work early, went to the gym, came home for dinner, and then went back to the office?"

"Yes."

"For how long?"

"Maybe an hour, an hour and a half. His secretary, Amber Smith, could confirm it. He requires she be there whenever he is working in the office—in case anything comes up." She crossed her arms and looked up at the ceiling. "He's particular about that."

She turned her attention back to Jake. "Stuart was here, and he took off just like that. It was quite rude, if you ask me. Luckily Stuart and I are friends. It could have been very awkward if it were any other of Conrad's friends, you know."

"Yes. You and Mr. Anderson seem quite close."

"Like I said, we go way back."

Sure seemed to be more to it than that.

"Well, that was interesting," Kayden said as Jake held the truck door open for her outside the Humphries residence.

"They're having an affair." He said it so matter-of-factly. How could he be so certain?

"How . . . ?"

"Years of experience," he said with weary resign.

"Oh." She waited until he climbed in the truck before proceeding. "You think they killed Conrad?"

"If they did, Stuart was right—it was stupid of Vivienne not to lawyer up."

"Wouldn't it look awful incriminating if they did?"

"Yes, but it's the wise thing to do."

She buckled in. "So what now?"

"We head to Rocktrex."

"Right." Talk about going way back. She wondered if Brody would be working and really hoped he wouldn't. She had no desire to see the man, and with Jake being so perceptive, he'd easily pick up on the fact that a past existed between her and Brody. A past she preferred to forget.

Reef watched as Piper cleared the empty plates.

Anna stood. "Let me help you with that."

"I got it, but thanks."

"Are you sure?"

Piper set them in the sink. "Positive."

Anna glanced around. "You have a lovely home here."

"Thanks. Would you like a tour?"

She smiled. "I'd love that."

Piper looked to Reef. "Do you want to do the honors or should I?"

"You go ahead. I'll tag along." It would be interesting to see her talk about their home and family.

Piper started in the kitchen, pointing out their dad's custom woodwork—the cabinets, tables and chairs, the pine paneling on the walls and ceiling. Her mom's hand-sewn yellow café curtains in the windows.

"So tell me about you," she said to Anna as they moved into the living room.

"Well . . ." Anna hunched her shoulders. "There's not much to tell."

"I'm guessing you're from California, since that's where Reef is living."

"Yes. I grew up just outside of Tahoe."

"Oh, so you're a skier?"

"No. I'm not much for the cold."

"Ah. A fan of summer sports."

"Not much of a sports fan either."

Reef could see the wheels churning in his sister's head. Just wait until Anna got to how she did spend her time.

"Where'd you two meet?"

"My father's church."

Piper darted a glance at Reef. "You met at church?"

"That's right." He watched the happiness spread across his sister's face, and it filled him with joy. "Anna's father is the preacher—Reverend Marsh."

"Your dad's a pastor?"

Anna nodded.

"And you two met at church?" Piper asked again.

Reef laughed. He understood his sister's confusion. The last time he'd willingly stepped foot in church he'd been a kid.

"Reef told me it'd been a long while since he'd been in church."

Reef wrapped his arm around Anna's shoulders. "Anna greeted me my first day at Calvary."

"Your brother is on fire for the Lord."

He'd heard that phrase before but never really understood what it meant. Being faithful with church attendance, he supposed. Joining a Bible study. That sort of thing.

"That's great," Piper said, her expression stunned.

"I told you I've been making some changes," he said. Serious, life-altering changes.

"Well, I'm thrilled you're both here. The wedding should be really special."

"I hear you're having one of your own soon," Anna said.

Piper lit up. "Just a couple months. We're going to have a forest wedding."

Anna's smile faded somewhat. "That sounds different."

"We're both so at home in the outdoors, we decided it'd be the perfect place. We're setting up a small outdoor chapel beneath the ever-greens for the ceremony, and afterward we'll have picnic blankets and baskets spread out for the reception. It'll be at night and we'll set up lanterns in the trees and dance beneath the stars."

"Sounds perfect for you," Reef said, squeezing Piper's shoulder. Just like her and Landon. "Maybe you'll even see your favorite animal."

"What's that?" Anna asked.

"Moose," Reef replied.

"Moose?" Anna's forehead pinched.

"I know it's not adorable to everyone, but they sure are to me," Piper said.

"Landon even built her a special overlook so she could keep an eye out for them."

"How cool." Anna smiled. "He must really love you."

"I'm very blessed to be so loved and to be marrying my best friend."

That would be nice. He and Anna were hardly best friends, but they'd only been together three months. The depth of relationship Piper and Landon had was years in the making. He and Anna would get there—even if at times it didn't feel like it. She was a great girl and a good Christian, and that's what mattered. Not some pie-in-the-sky dream of overwhelming love and passion like Piper and Landon's—and Cole and Bailey's. He and Anna would be fine. Just fine.

— 8 —

Spruce Harbor was a town of roughly two thousand people on the island of Imnek, which was northwest of Tariuk. A ferry system connected the two islands, along with Kodiak Island, to the mainland. It had been a while since Kayden had been to Spruce Harbor, and when she'd visited Brody's gym, she'd been pleased to learn he was away on a climb. Last time she'd seen her old flame had been two years ago, at an outdoor climbing event with several hundred people present, hardly giving them any one-on-one time, and that was just fine with her. She and Brody were in the past. Their relationship seemed a lifetime ago, and in a way it was.

Brody's gym, Rocktrex, was a converted four-story fish-processing warehouse that looked oddly out of place amongst the quaint historic buildings dotting the rest of the harborside downtown.

Norwegian immigrant Ole Enget had founded the town of Spruce Harbor in the late 1800s, not long after Scandinavian immigrant Peter Buschmann founded Petersburg along Alaska's Inside Passage. Both quickly became fishery towns steeped in Norwegian heritage, which was still highly evident in the town and its culture.

Painted flowers in the rosemaling tradition

adorned doorframes and wooden plates in various shop windows along the main road running through the heart of town. In the center of the town square sat the two-story Sons of Norway hall, where the Little Norway Festival kicked off each May. The locals dressed in Norwegian *bunaders* and performed folk dances. It was a fabulous festival that was not to be missed. Kayden and her siblings made a point of attending every year when possible.

Ole's other lasting heritage was the fishing industry, which was the main source of livelihood on the island. Every day ships poured out of the harbor in search of salmon, halibut, and cod. Every evening they returned with loads for the new processing plant on the far side of the harbor. The scent of fish always lingered in Spruce Harbor's sea air, much as it did by Yancey's main harbor.

Kayden led the way to Rocktrex, on the far end of Harbor Street. She wondered how Brody would greet her if he was there. Would Jake pick up on their past? Of course he would. Jake picked up on everything. It was annoying and—much to her embarrassment for finding it such —*extremely* sexy.

She was captivated by his strength, by his myriad of skills, and most frustratingly, by his mysterious allure. For years she'd been drawn to a man she wanted to despise—and on the surface she had. But now that she knew the truth, now that she knew he was a good man, a good man with a battered past, she couldn't help but be drawn to him all the more, and she'd never found anything more unsettling in her life.

Jake needed someone comforting, patient, nurturing—someone like Piper. Definitely not Kayden—not someone desperately trying to hide her own hurt.

The sun breaking through the clouds warmed them as they wound down the old stone wall lining the harbor and approached Rocktrex.

Jake paused with his hand on the gym door. "Ready?"

"Of course." She entered, her emotions in a flurry. Man, she hated that. If only she could control them on the inside the way she did on the outside.

She took two steps in and . . .

"Kaybear."

Jake swung his head in her direction with a grin. "Kaybear?" he asked. But Brody's arms engulfing her cut off her need for a response.

"Hey, Brody."

He released her, taking a small step back but still close enough to carefully appraise her.

Jake stiffened beside them.

"Man." Brody swiped a hand across his head. "Aren't you a sight for sore eyes."

She brushed her hair behind her ear, a bit

uneasy with the intensity of his stare. "Good to see you too, Brody."

"What's it been? A year or two?"

"Two. The Denali Championship."

"That's right. You put my bouldering team to shame." He smiled. His hair was darker and shorter now, but his eyes were still every bit as blue. "So, how you been? You look amazing, as always."

Brody had always been a charmer, though she preferred Jake's lingering glances to Brody's verbose flirting.

"I've been good."

"So glad you came in. It's been far too long. How's the fam?"

"Doing well. Cole's getting married the day after tomorrow and Piper in August."

"No kidding. To anyone I know?"

"Cole's marrying Bailey Craig."

"That's a name from the past. I remember them dating not long before you and me. But . . . she left town, didn't she?"

"Yeah, but she's back." Kayden swallowed, feeling the weight of Jake's curious stare washing over her. "And Piper's marrying Landon Grainger," she quickly added, hoping to shift the attention off of her.

"Pipsqueak and Landon?" He laughed. "Now, that's quite the pairing. Can't say I'm surprised, though."

"No?"

"Nah. There always were sparks between those two—even if it mostly took the form of jabbing at one another. Irritation and annoyance are sure signs of hidden desire."

Kayden forced herself not to look at Jake, praying he wouldn't see that truth about her—that beneath all the claims of distrust, the hope that he really was a good guy wrested feelings she never wanted to come to fruition. If Jake had been the man she'd accused him of being, when the truth of his character came out, the feelings would have dissipated eventually. But her plan had backfired. The truth of his character had come out and only made her care for him all the more.

"So you and your—" Brody looked Jake over for the first time—"*friend* ready to climb?"

"Oh, I'm sorry. Brody, this is Jake Westin . . . Cavanagh," she added in a rush.

"Well, that's a mouthful." Brody extended his hand.

"Jake works just fine." He shook the man's hand.

"Nice to meet you, Jake. You a climber?"

"Just starting out."

"He's being modest," Kayden said. "For a newbie, he's doing awesome." He'd gone from short top-line climbs to a few bouldering climbs to a couple smaller free climbs over the past few months, which meant he was a natural. Focused.

Determined. With incredible upper-body strength. The first time she saw his powerful arms gripping a handhold, her heart actually fluttered. It was like something long dead inside had sprung back to life. The fact that Jake was the cause still threw her.

"Cool. Let's get you guys on the wall," Brody said.

Here came the fun part. "Actually, Brody, we aren't here to climb."

"Just stopped in for a visit?"

Kayden looked to Jake, and he graciously took the lead, flashing his badge. "We need to ask you some questions about Conrad Humphries."

Brody looked at Kayden with a mixture of confusion and disappointment.

She shook it off. This was business. A man was dead. "Is there someplace we can talk?"

"Let's go to my office." He glanced back at a young man sorting harnesses. "Shane, take the desk for a few."

The young man, clearly eager to be done with his monotonous task, sprang for the counter, greeting a couple entering the gym. "Hey, folks. How can I help you?"

Brody gestured toward the side hall. "This way."

"After you." Jake gestured. For being such an outdoorsman, he sure knew his manners—must have been remnants of his upbringing in Boston's high society, which she still couldn't wrap her mind around. How did one go from high society to being nearly one with the outdoors? She would probably ask him someday, though she feared the more she learned about the man, the deeper her feelings for him would grow.

They moved along the outer edge of the main climbing area—four stories of tan walls with handholds in a vast array of colors. Neon-green tape labeled the difficulty level of each route.

A couple customers were climbing belay and one free-climbed, but the decent-sized bouldering area was empty.

She wondered where Conrad Humphries had spent the majority of his time.

Brody guided them down a short hallway to the door at the end. He opened it, ushering them inside. The office was approximately ten feet by twelve but was more cluttered than Piper's room—brochures and paperwork piled high on the desk, sample gear and products stacked on every other piece of furniture in the room, while boxes littered the floor.

"Sorry," Brody said, clearing off a chair for Kayden. "My office seconds as a storage room." He dumped the pile of water bottles on top of a leaning tower of climbing magazines beside her. He turned, looking for another chair.

Jake held up his hand. "I'm good, really. Don't go to the trouble." He positioned himself behind Kayden's chair.

Brody nodded, shifting his gaze back to her. "So, what's up?"

She leaned forward. "We're here to talk about Conrad Humphries."

"Conrad," Brody said with a sigh. "Such a shame. He was a great guy."

Her shoulders remained taut. "I'm the one who found him."

Brody clasped her hand. "Oh, Kayd, I'm sorry. That sucks."

Definitely wasn't pleasant, but she was used to death. "We need to ask you some questions."

Brody's face pinched. "Like what?"

"We're checking on his activity leading up to his climb." She glanced over her shoulder at Jake. "Jake's a deputy with Yancey's Sheriff's Department. He's investigating Conrad's death."

Brody sat on the only open edge of his desk. "What's to investigate? Conrad had a climbing accident."

Jake looked at Kayden, giving her the opportunity to respond, which she appreciated since she and Brody had a past—no matter how far in the past it actually was.

She took a steadying breath, knowing the news would affect everyone in the climbing community. It always stung when they lost one of their own, but murder was that much colder.

She cleared her throat. "I'm afraid it wasn't an accident."

Brody's eyes narrowed, his confused gaze shifting between her and Jake. "What?"

"His chalk was tampered with."

Brody shifted. "What do you mean *tampered with?*"

"I mean someone compromised Conrad's chalk."

"Let me get this straight. You're suggesting someone purposely compromised Conrad's chalk so he'd fall on his climb?"

"I'm not *suggesting*. Yancey's ME confirmed it this morning. An ingredient was added to Conrad's chalk that rendered it useless." Actually, the Dodecanol went a step further, causing the opposite of the chalk's intended effect, but they didn't need to share such specifics to get the point across. As Jake had explained, it was better to keep their information close to the vest, at least at this juncture in the investigation.

Brody slumped back. "I don't believe it. Who would do something like that?"

"That's why we're here. We need your help."

"My help? I wasn't on the climb."

"No," Jake said, resting his hands on the back of her chair. "But we've been told Conrad climbed here regularly."

"Yeah, so?"

"So do you think anyone in the gym knew about his Stoneface climb ahead of time?" she asked.

"Of course. Conrad talked about it nonstop."

He lifted his chin at Kayden. "You know how it is. When you have an upcoming climb, you're pumped to share."

"When was the last time Conrad was in?"

"The day before his climb."

So Vivienne had been telling the truth about that.

Kayden crossed her legs. "Who had access to Conrad's equipment that day?"

"Conrad."

"And?" she pressed. When he shook his head, she rolled her eyes. "Oh, come on. Everyone knows people just shove their stuff in one of the open cubbies when they shower or use the facilities."

"And . . . ?"

"And anyone in the building around the same time as Conrad could have tampered with his chalk."

Brody's blue eyes narrowed. "You're saying someone in *my* gym tampered with Conrad's stuff?"

Jake kept his voice calm and even. "We need to explore all the possibilities."

Brody shook his head. "I don't believe this. Don't believe *you* of all people"—he pointed at Kayden—"would come in here and suggest one of our climbers would do such a thing. Man, I heard you turned cold after you lost your mom, but I didn't believe it until just now."

Kayden ignored the painful barb from a guy she'd once cared for, and steeled herself, like always. "This has nothing to do with me. In fact, I find it odd you'd shift directly to outrage."

Brody linked his muscular arms across his broad chest. "What's that supposed to mean?"

"It means, if you really were Conrad's friend, you'd want to find his killer."

"You've got to be kidding me. You don't actually think *I* had anything to do with this?"

"She never said that," Jake said, "but it's interesting you'd go there."

"I didn't *go* anywhere. I'm ticked because this isn't how we handle things."

"We?" Jake asked.

"The climbing community."

"Are you suggesting people in the climbing community would cover for another?"

"Nah, man. I'm saying we're a tight-knit community. We watch each other's backs. We rely on each other. We don't hurt each other, or set them up to die."

It was true, but it appeared someone within the community had lost sight of that and crossed a terrible line.

"So you can't think of anyone who may have wanted to hurt Conrad?" Jake asked.

"No, man."

"Anyone showing an odd interest in him lately?"

"No." He paused. "Well . . . I suppose . . . when you put it that way."

"Yeah?" Kayden pressed.

"His buddy for the Stoneface climb."

"Stuart Anderson?" she asked, already not a fan.

"Yeah."

"What about him?" Jake asked.

"He was real insistent on the climb."

Jake's eyes narrowed. "What do you mean *insistent?*"

"I told Conrad I wasn't sure he was ready for Stoneface. It's an advanced climb, and Conrad was only a few years in."

"How'd he respond?" Kayden asked.

"He ran it by Stuart, and . . ."

"Stuart convinced Conrad he'd be fine?"

Brody tapped his nose. "You got it. He really pumped Conrad up. There was no talking him out of it after that."

Kayden shifted, looking back at Jake. Now came the really awkward part.

Thankfully Jake took the lead. "We were told Conrad bought his climbing supplies here."

"Sometimes . . ." Brody's words dropped off as his face slackened. "I don't believe this. Don't believe you." His intense expression bore into Kayden, and suddenly she was sixteen again— her and Brody sitting on her front porch swing, him leaning in to press his soft lips to hers for the first time.

"We've got to ask," she said.

"*You* didn't."

"Meaning?" She knew exactly what he meant. She could have sent someone else. Could have refused to ask her first crush, first boyfriend, if he'd played any role in Conrad Humphries' death.

"The old Kayden would know exactly what I meant." He shook his head with a sigh. "Can't believe the rumors are true."

Don't ask. "What rumors would that be?"

"That you're a cold b—"

"Enough!" Jake roared, shielding her with his body. "Answer the question. Did Conrad Humphries purchase his chalk here?"

"Not for the last three months."

"Where has he been buying it?"

"Natalie Adams' place."

"Imnek Island Adventures?" Kayden asked.

"Yeah. Natalie started carrying a new line of climbing equipment and she's been underbidding me ever since."

"Sorry about that," Kayden said. Owning Last Frontier Adventures, she knew the crunch of being lowballed by a competitor.

"Whatever." Brody shrugged with taut shoulders. "Our shop sales are a fraction of our intake, and I've got a lot of loyal customers. Only a small amount moved to buy from Nat."

"Any idea when Conrad last stocked up on chalk?" Jake asked.

"Nope. You'd have to ask Natalie."

Kayden looked at Jake. "Guess we know where our next visit is."

Jake desperately wanted to comfort Kayden after Brody's cruel remarks, but he was at a loss. How could he comfort her without making her feel even more uncomfortable?

She glanced back at the climbing gym. "Brody's reaction was off. He was far too defensive."

"You and he go a ways back?"

She slipped her hands in her faded jean pockets. "We were friends . . ."

"And then . . . ?"

"We dated in high school."

"But . . . ?" He was pushing his luck. She'd actually just shared more than she ever had with him intentionally.

"His family moved to Imnek my senior year."

The year her mom died. "That must have been hard." He swallowed, knowing she'd either take what he said next as the truth it was or she'd brush it off as if Brody's words hadn't stung. He cleared his throat. "What Brody said isn't true."

She frowned. "Which part?" She was clearly focusing on the case, not his comments directed at her.

Jake held her gaze, and the depth of emotion she never could hide in her amazing almond-shaped eyes nearly stole his breath away. "The part about you." He prayed she wouldn't look away, and shockingly, she didn't immediately break off eye contact. Simply gave a quick nod—leaving it at that.

Jake inhaled, studying her. What made her tick? What drove her? He excelled at reading people, and over the years he'd come to understand quite a bit about Kayden, but what intrigued him most was the part he couldn't read. He could predict how she would act, react, in almost every situation, but he couldn't for the life of him figure out *why* she was the way she was, why she reacted the way she did. It was tied to the loss of her mother, he was sure. But there was more, something deeper, related to that event that drove her. He would probably never know. It was for the man she would finally decide to open her heart to, and as desperately as he ached for it to be him, he feared it never could be.

Fear. He'd never fully experienced that emotion until the loss of Becca and the baby. Maybe if he'd had a little more fear before that, they'd still be alive. It's why he'd tried so carefully when it came to guarding his heart. But any fool could see when it came to Kayden, and the rest of the McKennas, he'd slipped up, let his guard fall. And the desperate fear he could lose the family he'd come to love, the woman he'd come to love, was like a stranglehold on his heart. *Suffocating.*

— 9 —

Jake walked beside Kayden, the sun glinting off his fair skin. There was so much she wanted to know.

"It's okay," he said with a lopsided smile.

"What is?" She prayed he wasn't bringing Brody up again. Brody's words had stung, but she'd shaken them off just like she did everything else. Jake's concern was thoughtful, and she'd fought hard not to crawl back into her fortress—actually answering his questions with honesty, but one step at a time was frightening enough.

He plucked a wild flower growing by the sidewalk and rolled its stem through his fingers. "I know you're curious."

Her brows pinched. *Where is he going with this?* "About . . . ?"

"Me." He smiled slowly, in a way he'd never smiled before, and it left her throat suddenly parched. He was so virile, so handsome . . . so . . . so much she shouldn't be thinking about.

He dipped his head. "It's okay to ask. If it's something I don't want to answer, I won't."

She laughed, the tightness in her belly relaxing.

He arched a brow, his lip twitching with a smile. "What?"

She shook her head. "Just sounds like something I'd say."

"Maybe we're more alike than you think."

She bit her bottom lip. "Maybe."

A knock sounded on his door. Reef smiled. He'd been wondering how long it would take. "Come in."

Piper stepped inside. "Getting settled?"

"Yes." He put the last of his things in the dresser, waiting for it.

Piper sank onto the bed. "She's very nice."

There it is. He glanced at the clock. Thirty seconds to bring up Anna. It was a new record. "Yes, she is."

"So how long have you—"

"Been going to church?"

"I was going to say *known Anna,* but sounds like they happened at the same time, so sure."

"Three months."

"She's—"

"Very different from the girls I usually date."

Piper threw a pillow at him. "You're taking the fun out of this."

He caught the pillow before it smashed him in the face. Her aim was getting better. "Sorry. I just know you too well."

"And I know you."

"And . . . ?"

"And I'm really happy for you."

"But . . . ?"

"But"—she shifted, sitting Indian-style—"I'm just curious."

He chuckled. "When aren't you?"

"True."

He sat on the bed beside her. "So what do you want to know?"

"What made you decide to start going to church?"

"My time here with you all. I saw the difference church makes in your life. I saw the direction my life was headed, and I knew I needed to make a change."

"That's great, but it's not church that makes the difference—it's Christ."

Semantics—not worth quibbling over now.

"And Anna?" she prodded.

"Is perfect."

"Really?"

He frowned. "Why do you say it like that?"

"She seems great, but I—"

"Just don't see her with someone like me?"

"Actually, I was going to say it the other way around. You're so full of life and adventure."

"And it's time that part of my life settled down."

"You can settle down in some ways without giving up your love of adventure."

"I'm not giving it up. I'm just toning it down." He stood, moving for the window. "You know, I'm surprised. I thought you'd be thrilled."

"I am. If you're happy, I'm happy. I just want to make sure you're truly happy."

"I'm happy, Piper." It was just a different kind of happy.

Piper stood. "Good. Then I'm happy for you. Anna is a lovely girl."

"Who we've left waiting long enough." He followed Piper back down the hall to the room Anna would be staying in—his old room. He was confused. He'd thought Piper would be thrilled, not concerned. He'd brought home a good girl. He was making good changes. Why the hesitation on her part? Why the questioning? So Anna didn't love adventure sports—or sports, period. That didn't matter in the grand scheme of things. The fact that she loved God was much more important. Didn't Piper get that? Or was he the one missing the mark again?

Jake followed Kayden into Imnek Island Adventures. They provided services similar to those of Last Frontier Adventures—equipping and guiding Alaskan adventures. Though, while LFA was co-owned and run by the McKenna siblings, IIA was a sole venture run by adrenaline junkie and outdoor enthusiast Natalie Adams.

Natalie was a nice enough gal. She and Jake's wilderness groups had crossed paths numerous times over the last couple years.

Natalie stood behind the counter, her sandy hair

dipping over her eye as she scanned a brochure. A fresh box of them sat on the counter beside her.

The shop was similar in size to Last Frontier Adventures and carried most of the same gear—dry suits, dive tanks, snorkeling gear, ski and snowboard equipment, kayaking and rafting supplies. Natalie's shop, however, lacked Piper's fun-loving tropical touches—the leis draped over the Last Frontier Adventure's display cases, the surfer posters on the walls, even the Hawaiian tunes playing over the speakers. Natalie's place looked like an Alaskan shop, while theirs looked like it could be in Hawaii or California.

"Hey, Natalie," Kayden said.

Natalie looked up, blowing the hair from her eyes. "Hey, Kayden, Jake."

"How's it going?" Jake asked.

Natalie shrugged. "Can't complain." She shifted her gaze to Kayden. "Heard you made a grisly discovery."

Kayden slipped her hands into her pockets. "Afraid so."

"Sorry to hear about Conrad. Always a bummer to lose a climber."

Or any human life. Jake understood camaraderie within the sport, but murder was murder. It was always terrible.

Kayden cut straight to it. "We've been told Conrad bought his chalk here?"

"Yeah." Natalie set the brochure back in the box and leaned forward.

"When was that? What day?"

"The afternoon before his climb at Stoneface."

"Are you certain about the timing?"

"Positive. He dropped by after work. I opened a new package. Gave him half. Used the other half for myself. We both had climbs the next day."

"Where'd you climb?"

"Over on Tariuk, too, but on the east side."

"And you had no problems with your chalk?"

"Nope."

"You got any of the batch left?" Jake asked.

"I'm sure there's at least a little. I'll go check. My chalk bag's in my locker."

Jake watched Natalie head for the rear of the shop. "It will be a huge break if she has any left, will help us determine when the Dodecanol was added—before or after it left Natalie's shop."

"How can we be sure what she shows us really is from the same batch? Especially if it comes up short on Dodecanol?"

"Booth can match the other components."

Natalie slipped back through the office door with a chalk bag in hand. "Sorry. There's hardly any left."

Jake studied the fine dusting of chalk lining the inside of the bag. He smiled. There enough. "You'd be amazed by what the ME can do with even a small amount."

"Oh. So you want to take it?"

"Yes, we do," he said.

Natalie swallowed. "Okay. I suppose that'd be all right."

"Great." He took the bag from her before she could change her mind and slipped it into an evidence bag. "Thanks."

Natalie nodded, her hands clasped tight.

"How well did you know Conrad?" Kayden asked, proceeding with the questioning. Jake smiled. She certainly wasn't subtle, and he loved that about her.

"Well enough, I suppose." Natalie moved back behind the counter, putting an effective barrier between them. "I taught Conrad to climb."

"Really?" Kayden slipped her hair behind her ear. "I thought he learned over at Brody's gym."

"He did. I was his instructor there."

Kayden leaned against the counter, her knee showing through the threadbare portion of her jeans. "You teach at Brody's?"

"Taught—until I started carrying climbing supplies in the shop."

Kayden's beautiful brown eyes narrowed. "Are you saying . . . ?"

"Brody fired me before I could blink." Natalie scooted the box of brochures to the side and rested her arms on the granite counter, picking up a pen lying there and twirling it between her fingers.

"Wow. That's harsh."

"Brody's all about loyalty. When he decides you're being loyal to him, he'll do anything for you. If he thinks your loyalty has swayed, he'll turn on you without a second thought."

"What about Conrad?" Jake asked, his curiosity piqued.

"What about him?"

"He started buying his supplies from you. Wouldn't Brody consider that disloyal?"

"I imagine he did, but it was just chalk."

She was right, it hardly seemed enough to kill over, though maybe his intention hadn't been to kill. Maybe it'd been a form of payback gone terribly wrong. "Don't suppose he'd try to teach Conrad and you a lesson?"

Natalie's eyes widened. "By tampering with the chalk I sold Conrad?"

Jake nodded.

She was silent a moment. "Nah," she said, shaking her head. "Brody can be a real jerk, but endangering another climber goes against all he stands for."

"Anybody else you can think of that could have wanted to mess with Conrad?" Jake asked, wondering if that was the direction they were headed—someone wanting to teach Conrad a lesson. A lesson that had gone horribly wrong.

"Yeah." Natalie exhaled with a smile. "Try his wife or mistress."

"Mistress?" Vivienne hadn't said anything about a mistress, but maybe she didn't know.

"Patty Tate," Natalie said.

"As in expert climber, two-time state champion Patty Tate?" Kayden had pointed her out on their last climb. Patty had quite the reputation for being a tough competitor and a fierce athlete.

Natalie tapped the pen against her flattened palm. "That's the one."

"How on earth did those two . . . ?" From what Jake knew of them, they seemed like an odd pairing.

"They met over at Brody's gym a while back. Been going strong ever since."

"How long is 'a while back'?" Kayden asked.

Natalie shrugged. "At least a couple of years."

"Years?" Kayden said.

"Did Vivienne know?" Jake asked, wanting to know if she'd purposely withheld pertinent information or if she was still in the dark about the affair.

"Oh, she knows."

"You sound very confident."

"Because I saw it."

"Saw what?"

"Patty and Vivienne having it out a couple months back."

So Vivienne did know. Interesting omission on her part. "Having it out, how exactly?" he asked.

"Vivienne's a shrewd woman, I'm pretty

sure she'd known for a while but let it go."

"How could a woman let something like that go?" Kayden asked.

"They've been married a long time. Maybe she was invested, maybe she figured it'd be a passing fling, or maybe she'd grown too used to the lifestyle. Who knows."

"What would have made her change her mind? I mean, why have it out with Patty if she'd known for a while?" Something had to spark the change.

"Because Conrad stopped being discreet. He brought Patty to the Spring Festival. Vivienne showed up, and if it weren't for Conrad's intervention, I think she'd have gouged Patty's eyes out."

"I'm pretty sure Patty Tate can hold her own," Kayden said.

"Regardless, it was loud and ugly and very public."

"Who'd Conrad leave with?" That was the key to where his ultimate loyalty lay.

"Vivienne." She smiled but quickly looked away from Jake, staring at her chipped nail polish instead.

"How'd that go over with Patty?" Kayden asked.

Natalie dropped the pen and retrieved a bottle of polish from under the counter. "I saw them together last week, so it must have been okay." She tapped the bottle against her hand, shaking it up.

Kayden shook her head. "I still can't picture Conrad Humphries and Patty Tate together."

"Why?" Jake asked, gathering his evidence bag.

Natalie's gaze pinned on it for a minute and then quickly shifted back to the bottle of polish. She definitely seemed concerned about the chalk sample she'd given him.

Kayden shrugged. "Patty's about ten years his junior, an accomplished athlete. She just seems to have her act together. Why she'd be interested in a married man . . . I don't get it."

"Definitely not the most likely pair," Natalie said, opening the polish.

Kayden looked at Jake. "Guess we know who we're visiting next."

"If that's Patty," Natalie said, using smooth strokes to apply the coral polish, "you're out of luck. At least until tomorrow."

Kayden frowned. "Why's that?"

"She's at the Mount Marathon race over in Seward."

So they'd come back to Imnek tomorrow.

Jake extended his hand. "Thanks for your help."

"No problem." She offered the hand she hadn't started polishing and darted a glance at the evidence bag in his hand, her shoulders tensing. She'd been distracted ever since she'd handed over her chalk bag, hesitant to make eye contact. What was bothering her? He couldn't wait to get the sample to Booth.

— 10 —

"Detective Cavanagh." Vivienne Humphries' condescending stare settled on Kayden as she stood beside him. "And the climber. How *lovely* to see you again."

Vivienne clearly didn't like her, but knowing what she now did about Patty Tate, she understood the woman's negative attitude toward female climbers, and in a way she couldn't blame her. She couldn't imagine how it would feel to be betrayed with an affair. Not after growing up with her parents—so faithful and deeply in love.

If she ever were to marry—and she only considered it in moments of pure fantasy—she wanted what her parents had had. She wanted to be married to her best friend, like Cole and Bailey, and Landon and Piper. Gage and Darcy were another story—more sparks and lit fuses—but for them it worked. And for the rest of them, it was highly entertaining to watch.

"What now?" Stuart said with an exasperated sigh as he trudged through Vivienne's foyer. In his lounge pants, T-shirt, and leather slippers, he looked mighty at home in another man's house.

Jake took the lead. "We need to ask Mrs. Humphries a few more questions."

"What more could you possibly need to know?" Vivienne asked.

"The truth about your husband's relationship with Patty Tate and why you didn't feel the need to mention it earlier?"

Vivienne opened the door with a sigh. "Come in. Let's get this over with."

They settled back in the front room, where they'd sat only hours ago, and Jake started again. "Why didn't you bring up Ms. Tate when we were here earlier?"

Vivienne crossed her legs, pinning her gaze on Kayden as she answered Jake's question. "Why do you think?"

She was embarrassed her husband had been having an affair, though the coziness she and Mr. Anderson displayed made Kayden again wonder if they weren't doing the same.

Jake leaned forward and cleared his throat, bringing Vivienne's attention back to himself. "Now that we're aware of the situation, what can you tell us about your husband's relationship with Ms. Tate?"

"I think *fling* is a more appropriate word."

"Fling?" Jake sat back. "I'd hardly call a two-year relationship a fling."

"Two years?" She chuckled. "That's absurd. Conrad had his occasional trollops, but they were always gone before I could blink."

Stuart shifted, avoiding eye contact.

Vivienne paled. "Stuart?" She cocked her head. "Tell them they're wrong."

"I'm sorry, Viv. The detective's right. Conrad had been seeing her for a while."

"And you knew?"

"Not the whole time."

She shifted. "But long enough." Her eyes narrowed. "I can't believe you didn't tell me. Why would you let me find out like this?"

Kayden watched the interchange, curious if they even remembered she and Jake were still present and taking it all in.

"Vivienne, now's not the time." Stuart glanced at Jake.

Guess that answered her question.

"Let's talk about how you found out about the affair," Jake said.

Stuart's shoulders stiffened. "I'm sorry, but what does any of this have to do with Conrad's death?"

"It's helpful to have an understanding of Mr. Humphries' relationships at the time of his death."

"Our relationship was strained, but we were working through it," Vivienne said.

"To your knowledge, had he ended his relationship with Ms. Tate?"

Vivienne's teeth clamped. "Would you stop calling it a relationship? I made it very clear that if Conrad wanted to remain in our marriage, he needed to end things with that tramp."

"And did he?"

"He said he would." She paused, and her eyes widened. "So if you're looking for suspects, you should be looking at Patty Tate."

"Why's that?"

"I'm sure she wasn't happy Conrad was ending things, and she's a climber."

"Meaning?"

"His chalk was compromised. That's what you said. Who better to mess with his chalk than another climber?"

"She's not wrong," Kayden said as they left the Humphries residence for the second time that day.

"On which count?" Jake asked.

"That another climber was likely involved. Adding Dodecanol to the chalk takes some sort of chemical expertise, but it also takes climbing expertise. The killer would have to know what chalk feels like and how it works, would know how high up Conrad would likely be when his hands got slippery enough to no longer be able to hold on. Only a climber would understand how chalk works over time. If it wasn't a climber who killed him, then the killer had an accomplice with climbing experience."

"So we have Stuart Anderson, Brody Patterson, Natalie Adams . . ."

"And we can't rule out anybody climbing at Brody's gym the same time as Conrad that day either," she said.

"We need to figure out what Conrad did first—climb at the gym or buy the chalk. And if he bought the new chalk first, did he use it at the gym that day or save it for his Stoneface climb?"

"According to Vivienne's timeline it sounds like he went straight to the gym after work, but we'll need to clarify."

"Along with establishing what he was doing that hour Vivienne believes he was at work."

"You don't think he really was at work?"

Jake shook his head.

"You think he was visiting Patty."

Jake shrugged. "We'll have to talk with her to know for certain."

"If so, that possibility would add a fourth name to our list of people with access to Conrad's chalk before his climb," Kayden said. "I hate leaving Imnek without talking to her."

"Unfortunately, we don't have a choice."

She sighed. "So what now?"

Jake glanced at his watch. "Let's drop back by Brody's, see if we can confirm where Conrad went first the day before his death."

The parking lot was fuller now that the workday was done. It was a good time for them to be returning. It was the same time, according to Conrad's wife, that he typically visited the gym. It would give them a feel for who else may have had access to Conrad's chalk and who he spent his early evenings with.

Jake held the door. and Kayden stepped inside. Jason Gellar, a fellow free climber, was working the front desk as they approached.

Jason glanced up from his work, and his smile faded.

Great. She grimaced. "Hey, Jason."

"Back to grill Brody some more? Well, you're out of luck. He's off for the night."

Kayden rested her weight against the counter, making herself comfortable. "No matter. You can help us."

"And why would I want to go and do that?"

"Because a climber is dead."

"And you actually think Brody had something to do with that?"

"We never said that."

"No. You just came in here insinuating someone from our gym may have compromised Conrad's chalk. Please. I thought you knew us better than that."

Jake stepped forward. "It's our job to ask the questions."

Jason rolled his eyes.

"Don't you care that a climber from this gym is dead?"

"Of course I do. But I wouldn't go around accusing his friends."

"Sadly it had to be someone with access to Conrad's chalk, someone close enough to him to get the murder weapon mixed in his chalk."

"I have no idea who'd do something like that, but I can tell you, it wasn't anyone here. We're family. We watch each others' backs." He pinned his gaze on Kayden. "We don't stab each other in them."

Man, Brody must have painted an ugly picture of their earlier interaction.

Jake once again stepped forward to shield her from Jason's ire. "Look, we need to confirm what time Conrad was here the day before his death."

Jason crossed his arms. "You have a warrant?"

"Are you saying I need one?"

"That's an affirmative. Brody said not to talk to you or show you a thing without a warrant."

"Very well. If that's how he wants to proceed, we'll be back with a warrant."

Jason squared his shoulders. "See you then."

Jake tapped the counter. "Those time logs better be unaltered when we get back, or you'll be charged with obstruction of justice. Got it?"

"Have a safe trip home," Jason said with a smug smile that made Kayden really uncomfortable.

"What was that all about?" she said as they exited the gym and headed back for Natalie Adams' shop. "I thought I knew him, but he just gave me the creeps."

The night was cool, lower fifties, and clear. The walk would only take a few minutes, but Kayden was thankful for the fresh air. "I'm surprised how hostile they're being. Don't they understand it makes them look like they are hiding something?"

"Brody and, clearly, Jason have an attitude."

"You don't mess with the climbing community." She understood the sentiment, but this was murder.

"Bingo."

"Don't they care that Conrad's dead?"

Jake rubbed his forehead. "I've seen this play out plenty of times. They believe things should be handled in a certain way."

"Hopefully, Natalie will continue to be helpful and we can find out what time Conrad was in her shop, then we can compare it with the gym logbooks when we come back with a warrant. I still can't believe Brody's insisting on one."

"Do you think he's hiding something or just trying to make a point?"

"I don't know. Everyone we've talked to seems suspect to me."

"That means you're doing it right."

"Because I'm ticking everyone off?"

Jake winked. "You got it, darling."

Natalie Adams' shop was closed for the night.

"That's odd." Kayden tapped the business-hours sign in the front window. "She isn't supposed to close until nine."

"Guess she decided to lock up early."

"Maybe our visit shook her up."

"She did seem awfully distracted after we took her chalk bag into evidence."

"You think she's trying to hide something?"

"She shouldn't have given me her bag if she was."

"But clearly she wouldn't have added the Dodecanol to her own chalk. That would be suicide. If anything, giving us her bag will make her look good. Her chalk, supposedly from the same batch, will come back clean, leading us to assume the Dodecanol was added later."

"Maybe it was, but it still could have been added by her. She could have split the chalk up, added the Dodecanol to Conrad's portion, and kept the clean portion for herself."

"But why kill Conrad? What would her motive be?"

"No idea. We'll have to dig a little deeper on Natalie Adams and her relationship with Conrad Humphries."

Jake's stomach growled. "Sorry," he said sheepishly.

"It's well past dinnertime. We should grab a bite before we head home."

"Got a place in mind?"

"Actually, I do."

The Roosting Nest was a restaurant and pub the climbers on Imnek frequented. A quaint establishment with fine-grain wood paneling and matching booths lining the perimeter, gold rails accenting the aged oak, and the walls covered with a series of gold-framed mirrors and photographs of locals climbing throughout the state.

Kayden entered first, Jake close behind her. The time spent with Jake, minus the subject matter, had been fabulous. She was sad their day was nearing an end.

"You've got to be kidding me."

She looked over to find Brody at a booth on their right. "Brody," she greeted him with a smile. No need to let him know his earlier words had stung. Stung, not because she cared what he thought, but because deep inside she feared what he'd said was true.

Brody slid out of the wooden booth and stood. "What are you doing here?"

Suddenly she felt everyone's gaze shift to her and Jake. He stepped closer.

"Grabbing a bite to eat," she said.

The scent of juicy hamburgers and crispy battered onion rings filled the room.

Brody linked his arms across his broad chest. "Right," he drawled.

How did she ever find this man attractive? "I can't believe you're insisting we get a warrant."

"And I can't believe you're interrogating your climbing family."

"Someone with knowledge only a climber would have is responsible for Conrad's death."

"You don't know that."

"Yes, I do."

"Then look at his climbing buddy from Anchorage, not your friends."

It'd been years since she and Brody had been friends, and that point was moot. Someone with access to Conrad's chalk had killed him. It was her and Jake's job to find that person, regardless of any ties she may have to them.

"You're being ridiculous, and you might want to consider that you're only making yourself look guiltier."

"Guiltier?" His voice rose. "So you really think I played a role in Conrad's death?"

A murmur spread through the patrons, looks of disgust on climbers' faces.

"I'm not saying that."

"Then what *are* you saying?"

"That if you're innocent, you sure aren't doing anything to help yourself."

"See," Brody said, addressing the crowd. "I told you she thinks one of us killed Conrad."

Jake stood behind Kayden, his hand now poised on her back as she continued. "It's almost a sure thing that someone with climbing knowledge killed Conrad. If you'd just cooperate, we could find his killer a lot faster."

Brody strode toward her and stopped just short of being in her face.

Jake stiffened behind her—his hand taut against her back.

Brody leaned in. "Go. Home."

She squared her shoulders. "I will—when we've caught Conrad's killer."

"You're no longer welcome here."

"Too bad, because I'm not going anywhere."

Brody glanced over at his buddies in the booth, chuckling.

Dinner had been tense, but Jake and Kayden had refused to leave the Roost until they'd eaten. Actually, *tense* fell short of describing the atmosphere, but Brody's intimidation seemed only to fuel Kayden's determination to find Conrad's killer.

Jake watched her hair flutter in the cool night breeze as they made their way down the pier to her Cessna floatplane. It'd been a long day, and he was ready to have Kayden out of Imnek for a while.

She moved to the front of the plane to start her preflight inspection but stopped short. "Real classy, Brody."

"What?" Jake stepped around to her side, and Kayden held up her flashlight in the dimming night sky—the light resting on indentations marring her props. Someone had taken a baseball bat or other heavy blunt instrument to the propeller.

"Great." She sighed. "Looks like we won't be leaving tonight."

"Someone did *what* to your plane?" Landon asked over the speakerphone.

Thanks to Imnek's sheriff, Jacob Marshall, Kayden and Jake had use of one of the deputy offices while they were stranded on the island.

They wouldn't be able to locate new props until morning, so they'd definitely be spending the night.

"Someone took a bat or something like it to the props," Jake said, standing to Kayden's right.

"Who do you think did it?"

"My guess is Brody and his buddies," she said, irritation flaring through her. She couldn't believe they'd messed with her plane.

"Brody Patterson?" Landon said, recognition in his tone.

"One and the same. He wasn't real keen on the questions we were asking."

"We got some backlash at the diner where the climbers hang out," Jake added.

"The Roost?" Landon asked.

Kayden smiled. "You got it."

"Can the props be repaired?"

"Not a chance. We'll have to arrange for new ones in the morning."

"And in the meantime?"

"We'll get a couple rooms at the hotel down-town. It'll actually save us a trip back over here tomorrow to speak with Patty Tate."

Kayden hated to miss out on the last-minute preparations for Cole and Bailey's wedding, but there were plenty of helpers to fill in, and it was important they keep at the case. The sooner they solved Conrad's murder, the better.

"So what are you guys thinking?"

"Though the circumstantial evidence surrounding him doesn't look good, I'd be surprised if Stuart Anderson turns out to be our man," Jake said, leaning against the file cabinet, his arms crossed, a smattering of whiskers covering his cheeks and jawline.

Her dad had always had the same five o'clock shadow. If he were still around, he'd like Jake. The two had more in common than she'd let herself realize—reserved, understated, intelligent, patient, more at home outdoors than indoors.

"Care to elaborate?" Landon asked.

"He's too preoccupied with himself, too impulsive, to pull off something like this by himself," Jake said.

"Kayden, what about you?"

"I agree with Jake. I don't see Stuart masterminding this. I'd put my money on the wife." Kayden rolled her shoulders, trying to ease the tightness. "She would need help with the chalk, though, so I suppose that might bring us back to Stuart."

"Tell me about her."

"She's smart, savvy, shrewd."

"To a point," Jake said. "She says she didn't know her husband had been having an affair for years."

"That's right. Vivienne's surprise over the duration of the affair seemed quite genuine. Perhaps she knew he'd been fooling around but didn't realize it'd been with the same woman for the entire time."

"So you think the wife and Stuart Anderson may be working together?" Landon asked.

"I definitely have my suspicions on that count," Jake said. "It seems pretty clear the two are more than friends."

"You think *they're* having an affair?"

"It sure seemed that way," Kayden said. "If not, they've got a very peculiar friendship."

"Interesting." Landon's voice garbled momentarily on the other end. "If that's the case, the pertinent question may be which affair started first."

"We can ask around tomorrow. See if we can get a more concrete timeline nailed down." Jake stepped from the cabinet, moving toward the back of her chair.

She struggled to keep her attention on the conversation, but her focus shifted to Jake's presence behind her. She wasn't willing to give in to it, but his nearness caused an undeniable pull.

"Let's run through tomorrow's agenda."

Jake went through the list of people they'd be visiting—Patty Tate, Natalie Adams, and Brody. Without any hard evidence of his involvement in the vandalism of her plane, he'd get away with it, and she hated the injustice.

"I'll get you that warrant as soon as possible," Landon said. "Sheriff Marshall is connecting me with an Imnek judge in the morning. We'll see if we can't expedite things and get you a look at Brody's books."

"Thanks," Jake said.

"You two did a great job today. Now, get some rest."

Kayden nodded. Rest sounded very good.

Something was rattling. What was Piper up to now? Kayden rolled over, covering her head with a pillow.

The noise shifted to hissing.

Go to sleep, Piper. We need . . .

We. That's right. She was in Imnek, with Jake. He was in the hotel room across the hall. She wasn't home. . . . So who was making noise outside her room?

She opened her eyes and cast the pillow aside. 5:11 a.m. Too early for maid service.

Rubbing her eyes, she sat up. Listened. There it was again. Hissing.

Slipping off the covers, she padded to the door and peeked out the peephole. *Empty.*

She glanced to the sliding door. The hissing had stopped, but she thought it had been coming from that direction.

Grasping ahold of the curtain, she peeled it open . . . and stumbled back.

You're both dead. You just don't know it yet.

The words were scrolled across the sliding glass door in red spray paint, dripping letters reminding her, eerily, of blood.

Brody had gone too far.

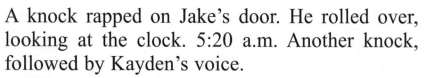

A knock rapped on Jake's door. He rolled over, looking at the clock. 5:20 a.m. Another knock, followed by Kayden's voice.

"Jake, open up. It's me."

Kayden?

He shot up in bed. "Coming." He raced for the door. Kayden was an early riser, but not this early. If she was knocking on his door, something was wrong.

He yanked the door open to find her in her PJs. A lilac tank top and pastel polka-dot bottoms. Probably not her first choice in nightwear, but they hadn't planned an overnighter, so she'd had to pick up something at a local store. Maybe they didn't have a large selection, but to be honest, he liked the soft colors on her. She looked beautiful but shaken.

She stared at him, her gaze lingering on his bare chest and then shifting to his face. She blinked, a soft flush creeping up her cheeks.

"What's wrong?"

"Wrong?" she swallowed. "Oh. Right. Brody and his crew of miscreants left a message for us."

He should have known. The level of their antagonism and bravado at the Roost signaled something more was coming.

"Where?"

"My room."

"Let me grab a shirt."

Pink flushed her cheeks once more. Was Kayden McKenna actually blushing? And was it truly because of him?

He fought the smile tugging at his lips and slipped into his navy T-shirt.

Following her back to her room, he noticed her tight shoulders. Whatever message Brody left, it had jolted her.

Obviously he hadn't been clear enough in signaling his protection of Kayden—hadn't conveyed the depth he'd go to to keep her safe. He'd have to pay Brody another clear and profound visit. When it came to Kayden McKenna, Brody would back away or face Jake's wrath.

Kayden stepped to the sliding door and pulled back the curtain to reveal words scrawled in red.

You're both dead. You just don't know it yet.

She'd taken time to close the curtain. Brody's threat had really gotten to her.

"It's time I had a one-on-one with Brody."

Sheriff Marshall accompanied Kayden and Jake to Brody's gym after visiting his home and learning from his girlfriend that he'd already headed to the gym for a preopening climb with some friends.

The girlfriend seemed rattled by their appearance at her door so early in the morning but not entirely surprised. Had Brody warned her they'd be coming?

They entered the gym to find Brody, Jason Gellar, and Natalie Adams, of all people, climbing—along with a young man Jake didn't know.

"Well, that's an interesting turn of events," Kayden said with a smile.

Jake rocked back on his heels. "Very interesting, indeed." And definitely not in line with the picture Natalie had painted of Brody firing her. For ex-boss and employee, the two seemed quite jovial and cozy climbing side by side.

Sheriff Marshall stepped forward. "Brody, we need you to come down. You've got some questions to answer."

Brody looked down, the creases on his face tight. "You brought the sheriff?" He glared at Kayden.

"What'd you expect after you vandalized my plane and threatened our lives?"

"I never threatened you."

"The graffiti on my hotel door says differently."

Brody frowned. "What are you talking about?"

Jake slid his hands in his pockets. The man was good at feigning innocence—he'd give him that much.

Brody worked his way down the wall with grunts of irritation. "This is ridiculous."

"Your *behavior* is ridiculous," Kayden countered.

He stepped to her. "I could say the same about yours."

Her gaze shifted to Natalie descending the wall. "I'm surprised to see you here."

Natalie jumped the final few feet to the floor and brushed the chalk from her hands. "Just getting in an early-morning climb."

"It's interesting seeing you here before hours, climbing with Brody, especially after he fired you."

"Fired?" Brody laughed. "You told them I fired you?"

Natalie planted her hands on her hips, white palm prints distinct against her black yoga pants. "You let me go right after I started selling climbing supplies. What else would you call it?"

"Our business took a dip, and I had to cut back on instructors."

"So I lost my spot?"

"You have another means of regular income. My other instructors don't. Teaching is their only income other than winnings from events, which we both know doesn't make for reliable income."

"So you weren't mad at me for carrying climbing supplies?"

"I wasn't thrilled. It's cost me some business, but I didn't let you go because of it. Come on, Nat, if I was mad at you, you'd know it."

Natalie blew a stray hair from her face. "Huh."

"Now that you two are all buddy-buddy again," Jake said, "let's address last night's vandalism of Kayden's plane and, more importantly, the threat."

"What threat?" Brody shrugged his arms. "All I said was she wasn't welcome anymore. That's a fact, not a threat."

"We're talking about the message you spray-painted on my hotel room door," Kayden said.

Brody stared at her with what appeared to be genuine surprise. If it wasn't Brody, then who had left the creepy message? Uneasiness rattled through Jake.

" 'You're both dead. You just don't know it yet.' " Kayden cringed a bit as she repeated the threat.

"What?" Brody burst out laughing. "Seriously? You think I'd do that? Come on."

Kayden rested her hands on her hips, her shoulders squared. "I suppose you also didn't bang up my propeller?"

Brody swallowed.

That is guilt, Jake noted. But he'd shown none over the spray-painted message. Had that been someone else?

"Look . . ." Brody raked a hand through his cropped hair. "I was at work yesterday until six, and then I was at the Roost. The boys can vouch for me."

The same boys who'd probably helped him damage Kayden's props, so in other words, they'd lie for him about his whereabouts.

"And at five this morning?" Kayden pressed, her ire fully riled.

"I was in bed, with my girlfriend."

"And how do we know you didn't sneak out and slip back in before she woke?"

"Ask Rachel. Her alarm goes off every morning at five, and she hits the stupid Snooze button for a good forty-five minutes. Trust me, she'd notice if I wasn't there."

Jake looked at Kayden. If Brody's girlfriend confirmed his alibi and no other physical evidence surfaced, they couldn't touch him.

Kayden slammed the rental-car door after speaking with Brody's girlfriend, Rachel. "Of course she'd confirm his alibi." Frustration seared inside, making her restless and agitated. He was going to get away with his bullying.

Jake rested his hand on the open car door.

"For what it's worth, she didn't appear to be lying."

"What are you saying?" He didn't believe Brody, did he?

"That I don't think Brody is responsible for the graffiti."

That hit her like a ton of bricks. "What? If not Brody, then who?"

"One of Brody's friends or the killer."

"And you don't think Brody's the killer?"

"Do you? Deep down, do you really think Brody's capable of murder?"

She pondered that. It'd been years since they'd been close, and Brody's reaction had raised questions in her mind, but deep down she couldn't see him killing someone. But that wasn't her area of expertise—it was Jake's. "I don't know. It would surprise me, but I've been surprised before."

"Trust me, I hear you." He exhaled. "But think about it. Nothing would please Conrad's killer more than to get us running around trying to catch whoever caused the vandalism rather than working on Conrad's case.

"I think Brody and his buddies are definitely to blame for the damage to your props, but the graffiti . . . When you called Brody on it, he truly appeared to be shocked. I don't think he did it. I think the killer did it to keep us focused on Brody—knowing we'd go right to him."

"So the killer is close by. Close enough to see what's happening with Brody."

"It's a small island. It wouldn't be hard to keep tabs on things."

She sighed with frustration. "So what now?"

"We work the case. We head over to Natalie's shop and confirm exactly when Conrad purchased the chalk."

Kayden shook her head. "I can't believe Brody still won't let us look at his books without a warrant. What a loser."

"We've called him out more than once in front of his peers. Refusing to let us take a look makes it feel as if he still has some measure of control. Plus, he just wants to give us a hard time, make our job more difficult."

"It's only going to work until the warrant comes through."

"Sheriff Marshall assured me we'd have the warrant before the day is out. It's only a matter of time before we get a look at the gym's time logs."

"That will make Brody even more fun to deal with."

"Good. Then maybe he'll lash out again. And this time we can catch him in the act."

"How?" They couldn't prove he'd been involved with either case of vandalism thus far. How would they be able to catch him in the act the next time?

"Sheriff Marshall has a deputy watching him.

If Brody does anything to scare us off, he'll be caught red-handed."

"Nice." She couldn't wait to see the look on Brody's smug face when that happened. She'd thought she knew him, and he'd turned out to be a totally different person than she'd remembered. Had he changed so drastically, or had she never really known him at all?

She took a moment to study Jake. For years she'd thought she had him pegged, and she'd been dead wrong. There was no bravado with Jake— just skill and humble mastery. She respected his strength, and not just bodily strength, though seeing the defined muscles of his torso, his sculpted stomach and arms . . . Her heart had definitely skipped a beat. Hers. Who would have ever thought?

"You all right?" he asked. "You're looking a little flushed."

She stretched out, trying to ease the tightness in her body. "Just frustrated." In more ways than one.

— 12 —

Natalie greeted Jake and Kayden with less enthusiasm than the last time they'd entered her shop, but she managed a level of politeness— even if it was remote.

"Back again?" She shifted her weight, rubbing her arms. "I hope the chalk tests came back okay?"

"We're still waiting to get the samples to the lab," Jake explained.

"Oh. So why are you here?"

"We need to confirm when Conrad bought his chalk."

"I told you . . ." She leaned against the counter. "The day before his death."

"We need you to be more specific."

Her eyes narrowed. "As in . . . ?"

"What time of day."

"Again," she said, her tone becoming more clipped, "he came in after work."

Kayden leaned against the counter beside her, propping her elbows on the countertop. "We're trying to determine which came first—Conrad's buying the chalk here or visiting Brody's gym for a climb."

"But Brody won't let you look at his books." For supposedly being at odds, she seemed to know quite a lot about him. What was up with that?

"Not without a warrant, but we'll have one soon enough," Jake said. "What we need from you is the actual time Conrad was in your shop. Buying his chalk."

"I don't remember that precisely."

"You must keep a record of purchases," Kayden said. They did at Last Frontier Adventures.

"Yeah." Natalie shrugged.

"So look up Conrad's purchase."

"All right. I suppose." Natalie moved to her computer and shuffled through the day's purchases, her countenance a 180 from yesterday. What had happened to shift her willingness to comply? Had Brody said something to her— told her they needed to stick together? Natalie scrolled down the screen and gestured for Jake to look at the screen. "Looks like he purchased the chalk at five-thirty."

"Vivienne said Conrad left work early that day, so chances are he climbed first," Kayden said.

But they'd still need to look at Brody's book and get confirmation from Conrad's secretary as to what time he actually left the office.

"Thanks, Natalie," Jake said.

"Uh-huh." She stepped from the computer, linking her arms across her chest.

Why was she so uneasy? Because they'd caught her climbing with Brody? Because they now had the time the chalk was purchased? Because the results of the chalk weren't in yet? What did she think they'd discover?

Jake pulled their rental car to a stop outside Patty Tate's home. While waiting on the warrant, at least they had something useful to do in the meantime—interview Patty Tate—and Kayden was thankful for that. Brody had resurrected old feelings, memories. Not for him, in the least, but for the person she'd been before her mom's death, before her mom's illness had taken hold, ravaging her once-vibrant and healthy body. Kayden had been different then—more relaxed, fun, untarnished. She suddenly ached for those days, for what she'd lost, and most especially for her mom. It was amazing how the effects of loss lingered, even after so many years.

She glanced over at Jake, wondering if he'd been different before Becca's death. Had he been more carefree? Carried less weight on his shoulders? How had his wife's death changed him? And did he miss his wife as much as she missed her mom?

She sighed. The two of them made quite the broken pair, and strangely, there was something of beauty in that.

Getting no answer at Patty Tate's front door, Jake guided Kayden around the rear of the home, where they found Patty at work in her greenhouse. The air inside smelled earthy and damp. Trays of baby seedlings up through full-grown plants sat on roughhewn tables made out of plywood and sawhorses.

Patty looked up at their approach. She was shorter than Kayden, but not by much, though far more muscular. Patty was of the climbing school of thought that big muscles meant faster climbing times, whereas Kayden believed in overall health and graceful dexterity and strength. Patty's curly dark-brown hair was pulled up in a lopsided bun, swirly strands sticking every which way. Her arms were covered with potting soil up to her elbows. She wore a loose-fitting geometric print T-shirt and tan capris. "Kayden McKenna."

"How's it going, Patty?"

"Can't complain. Won the race up Mount Marathon. Surprised you weren't there."

"My brother's getting married tomorrow. Didn't want to schedule anything so close to the wedding." Again she wished she'd been able to help out this last day before the wedding, but surely Bailey understood.

Patty shrugged. "Sucks to be you."

Wow! She was every bit the peach Kayden recalled her being.

Patty lifted her chin at Jake. "You must be the cop."

"Deputy Cavanagh."

"Brody said you two would be by."

Of course he had. It appeared he was doing anything he could to make the investigation more difficult. Why was that?

"We'd like to ask you a few questions about your relationship with Conrad Humphries," Jake began.

"What about it?" Patty brushed her hands off and came to stand with her back against the table in front of them.

"Mom, I dumped the latest in your workshop."

A young man, probably seventeen or eighteen, stood in the doorway. Tall, lean, dark hair like his mom, but green eyes instead of her blue.

"Thanks, Shane."

Shane eyed the two of them.

Kayden tried to place where she'd just seen him.

"Didn't know you had company," he said.

Jake stepped toward him. "Didn't we see you over at Brody's gym?"

"Maybe."

"Shane works there part time," Patty said.

"That's right." Jake snapped his fingers. "Brody asked you to watch the counter while we spoke yesterday, and you were there again this morning."

Shane remained silent.

"You like working there?" he asked.

Shane shrugged. "Pay's okay, and I get to climb for free."

"So you're a climber like your mom?"

"Like a lot of people."

"Ever climb outdoors?" Kayden asked.

"Yeah." He expelled a huff. "I'm not just some gym monkey wannabe."

"Cool."

Patty glanced at her phone. "If you don't hurry, you're gonna be late for work."

Shane slid on his sunglasses, lifted his long-board, and spun the wheels. "Later."

"It's nice both you and your son enjoy

climbing," Jake said to Patty once Shane was gone.

Kayden had watched him do the same thing with Vivienne Humphries, trying to find something nonthreatening to talk about, to establish a rapport.

"Been taking him with me since he was a toddler. It's second nature to him."

"That's nice."

"Look. I know you're not here to talk about me and my kid. Let's just get this over with, so we can all get on with our day. All right?"

"Of course," Jake said, moving straight to it. "We've heard you and Conrad were an item."

Patty chuckled. "That's one way to look at it."

"How d'you look at it?" he asked, resting his boot on an overturned bucket.

"Conrad and I came from different worlds. When he first came in the gym a couple years back, he was this uptight type-A business dude. Even his climbing was tense. I told him he needed to learn to relax."

"And did he?"

"We'd talk while we climbed, talking turned to flirting, and after a while . . ."

"You two ended up in bed."

"Yeah."

"Did you know he was married?" Kayden asked.

"Yeah. Conrad was totally up front with me."

She grabbed a watering pot and carried it to the sink.

"Meaning?" Kayden pressed.

"He didn't sugarcoat things, didn't lie just to have his way. After years of marriage to a liar, it was refreshing to hear the truth for a change."

How could she equate marital infidelity with truth?

Patty filled the watering can, shut off the faucet, and moved to the first row of seedlings.

"How long had you and Conrad been having an affair?" Jake asked.

"A couple years."

"And it didn't bother you that he remained married?" Kayden asked. "That he didn't leave his wife?"

"Leave Vivienne?" She laughed. "He wasn't going to leave Vivienne."

"Why's that?"

"Because she'd take him to the cleaners, because he liked the image of the perfect society family, because I think on some level he still loved her. He held on to feelings for a long time."

"To your knowledge, was Vivienne faithful to Conrad?"

"I don't know. When she confronted me at the festival—which I know you've heard about—she swore *she'd* never cheat. Said she still loved Conrad too much, but I had my suspicions."

"Based on what?"

"Seems to me if you know your man is cheating and you plan on staying in the marriage, you're going to find a way to have a little fun on the side. Payback, if you know what I mean. It's what I'd do—if I chose to stay in the marriage, that is."

Yep, Patty was a winner. "But you wouldn't stay in the marriage?" Kayden said. She could see it. Patty wasn't the sort to stick something out if she wasn't happy.

"Uh-uh. No thank you."

"If Vivienne strayed, any idea who she might stray with?" Spruce Harbor, like Yancey, was a small town. Word of affairs, of any gossip, spread like wildfire.

"Nuh-uh. I never heard of her being with anyone, and they had an all-female household staff. Conrad didn't want Vivienne getting even with the lawn boy."

"So he was worried she'd cheat?"

"No, not really. He just took preventive measures to ensure she didn't."

What kind of sick dynamic was this? "I'm sorry, but if he was cheating, why did he care if she strayed? If he was worried about her taking everything in a divorce, wouldn't her cheating make that unlikely?"

"You've got to understand Conrad. He was all about control. Control of his environment. Control of his image."

"Control and free-climbing appear at odds with one another," Jake said.

"Nuh-uh." She looked at Kayden. "Ask her, she'll tell you. Free-climbing is about the ultimate control. Mastery over something you were never meant to do. Mastery over the odds. You master that and there's nothing you can't conquer."

Jake looked at Kayden, studying her response.

She shifted the focus back to Patty. "So tell us about your confrontation with Vivienne at the festival."

"Yeah . . ." Patty shrugged a shoulder. "First time Vivienne had seen us together—that's all."

"Vivienne says Conrad broke it off with you after that."

"Yeah, right."

"So you're saying Conrad didn't end things?"

"No, Conrad wasn't going anywhere."

"You have any idea who may have wanted to harm Conrad?"

"I'd put Vivienne at the top of that list. He humiliated her by showing up at the Spring Festival with me—making us public. She was furious. Said she'd kill him. If that's not motive, I don't know what is."

— 13 —

"Let me guess," Kayden said, climbing in their rental car. "Back to Vivienne's?"

"Looks like it." It was the next logical step, but Jake needed a bit of time to pull the puzzle pieces together before questioning Conrad's widow again. "Why don't we grab a bite to eat first. I'm starving." It had been a long morning.

They settled in a front booth at Spruce Harbor Deli, a tiny establishment on Spruce Avenue—the main street running through the downtown district. A decent crowd bustled in and out, and Kayden swore they had the best breakfast burritos, served fresh all day.

The waitress started them off with water, and they both ordered a cup of coffee—black. It was Kayden's one indulgence, if you considered one cup of black coffee a day an indulgence.

"Everything's organic," she said, handing Jake a menu.

No wonder she liked this place so much. Kayden was a health nut, running ten miles a day, eating nearly all organic foods and daily green smoothies. It was almost as if she believed if she worked out enough and ate just right she could prevent . . .

He was an idiot. How had he missed such an

obvious clue for so long? Kayden was so stringent about her health and everyone else's because she was terrified of getting sick like her mom.

His heart ached for her. He knew she and her mom had been close, and had assumed her guardedness was tied to her mom's death, but this opened up a side of Kayden he hadn't seen before. Now he understood why she worked so hard to stay healthy. She feared getting rheumatoid arthritis like her mom.

"What'll it be?" the waitress asked.

"Santa Fe burrito for me," Kayden said.

"I'll take the same," he said without even bothering to open his menu, his thoughts on Kayden and the fear she must be struggling with.

Her brows pinched together. "Something wrong?"

"No." He cleared his throat. "Not at all." It certainly wasn't something she would want to talk about—maybe never, but for sure not in the middle of a crowded restaurant. He lifted his coffee mug and took a sip.

"So who do you think is lying?"

He gurgled on his coffee, burning his hand in the process. "What?"

"Who do you think is lying about Conrad having broken off the affair, Patty or Vivienne?"

Oh. "May not be either."

She nodded. "So, Conrad?"

"Could be he told Vivienne he was breaking it off to placate her."

"But never said a word to Patty."

Jake took a slower sip of coffee this time and nodded.

"What a sad existence."

"Whose?" he asked over the rim of his cup.

"All of them! Patty and Vivienne were in a relationship with a man who didn't care enough about his wife to be faithful or enough about his mistress to leave his wife, and they're both just okay with that. I mean, who does that?"

"You'd be surprised." Jake shifted as the waitress set down their plates.

"Can I get you anything else?"

When Kayden shook her head, Jake said, "We're good. Thanks." And as the waitress walked away, he asked, "Would you like me to pray?"

"That would be nice. Thanks."

Jake lowered his head. "Father, we thank you for this meal, for your provision and guidance on this case, and for this time together. Amen."

"Amen." Kayden busied herself with laying her napkin across her lap. "So what did you mean when you said I'd be surprised?"

Jake swallowed his bite of burrito—scrambled eggs, diced potatoes, chorizo sausage, pepper jack cheese, and green chiles. It was outstanding. He swiped his mouth with a napkin. "I've just seen it before on cases."

"Any of them stick in your mind?"

"A woman named Angela Markum, for one."

"That name . . ." Recognition dawned. "The college president's wife?"

Obviously she knew whom he was talking about. When Darcy filled the McKennas in on his past, she'd no doubt told them about the case that had flipped his world upside down. "Yeah."

"Her husband cheated on her with the co-ed he murdered?"

"Yes, Joel Markum. And he had affairs with a handful of others that we know of. But no other murders, as far as we know."

"Did his wife know? I mean . . . all along?"

"She knew. Even stepped in and helped dispose of Candace Banner's body after Joel killed her."

"How could his wife do that? Why would she put up with it? And why would she cover for him?"

"She liked her life, liked the style to which she'd become accustomed, liked the image and prestige."

"She was married to a monster."

"A monster she nearly helped get away with murder."

"Do you think someone is helping our killer in this case? I mean, do you think there's an accomplice?"

"Could be. Just depends on the killer."

"What do you mean?" She added Tabasco to her burrito.

"Well, let's say, hypothetically, if Vivienne wanted Conrad dead for cheating on her, she would have had to enlist Stuart or someone else with climbing expertise to help her."

"But if Stuart wanted Vivienne for himself, he could have easily acted alone. He doesn't appear to possess the needed level of sophistication, but that could be an act."

"Patty Tate also could have easily done it on her own."

"Which brings up the question of motive." Jake took the bottle of hot sauce from Kayden and added a few shakes to his burrito before folding it back up.

"Maybe Conrad really did break things off with Patty, like Vivienne claimed, and Patty didn't take it so well."

"Could be. We need to keep digging until we uncover the truth."

"And what if we don't?"

"Don't solve the case?"

"Yeah. What if we never find the truth or the killer?" she asked.

It was a cop's worst nightmare, not to mention the victim's family. Unfortunately he'd experienced that as both a cop and a husband.

— 14 —

A thrill sifted through Kayden as they reentered Brody's gym with a warrant in hand. She couldn't wait to see Brody's smug face settle when they served it to him. If there was one thing she couldn't stand, it was a bully.

Brody caught sight of them. "You two again? What do I have to do?" He moved at a clipped pace toward them. "Toss you out of here?"

Jake squared his shoulders "I'd like to see you try."

Brody stiffened, only a handful of inches remaining between the men.

Jake didn't budge, didn't flinch.

"We've got the warrant, Brody," Kayden said, trying to diffuse the tension before the two men came to blows, not that she'd mind seeing Jake knock Brody on his behind, not after his relentless intimidation tactics.

Brody's jaw tightened, and a curse slipped out. Anger flared crimson in his cheeks as everyone in the gym paused to look on.

"This could have all been avoided if you'd just cooperated," she said, not intending to embarrass the man in front of his clientele.

"Or if you'd minded your own business." He tossed the logbook across the desk.

Jake quickly scanned the contents, then handed the book to Kayden with his finger pointing at Conrad's signature.

Conrad Humphries had signed in to the gym at three forty-five the day before his murder.

So he'd climbed first and then purchased his chalk, which narrowed the suspect pool significantly. Conrad hadn't left his chalk in his cubby for someone to doctor with Dodecanol, because he hadn't purchased the chalk yet.

"Are we done here?" Brody cocked his head.

Jake handed him the book. "For now."

"That felt good," Kayden said upon leaving Brody's gym.

Man, she had a gorgeous smile—it lit her entire face.

The afternoon was warm, nearly seventy and sunny. Kayden wore the same outfit she had yesterday, because of their circumstances, but it looked just as good today as it had the day before.

She'd left her hair down, and Jake fought the urge to run his fingers through the auburn lengths—so shiny and smelling of apricots.

He'd balked at the fruity scent of the hotel shampoo, but on her it was intoxicating. He let the case ease from his mind momentarily and simply enjoyed walking beside her to Conrad's office.

It felt good to finally get a solid piece of the

puzzle locked in place. Their timeline was beginning to come together. Now they needed to speak with Conrad's secretary to confirm when he left work that day and when he returned that night.

As they entered the plush office, a woman he assumed was Amber Smith, Conrad's secretary, was sitting at the first desk. An open printer-paper box sat in the center of the large mahogany desk, and the woman tearfully slipped items inside.

"Miss Smith?" Jake said.

She looked up from her task and swiped at her eyes. "Yes?"

"Deputy Cavanagh, and this is Kayden McKenna. We're here to ask you some questions about Conrad Humphries."

Her hand stilled on a glass paperweight—a duck. "What kind of questions?"

"We're trying to determine how Mr. Humphries spent his last day prior to the climb."

"I see." She placed the glass duck in the box and reached for the stapler. "Conrad came in to work at eight o'clock, as usual, but he left early, around three thirty, to go climbing."

"And did he return to the office later that evening?"

"No."

"I mean later that night. Around nine?"

"No."

"You sound certain."

"I'm positive."

"How can you be positive?" Vivienne had claimed that Amber was always in the office when Conrad was working, but who could say he hadn't gone in without calling her back in.

"He would have made me come in if he was going to be working here—it's just his thing. But he didn't have to, because I was here until ten that night."

"Why so late?" Kayden asked.

She dropped the stapler in the box and reached for the tape dispenser. "Conrad's business hasn't been doing so well lately. He hit a slump. It's happened before, and he always got through it, so I always stuck it out, but this time he had to fire Kim."

"Who's Kim?"

"Conrad's bookkeeper."

Jake looked at Kayden. Perhaps a woman scorned? "Why'd he fire Kim and keep you, if you don't mind me asking?"

"I've been with Conrad longer, and I don't think she would have been willing to pick up the assistant duties. I'm good with most of the bookkeeping tasks, but sometimes I had to work late to get things finished." She set the tape dispenser in the box and glanced around the now empty desk with what appeared to be longing. She really liked her job or her boss.

"Was Kim upset?" Jake asked.

"Of course, but she understood."

"What kind of terms would you say they parted under? Good, bad, neutral?"

"Neutral. Like I said, she was upset, but what was Conrad to do?"

"When did he let her go?"

"Last month. So I've been staying late a couple nights a week to cover the load, and the night before Conrad's death happened to be one of them. I wanted to get caught up before the weekend."

"And you're positive Conrad never came by?"

"Positive." She shifted. "Why do you think he did?"

"His wife told us he left the house at nine for an hour, supposedly for the office."

"Oh." Amber bit her bottom lip.

Jake took a stab. "You think he was visiting Patty Tate?"

She swallowed. "You know about *her?*"

Jake nodded, intrigued by Amber's condescending tone when mentioning Patty. A little jealousy brewing there, perhaps?

"Then, yes, with Patty would be my guess, but wherever Conrad was, it wasn't here."

"Well, thank you for your assistance, Amber. Have a good afternoon."

"So his business wasn't doing well," Kayden said as they stepped out of the chilly office and back into the sunshine.

"Perhaps Vivienne found out and decided to cash in on his life-insurance policy."

"How do you know Conrad had a life-insurance policy?"

Jake slid his sunglasses on. "Men in Conrad Humphries' position always have a life-insurance policy. I'll put a call in to Landon and have him look into it."

"Sounds good. And Kim?"

"We'll have to see if she really left under decent terms."

Kayden nodded and they made the short walk back to Brody's gym to retrieve their rental car for the ride over to Vivienne's.

Kayden hitched at the sight of the white envelope stashed under the wiper blades. She looked at Jake. "A nasty note from Brody?"

He grabbed it, pulled out the note, and his jaw tightened.

He crumpled it, threw it down, and headed straight for Brody's door.

Kayden retrieved the paper and smoothed it out.

I see the way you look at her. Oh, the pain you'll feel when I inflict it on her.

Brody was a lunatic. She shoved the note in her pocket, knowing Landon would want it for evidence, and followed Jake back inside.

He had Brody by the throat, and Jason Gellar was leaping across the desk to try to intervene.

"You lay so much as a finger on her and I'll see you behind bars." Jake clutched harder.

Jason grabbed his shoulder, and Jake released one hand from Brody, keeping the other firmly grasped on his neck. Taking Jason's arm, he executed a move that had Jason on his knees with his arm pinned behind his back and his hand poised to break if Jake pulled.

"Cavanagh." Deputy Franklin, the man Sheriff Marshall had put on Brody, rushed forward. "What are you doing?"

"He threatened Kayden again."

"I . . . did . . . not . . ." Brody wheezed out.

"When?" Franklin asked, confused. "I've had eyes on him all day."

Kayden pulled the note from her pocket. "He left this on our car."

Brody sputtered.

"Jake." She tilted her head at Brody, who was turning a deep shade of red.

With a firm glare, Jake released his hold.

Brody clasped his throat, coughing. "Are you . . . insane?"

"When do you think he left it on your car?" Franklin asked as Jake released his hold on Jason.

Jason slowly rose from the floor, staring at Jake with a mixture of anger and admiration.

"It had to be while we were at Conrad's office."

Franklin glanced at his watch. "You've been

gone less than an hour, and I've had Brody in my sights the whole time. He didn't leave the gym once or hand a note off to anybody. He's not your guy."

"I told you," Brody grunted.

A shiver snaked up Kayden's spine, just as it had with the spray-painted message. Brody trying to intimidate them was one thing, but if someone else was leaving the messages . . . were they serious threats? Was the killer really after her and Jake? Trying to silence them before they were caught? She looked at Jake. How much danger were they in?

Jake knocked on Vivienne's door, adrenaline still burning through his veins. Whoever sent that message wasn't bluffing. He felt it in his gut. They had to catch the killer before he or she got to them.

The door opened and Vivienne's housekeeper, Amelia, greeted them with a smile. "Detective Cavanagh." She looked to Kayden. "Miss McKenna. Nice to see you again."

"Thank you, Amelia. Is Mrs. Humphries in?"

"No. I'm afraid not. She and Mr. Anderson flew to Kodiak."

"Really?" To get away from the sorrow? The investigation?

"Who's at the door?" a young male asked.

"Deputy Cavanagh. He—" Amelia began.

"My mother's not here." Phillip Humphries, Conrad and Vivienne's younger son, swung the door open wide. "And don't you think you've put her through enough already?"

"I'm sorry if we've upset your mother or you," Jake said, "but it's my job to figure out who killed your dad."

"Well, it wasn't my mom. So leave us alone." He slammed the door in Jake's face.

Jake moved to knock again, but the door opened. Amelia snuck out and closed it quietly behind herself. "You must excuse Phillip. He's taking Mr. Humphries' death quite hard."

It probably didn't help that his mom had taken off to Kodiak with Conrad's best friend. "Of course," he said. "Do you know when Mrs. Humphries will be back?"

"Not until late tonight. If you want to speak with her, you'll have to come back in the morning."

Tomorrow was Cole and Bailey's wedding, which meant they'd need to return the day after. He was thankful they'd have a day away from Imnek. The place was getting under his skin. He wanted Kayden safe and on home turf. "Thank you, Amelia."

She nodded and stepped back inside the house.

"Seems odd for a grieving widow to take off with the deceased's best friend for the day and just leave her kids at home right after they lost their dad," Kayden said.

"In most cases I'd agree. . . ." Jake looked back at the house and caught sight of Phillip watching from the upstairs window. "Sadly, based on Vivienne and Stuart's behavior thus far, I can't say I'm surprised."

"What do you think they're doing on Kodiak?"

He arched a brow.

"So soon after Conrad's death? Wow, no shame there."

"I could be wrong. Maybe they wanted some time away from us in order to get their stories straight."

"So . . . you think they killed Conrad?"

"I don't know, but their taking off certainly doesn't help their case." He tried picturing Vivienne or Stuart leaving the threatening messages. Were either of them a cold-blooded killer, ready to kill again if need be?

After getting a replacement propeller for her plane, the trip back to Yancey passed quickly, and Kayden found herself reluctant to leave Jake's presence. Though they'd both be attending the rehearsal and dinner following, it would be different. It wouldn't be just the two of them, and while that should cause her relief, it left her wanting more.

They'd spent more one-on-one time together in the past few months, in the past few days, than they had in all the years they'd known each other. She enjoyed their time alone way too much and was already starting to rely on him, which was dangerous. She didn't want to need anyone. Not again.

— 15 —

Reef sat with Anna on a blanket overlooking the ocean. The rehearsal had taken place at Grace Community Church, where his family attended, and soon the wedding party would be returning for the rehearsal dinner—rehearsal clam bake, to be precise. Darcy and a handful of family friends had hung back at Kayden and Piper's, where the party was being held on the shore. Earlier they'd set up beach chairs in large circles around a series of fire pits. Picnic tables lined the grassy space between the shore and the house, and the scent of fresh seafood wafted on the ocean breeze.

Reef glanced over at Anna shivering in her yellow sundress. Alaska was a far cry from her California home. He slipped off his sweater and offered it to her.

She took in his white T-shirt and cargo shorts. "Are you sure you'll be warm enough?"

"I'll be fine. If not, the house is right there. I can always grab a sweatshirt."

He helped her slip on the navy cable-knit

sweater, the sleeves drooping a good three inches past her hands. She was so delicate.

"I'm anxious to meet Kayden and Jake. He sounds interesting."

So far she'd met the rest of his siblings, their significant others, and a handful of townsfolk— all very curious to see what kind of lady the wild McKenna boy had brought home.

"They're back," Darcy said, moving up the hill to greet Gage.

Reef stood and helped Anna to her feet. He spotted Jake first, opening his truck door for Kayden. Reef raked a hand through his hair. He still couldn't believe Jake's past. It seemed the thing of movies, not real life. His heart went out to the man. All those years of having his character questioned and doubted by Kayden. He wondered how his sister viewed him now.

Kayden turned toward him, beautiful as ever— long dark hair, high cheekbones, and large almond-shaped eyes. Just like their mom. It was like peeking back into his childhood.

"Hey there," she said as she approached.

"Hey." He gave her a hug—quick, like she preferred.

"There's someone I want you to meet." He turned to Anna, introducing her.

"It's nice to meet you, Anna," Kayden said. "I hope you aren't finding our family to be too overwhelming." She glanced over her shoulder at Cole and Gage already goofing around with a Nerf rocket launcher.

"Everyone's been wonderful," she said.

Reef waved Jake down from his perch on the hill.

"How's it going, Reef?"

"Much better than last time I was here."

Jake smiled.

"I don't know if I ever really thanked you for your part in clearing me."

"Happy to help, small as that part was."

He was being too modest, but that was Jake. Though he'd been traveling for most of the time Jake had been in Yancey, Reef recognized him as a man to be admired.

"I hear you and Kayden have an interesting case going."

Jake looked back at Kayden. "That's one way to put it."

"We spent the better part of two days questioning Patty Tate, Natalie Adams, and Brody Patterson," she said.

"Brody? I haven't heard that name in years. How's he doing?"

"He owns the climbing gym over on Imnek. Seems to be doing okay."

Reef smiled. "Bet he enjoyed seeing you."

"Actually . . ." Kayden shuffled her feet along the sand. "He wasn't too happy with our questions. Took it out on my propeller."

"He's the one who did that?" Piper had mentioned what had happened, but not who was responsible.

Kayden nodded.

"Can't say I'm surprised." The extreme-boarding community was the same as the climbing community. People looked out for their own, and talk stayed within the core. No outsiders. And Jake was an outsider, even if he'd taken up climbing. He wasn't truly one of them, not yet.

"We're heading back over day after tomorrow."

"Doubt you'll get people to open up." When Reef's friend and fellow extreme athlete Karli Davis had been murdered and he was a suspect, few spoke, and when they did, their words weren't pretty.

Kayden glanced at Jake with a smile. "He has a way of getting what he needs from people."

Reef stared. Had his sister just paid Jake a compliment? "Any suspects?" he asked, shaking off his shock.

"A few." She shrugged.

"Hopefully we'll be able to narrow it down after Booth finishes running the sample we brought back," Jake said. "And after we spend another day on Imnek, of course."

"I'm pretty sure you're not going to get a good reception."

"Based on our experience so far, I'd say you're definitely right."

Kayden woke to the ringing of her cell.

Blinking, she glanced at the clock. 5:11 a.m. This had to stop. If this was another one of Brody's pranks . . .

She looked at her phone, not recognizing the number. "What?"

"I'm watching you." The voice was muffled and robotic—computerized. "You'll be so beautiful in death."

"Who is this?"

"Your end."

Click.

She tossed the phone on her nightstand, resisting the overwhelming urge to call Jake. Today was her brother's wedding. She didn't want to do anything to take away from Cole and Bailey's joy. Didn't want people focused on Brody's prank rather than the festivities, but the tone of the pranks was growing darker.

She tried to settle back into bed. Jake had warned her to anticipate some blowback, but for the first time in a long time she was truly scared.

Unable to sleep, she pulled on her robe and headed downstairs. She brewed a cup of coffee and headed out onto the porch swing to enjoy the sunrise.

Yellow and orange in hue, the sun shone brilliantly as it crested over the horizon, bringing the breadth of their property into view.

A fresh layer of dew graced the grass, dampening the earth, blanketing the . . . She stared at the markings trailing across the lawn and stopping beneath her bedroom window. Boot prints.

She stood and followed them across the yard into the trees and back out to the road. Somebody *had* been watching her. Had the killer called her from outside her home?

Fear coursed anew through her.

— 16 —

Kayden took a deep, steadying breath before taking her first step down the aisle.

Pastor Braden waited at the end underneath the wooden arch her brothers built and Piper had draped with a beautiful white linen swag that swayed in the ocean breeze. To Pastor Braden's left stood Cole, then Gage, then Landon, and finally Jake. All four so dapper in their crisp white dress shirts, sleeves rolled to the elbows, shirts untucked, hanging over new khaki pants rolled up to their ankles with bare feet in the sand. It was the perfect shabby-chic beach wedding.

Instead of matching rows of white chairs, they'd raided their homes for their dad's handcrafted chairs, along with more from Bailey's antique shop—the Russian-Alaskan Trading Post. What they had gathered provided an eclectic yet beautiful collection of handcrafted pieces and historical treasures. The end chair in each row was decorated with an abundant bouquet of wild flowers tied with bright turquoise ribbon—the colors bursting in a vivid path lining the walk that would forever change Cole and Bailey's life. In less than a half hour Bailey Craig would become Bailey McKenna.

Kayden couldn't imagine what it would be like to become one with a man, but that's how the Bible described the union, and that's how her parents lived out their marriage. Unfortunately, seeing the incredible agony her mom had suffered at the loss of her husband, at the loss of her other half . . .

Kayden's hand tightened on her bouquet.

She refused to ever set herself up to experience such pain. She continued walking down the grassy aisle to where it met the sand.

The sun was warm, the air a gentle sixty-three degrees. Cole smiled as she approached. He looked so handsome and happy. She tried to keep the creepy morning wake-up call and footprints out of her head, but the eerie voice lingered.

Jake flashed a worried look her way. How could he always tell when she was upset? She smiled, trying to throw him off, but something in his expression said he wasn't buying it. She looked away, focusing on Landon instead as his stare fastened on something behind her. On some*one,*

151

rather—Piper. Abundant love and happiness swelled in his eyes.

Who would have thought her little sister would find love so early in her life? It wasn't really surprising, though. Piper was warm, open, caring, giving—such a stark contrast to herself.

And Landon . . .

A smile tugged at her lips. Despite her aversion to their incessant PDAs, they were perfect for one another, and it warmed her heart to know her sister would be loved, cherished, and well taken care of.

Piper took her place beside Kayden as the matron of honor—Bailey's best friend from Oregon, Carrie Matthews—followed down the aisle.

The music shifted, signaling Bailey's arrival. Cole straightened, his entire countenance beaming. She was overjoyed for her big brother, and for sweet Bailey. She watched as her future sister-in-law walked down the aisle on Gus's arm. Her gown was long and flowing—white satin that gently hugged her curves with a simple V neckline and an understated elegance. Her hair was in a soft, loose updo with a white calla lily tucked behind her ear.

Kayden glanced at her brother, at the love shining in his eyes for his bride-to-be. She ached for that, for someone to look at her with such overwhelming love—but it could never be.

Cole's heart seized at the sight of his bride. His *bride*. Bailey Craig. The woman he'd loved since he was a teen was about to become *his* bride.

He glanced up at the heavens—*Thank you, Father*—then back at Bailey. Blond tendrils spilled out of her side bun and down across her creamy shoulders. He was sure her gown was lovely, but he couldn't pull his eyes from hers— blue and overflowing with love for him. *For me.* He was so very blessed.

Gus, family friend and Bailey's adoptive uncle, handed her off, and together they turned, hand in hand, to face Pastor Braden. This was it. He'd found his happily ever after, and she was standing right beside him.

Pastor Braden began with a prayer and then a passage of Scripture—Ephesians 5:25. " 'Husbands, love your wives, just as Christ loved the church and gave himself up for her.' "

He would. He would strive every second of his life to love Bailey as Christ loved the church.

But I can only do it through your strength, Father. Equip me to love her as you created me to. May our lives and our marriage glorify you always.

The rest of the ceremony went by in a blur, so much emotion welling inside him, in the words of love he spoke, in the words of love she spoke to him. Her hands were trembling as he slid the ring on her finger, but the joy in her eyes said it was all out of love. She placed the band on his finger and Pastor Braden said, "You may now kiss your bride."

My bride. The greatest joy he'd ever known, next to accepting Christ as his Savior, swept over him as he pulled Bailey into his arms and kissed his wife for the very first time.

"Mrs. McKenna," he whispered against her petal-soft lips.

She smiled, making his insides Jell-O. "I like the sound of that."

He grinned. "How about this?" He moved his mouth to her ear and whispered words of love only a wife should ever hear, and joy filled him as her smile widened, brushing her cheek close to his. A giggle escaped her lips.

Round tables with white linen tablecloths dotted the grounds, candles glowing in glass pillars at the center of each. Well over a hundred guests were in attendance, everyone smiling and enjoying the festivities.

Jake watched from the periphery as usual. The McKennas' property had been transformed once again—this time into an oasis beneath the stars.

Growing up with his well-to-do parents, he'd been to his fair share of elegant dinners and dances, but all that paled in comparison to the beauty before him and the rhythmic sound of waves tossing behind him.

Cole had doted on Bailey throughout dinner, and his bride shined. Memories of his wedding day flooded Jake's mind, and he wished he'd been more mature, more loving, more enraptured. He and Becca, while they loved each other, had been so young, and having recently become the youngest homicide detective in Boston history, he'd been far too cocky. He hadn't known the first thing about being a good husband, but he'd tried his best, until the co-ed case fell in his lap and he'd become obsessed. He'd let Becca take a backseat to his career, and in the end she'd died because of it—because of him. How he regretted his arrogance, regretted a great many things.

And now he regretted not admitting to Kayden how he truly felt about her—about the depth of love coursing through every fiber of his being for her. The arrogance had been knocked out of him long ago. He was far more mature now, and when it came to Kayden . . . *enraptured* didn't even come close. But because he loved her so much, he remained silent. She wasn't interested in him like that. Despite the gentle looks he caught now and again, she never indicated anything more. It was better than her previous animosity and distrust, but it wasn't love.

"The bride and groom will share their first dance as man and wife," the bandleader announced.

Cole and Bailey stepped onto the dance floor they'd set up on the sand—taking great pains to level it out perfectly and place it high enough on the beach that the shifting tide wouldn't touch it. Old-fashioned glass bulbs fanned out in strings over the dance floor, and white Chinese lanterns dotted the perimeter. "Greatest Story Ever Told," by Oliver James, played as the two danced.

Jake's gaze shifted to Kayden, watching from across the dance floor, the light of the lanterns shimmering off her golden skin and radiant complexion. The turquoise bridesmaid dress suited her perfectly, her long brown hair nearly covering the open back.

The song concluded, but Cole and Bailey remained wrapped in each other's arms.

"The bride and groom request the bridal party join them on the dance floor."

Kayden's gaze locked on his.

He smiled to squelch his nerves, but they only jangled harder. This was it. His excuse to dance with Kayden. Surely she wouldn't refuse. She kept her focus on him as he made his way around the dance floor to her side. Piper and Landon were already dancing, and Gage was taking Carrie Matthews' hand.

Kayden's hand. He'd finally be able to hold her hand, to touch her skin, to feel her near him—if only for the length of the song. And it was a great one. "You and Me," by Lifehouse.

His heart hammered in his throat as he stepped toward her, closing the distance between them.

She looked . . . nervous. Was she that uncomfortable about dancing with him?

"Hi," he said, reaching her side. *Hi? Wow.* He was the master of vocabulary tonight.

She brushed her hair behind her shoulder. "Hi."

"May I have this dance?" He held out his hand, praying he wasn't shaking as badly as he felt he was.

Without a word, she placed her hand in his— lithe fingers, velvety skin. She felt more delicate than he'd imagined. Not what he'd expected from a climber's hands.

He led her onto the dance floor, wishing he could lead her all the days of his life, but he'd settle for this perfect moment in time.

He cradled his hand along the supple curve of her back, just below the tip of her lush hair, the silky strands tickling the top edge of his fingers.

He placed her free hand on his shoulder, and they began to move in step with the melody, in step with each other.

The lights overhead reminded him of fireflies in the night during his summers spent with his grandparents down along the western shore of Maryland. His parents had shipped him out to his mom's parents while they took cruises, visited spas, and toured Europe.

Many children would have been hurt by being left behind, but he'd loved every minute of it. His grandpa had taught him how to fish, to track, and to camp. His grandmother had taught him about comfort, laughter, and joy—all of which were sorely missing from his proper parents' lives. Best of all, his grandmother had taught him to dance.

It started one night after he was supposed to be in bed. He heard music—the throaty crooning of Patsy Cline—and had snuck down to catch his grandparents dancing on the front porch beneath the full summer moon.

Grandma's favorite song had been "Fly Me to the Moon," because Grandpa had always spun her—just as Jake was spinning Kayden now, her long lush hair flowing. The soft hint of a smile on her lips warmed him, and his head spun faster than his body. How did she do that? Utterly captivate him . . .

She was breathtaking, and he prayed this moment would never end.

She lifted a glass off a passing tray. Quite a party the McKenna clan threw. She'd been hearing as much. Shame they didn't serve alcohol. She could use a stiff drink, but no matter. She took a sip of the wretched ice tea and moved closer to the dance floor, closer to them—the source of her problem. But not for long.

"Don't they make a handsome couple?" a man said beside her.

"Yes." She took another sip as Jake twirled Kayden around. Too bad they wouldn't live long enough to pursue a relationship. *Such a pity.*

— 17 —

The next morning, the whole family and a few friends gathered on the dock to see Cole and Bailey off for their honeymoon. Kayden would fly them to Anchorage before heading over to Imnek with Jake to continue their investigation.

Piper had decorated the inside of the plane with balloons and streamers as a fun send-off, but Kayden would be taking them down as soon as she dropped Cole and Bailey off at Anchorage International. She wasn't flying around all day with pink and purple fluff.

"I know you two will have an amazing time," Piper said, hugging Bailey. "I can't believe you're going to Australia. Take lots of pictures of koalas for me." If anything came in second to Piper's love of moose, it was koalas.

"I will," Bailey promised.

"Okay, Piper, let them go," Kayden said. "They'll only be gone two weeks."

Piper made her annoyed face. "I know. I'm just *so* excited for them."

And she was going to miss them. Kayden could read it on her sister's face. It was sweet how much she loved them all and enjoyed being with them, but it was only for a couple of weeks.

She turned to Cole. "We better get going if we're going to make your flight."

He nodded and scooped Bailey up in his arms. "Time to go, Mrs. McKenna."

Bailey laughed. "I think you can stop carrying me over thresholds now."

"Nope. You get the special treatment for at least another day, maybe another week." He pressed a long kiss to her lips.

"Okay, lovebirds." Kayden tried scooting them along while keeping her gaze off Jake. What was wrong with her? Every time she saw one of her siblings express affection with their partner, her mind went directly to Jake—wondering what his lips would feel like, longing to be back in his strong arms, to feel his hand splayed on her lower back while they danced.

Stop it! You will not swoon over Jake. Over anyone, for that matter.

But that was just it. She'd had boyfriends growing up, but she'd never *swooned* over anyone. Not until now. Not until Jake.

Kayden lifted off from Anchorage International Airport. They'd seen Cole and Bailey off to their connecting flight for Sydney, and after refueling and grabbing a bite of breakfast, she and Jake were on their way to Imnek. An entire day of just her and Jake together, with all the raw emotions of last night's dance still welling inside. *Great.*

"Some wedding," she said, feeling the need to fill the silence.

"Yeah." He smiled. "I especially liked the dancing."

Her mouth went dry, and she blindly scanned the instruments, even though the plane practically flew itself, struggling to think of something light-hearted to say. "Yeah. Gage puts on quite the show. I particularly enjoyed his 'Thriller' rendition."

Jake laughed. "That was hysterical."

Gage always was the life of the party. "And did you notice how he raced to Darcy's side after his obligatory dance with the matron of honor was over?" It was so sweet.

"Obligatory?"

"Yeah, you know, the obligatory wedding dance."

"Right. Obligatory." He shifted back in his seat. "I got it."

What was he . . . ? *Oh. Real smooth, Kayden.* She'd just made it sound as if she'd only danced with him out of obligation. In a way it was true. She never would have gone up and asked Jake to dance on her own, but what she'd felt during the dance was far from obligation. Her heart was still racing. When he'd cradled her back in the palm of his hand . . .

Gooseflesh rippled up her arm.

"You cold?" he asked, always too perceptive.

"No. I'm fine."

"I've got a jacket."

"No. Really. I'm not cold."

He studied her a moment, no doubt taking in the flush on her cheeks.

A slight smile curled on his lips, and she knew she'd been had. Fortunately he was a gentleman and didn't call her out, but the smirk dancing across his lips was painful enough.

She still hadn't told him about the creepy phone call or the footprints outside her window, and she almost wanted to let it just slide, knowing it would only distract him from the investigative plans he had for the day, but he'd want to know.

"Jake."

He looked over, his green eyes dazzling in the sun streaming through the Cessna's front window. "Yeah?"

"I need to tell you something."

He shifted toward her. "Okay."

"I would have said something sooner, but I didn't want to distract from Cole and Bailey's day."

"I knew it."

"What?"

"I could just tell something was bothering you." He rested his hand on the back of her seat. "What happened?"

She explained the phone call and footprints, then tried to read his stoic expression.

Jake clamped his hand on the headrest, his knuckles bulging. "Brody's just going to keep pushing until he ends up behind bars."

"That's just it." She swept her hair over her shoulder. "I don't think it was Brody."

"What? Why not? Because we didn't catch him leaving the note on our windshield?"

"You still think he left the note?"

Jake looked down.

"You don't—the pieces don't fit—so why is it so hard to believe the creepy call was someone else too?"

Jake looked at her, concern filling his face. "Because Brody's easy. Containable."

"And whoever called me?"

Jake swallowed. "Why do *you* think it was someone else?"

"Because it felt different."

"Like the spray-painted message?"

"Yeah. The banged-up propeller rang true for a bunch of guys buffed up on alcohol and testosterone—stupid, but not dangerous—but the messages, they felt darker."

Jake sighed, releasing his grip on the seat and folding his hands in his lap. "I agree."

"Then who do you think is sending them?"

"Conrad's killer."

"Meaning . . . Viv and Stuart?"

"They're a strong possibility."

"But . . . ?"

"I don't know." He shook his head. "I'm loath to trust my instinct after—"

"Rebecca." She reached out, touching his arm.

He closed his eyes, resting his hand over hers.

"I'm sorry," she whispered.

He nodded, letting the moment pass silently.

— 18 —

Jake wasn't sure if he was thankful for the interruption of his ringing phone or not. The moment he and Kayden had been sharing was one of the most profound of his life. She'd reached out to him in more ways than one, and his heart hadn't stopped hammering since.

"Cavanagh?" he said, the name becoming his own again.

"It's Booth."

"You got the results?"

"I could be calling to check up on you two kids," he said with humored pleasure.

"Kids? You aren't that old, old man."

"Old enough to be your father, but that's not why I'm calling."

"Tell me you've got good news."

"It's definitely good news for Natalie Adams."

"The sample was clean."

"Yes indeed."

"And you're sure it came from the same chalk block as Conrad Humphries'?"

"Exact match, minus the Dodecanol, of course."

"And you're positive?"

"Ran them twice."

It was good news for Natalie Adams, though who was to say she hadn't separated the chalk earlier than she claimed and added the Dodecanol? But what would her motive be?

Booth cleared his throat. "Thought you'd sound happier."

"Just not sure we've ruled anyone out." And the threats kept coming.

"Any luck with the suppliers?"

"No. Landon's still working that angle, trying to track any Dodecanol shipments made to Imnek in the last few months. At least we've been able to cross several off the list."

"How many more to go?"

Jake sighed. "A couple dozen."

"Landon's tenacious. He'll keep at it until he gets answers." Booth chuckled. "Reminds me of someone else I know."

As Jake hung up, Kayden said, "Samples were clean?"

"You got it."

"So where does that leave us?"

"We know the Dodecanol was added after arriving at Natalie's. I'm going to call Landon and get a warrant to search all areas of her shop and home, but I suspect we won't find anything."

"Then why go through it, and will you even be able to convince a judge to issue one now that the sample has come back clean?"

"Because we need to be positive, and it won't be easy." He smiled. "Actually, it might be a whole lot easier just to ask."

Jake had been right. Rather than insisting on being served a warrant in front of her staff or patrons as Brody had been, Natalie agreed to let Jake and Kayden search her work and home as long as she was present. Both had turned out clean—no sign of Dodecanol. Without its presence—or apparent motive—it was time to take Natalie Adams off their list of suspects.

"Where now?" she asked as Jake stepped to the driver's side door of their rental car.

"Back to Vivienne's."

"Any luck obtaining a warrant to pull her and Stuart's credit-card statements?"

"Landon went to the judge this morning."

"You really think if they did it, they'd be stupid enough to pay for Dodecanol with a credit card?"

"It's not something you can just walk into any store to get, and I doubt even if you could that the killer would go local. Imnek is too small a town for something like that. But just in case, Landon's running Dodecanol suppliers, searching for any deliveries to Imnek in the past six months, plus canvassing any local businesses that might have carried it."

"I heard you telling Booth. So no luck so far?"

"Only in crossing half a dozen suppliers off the list."

"I know it's frustrating, but it's still progress— narrowing down the suppliers. Are you also checking for deliveries to Anchorage?"

"Yes, specifically to Stuart Anderson's home and business addresses. He could have easily brought it down with him."

"The killer would need a decent amount of time with Conrad's chalk. Time to effectively blend the Dodecanol in," she said.

"How long would you say?"

"Twenty minutes, maybe more."

"So the killer would need access to wherever Conrad kept the chalk at home."

"Or they tampered with the chalk somewhere along his route. If he left his car long enough, unlocked, they would have had access to the chalk sitting in his vehicle."

"Vivienne said he went back to the office, which we know isn't true according to his secretary." Jake pulled a U-turn. "On second thought, let's pay Patty a visit first, see if Conrad was with her that night."

Once again they found Patty's bungalow-style house empty and took the winding stone path around to her backyard. The sun lit her silhouette in the greenhouse, and they rapped on the open door.

She glanced up from her work. "Great."

Jake stepped inside. "We've got a couple more questions for you."

"Lucky me." She brushed soil from her hands. "What is it this time?"

"When did you last see Conrad?"

"The night before his climb."

"Where?"

"Here at the house."

"How long was he here?"

"I don't know." She shrugged. "Maybe an hour."

"How'd you spend the hour?" Kayden asked.

Patty tilted her head. "How do you think?"

Kayden felt her face flush and was thankful when Jake continued the questioning without apparent reaction.

"We're trying to determine a timeline for the day before Conrad's climb," he explained. "We know he worked most of the day but left a few hours early according to his secretary. He swung by Rocktrex for a couple practice runs, stopped by Natalie's for chalk, went home for dinner, and then according to Vivienne, went back to the office. But you said he came here instead."

"What time did he arrive?" Kayden asked.

"Around six."

"Six?" That wasn't right. Vivienne said Conrad

had left after dinner. Around nine o'clock. "Are you sure?"

"Yeah. I invited him to join me and Shane for dinner afterward, but he had to go."

"Go where?"

"Home. Apparently Vivienne was making dinner for him and Stuart."

So he'd dropped by Patty's between buying his chalk at Natalie's shop and heading home for dinner with Stuart and Vivienne. "Did Conrad come back later?"

"Nope."

"His wife said he went out around nine for an hour or so. He claimed he was going to the office, but he didn't. We assumed he was with you."

"Afraid not."

"Any idea where he might have gone?"

"No clue."

Was it possible Conrad was seeing someone in addition to Patty Tate? Or had his work taken place someplace other than his office? And if so, why?

They were starting to lose traction. As questions were being answered, new ones were taking their place. The ex-employee-Kim angle had turned out to be a dead end. After losing her job with Conrad, she'd gotten a much higher-paying one over on Kodiak. She sounded thrilled and didn't express any ill will toward Conrad, according to the Kodiak deputy who had tracked her down and questioned her for them. When it came to Mrs. Humphries and ill will toward Conrad, Kayden had a feeling it was about to get much worse.

— 19 —

"Back again," Vivienne said through clamped pearly white teeth. Clearly someone had been using whitening strips. Perhaps leaving them on for a tad too long, or perhaps the deep red lipstick she wore made them appear brighter.

She glared at Kayden. "And I bet with more questions?"

"I'm afraid so." Jake looked past Vivienne, expecting to see Stuart. "Is Stuart here?"

"He's in the shower."

Jake's brows heightened.

"In the guest shower," she said with an unmistakable edge. "He's staying in our guest suite until the funeral."

"How thoughtful of him." At least they'd be able to question Vivienne alone, without any protests from Stuart.

"I assume these pleasantries aren't the questions you were referring to?"

"No."

"Fine. Let's get this over with. I have a nail

appointment in a half hour." She led them back into the parlor.

And her appointment would give them the opportunity to chat with Stuart alone. *Perfect.*

Jake decided the direct method was probably best. "We spoke with Patty Tate."

Vivienne glanced at her nails. "Oh?"

"She claims Conrad never broke things off with her."

Vivienne crossed her legs. "She's lying."

"How can you be certain?" Kayden asked.

"Because Conrad gave me his word."

Jake almost laughed out loud. How could the word of a cheater hold any weight? "I don't mean to be insensitive, but how do you know Conrad wasn't lying to you?"

An expression crossed Vivienne's face—a mixture of consideration and rejection warring for purchase. "He wouldn't do that."

Jake leaned forward. "I hate to be blunt, but I have to ask. Were you having an affair?"

Vivienne stiffened. "I don't see how that's any of your business."

That pretty much answered his question.

"It's pertinent to our investigation."

"Vivienne," Stuart said, entering the room freshly shaved and showered. "I insist you refrain from speaking with them without your lawyer present. This has gone far enough."

"I believe I will take Stuart's advice." Vivienne

stood and walked toward the door. "This conversation is over."

As soon as they exited the Humphries residence, Kayden said, "She might as well have admitted she was having an affair."

"The fact that she refrained from lying is wise on her part." Jake hesitated and looked back at the house.

"But . . . ?"

"I don't know. There's something lingering beneath the surface, but I can't put my finger on it." Something was off.

"With Vivienne and Stuart?"

"With this entire case."

— 20 —

Kayden settled on the loveseat in the family room, and to her surprise, Jake sat down beside her. Not that she was complaining, but it was the first time he'd done so when other seating was available. He was getting as comfortable around her as she was with him, and while a part of her loved it, it was scary. She needed to be careful. It was obvious Jake had strong feelings for her, and as much as she wanted to reciprocate those feelings —even if she did on the inside—she couldn't pursue them. She'd made her decision years ago, and she needed to stick to her resolution.

"How are the suspects looking?" Landon asked. The house was abuzz with all the siblings there, except the honeymooners.

Jake reclined. "To cover everyone . . . we have Brody—who is doing his best to look guilty, even though he most likely is not—Stuart, Vivienne, her and Conrad's two boys, the maid, Patty Tate, and possibly her son, if he was home with access to Conrad's chalk when Conrad visited Patty."

Kayden shifted to face him. "You can't possibly think Conrad's own boys or Patty's teenage son had anything to do with his murder, or the maid, for that matter, do you?"

"We can't rule anyone out without fully investigating. Conrad and Vivienne's boys don't climb, according to Vivienne, so they seem unlikely. Patty's son works at Rocktrex, so he'd have the knowledge, I suppose, but what possible motive could he have?"

"None that I can imagine," Kayden said.

Jake exhaled. "What we need to account for is Conrad's lost hour."

"Lost hour?" Landon asked, sitting on the couch beside Piper.

"According to Vivienne, Conrad left the house at around nine o'clock for an hour or hour and a half. He told her he was going to work. . . ."

"But he didn't?"

"His secretary says he wasn't at the office."

"So where was he?"

"Not with Patty Tate, according to her. And I can't imagine why she would lie about the timing," Jake said, shifting so he was even closer to Kayden.

She knew she should move, but she really, *really* didn't want to.

"Maybe Conrad went back to Rocktrex for another practice run," Jake said. "If so, then everyone present at Rocktrex at the time would have had access to his chalk. We never checked the logbook for that night. Only that afternoon."

"But why would Conrad go back?" Her brows arched. "You think he was nervous about the climb?"

Jake nodded. "He probably knew he was pushing his limits."

He had to have. She couldn't imagine someone with his level of experience being confident about a route as dangerous as Stoneface.

Jake set his coffee mug on the table as Darcy offered him a tray of chocolate-chip blondies. He grabbed one and placed it on his napkin. "Thanks. They look delicious."

"Kayden?" she asked.

She didn't want to hurt Darcy's feelings, but she didn't do desserts unless it was fruit or sorbet or had only natural ingredients. "I'm good, but thanks. They do look delicious."

Darcy smiled and moved on to Reef, who politely handed one to Anna before taking one for himself. Piper was right. He was changing. It was good to see and good to have him home. He was more like the sweet kid she remembered than the sullen young man he'd been for years. Anna was obviously good for him.

Gage snatched three blondies from the plate before Darcy sat down. "What?" he said, about to swallow one whole. "I'm a growing boy."

Kayden left off her usual "You got the *boy* part right." She was too focused on the case at hand and on Jake by her side. "So, now what?"

"We'll be paying Brody another visit, to see if Conrad went back to the gym that night."

"Brody will love that."

"We've got a warrant. He can balk all he wants."

"Speaking of warrants . . ." Landon swallowed his bite of blondie. "I got mine too. We can go through Vivienne's and Stuart's credit-card records."

Kayden shook her head. "Still seems dumb to me that they'd use their credit card to buy the Dodecanol. They had to know it would be traceable."

Jake rested his arm along the couch back. "It's not like you can order something over the Internet or phone with cash, and it's too obvious to purchase it anyplace local."

"I suppose you're right." She'd always given him a hard time about his surprising knowledge of criminal behavior, but after Darcy's revelation, Kayden now knew the story behind it. She didn't plan on questioning his knowledge ever again.

The rest of her family occupied in a lively game of Pictionary, Kayden snuck out to the porch swing with her cup of homemade all-natural cocoa.

She sank down onto the swing, always feeling closest to her mom there. It was the same weathered porch swing her mom had swung on with her when she was little. And it was the last place they'd had one of their talks before her mom's passing. It was an evident reminder of her mom and the close relationship they'd shared. She treasured it and spent a little time out on it each evening, weather permitting—though she wasn't one to mind a little rain or snow.

She pumped with her legs, getting the swing going.

"Mind if I join you?" Jake asked, stepping onto the porch.

She jolted, hadn't heard the kitchen door creak open. The man was stealthy. Too stealthy. If she wasn't careful he'd completely steal her heart—if he hadn't done so already.

She slowed the swing to a stop and scooted over.

He sat down beside her, the swing moving under his motion. "Nice night," he said in his luscious baritone voice.

Heat flushed her cheeks with a sudden rush, and she glanced up at the stars beaming bright overhead. "It's beautiful."

Feeling his intent gaze on her, she turned to stare at him, but he didn't look away.

"Not up for Pictionary?" she asked, trying to ease the tightness in her belly that seemed to come whenever Jake was near, or when someone brought up his name, or even when she smelled his cedar aftershave. . . .

He grasped the swing chain with his left hand, propping his elbow on the armrest. "I'm not into games."

Why didn't she think they were still actually talking about board games? "None at all? Maybe cards are more your style?"

"Directness is more my style."

"Now that *your* truth is finally out?"

He exhaled. "I'm sorry about that. About not being upfront with you all before. I was just trying to put the past behind me, to . . ."

"You don't have to explain." Certainly not to her. Not after the way she'd treated him for so many years.

"But I want to be upfront, with *you.*"

"I appreciate that." But she knew he hadn't been hiding things as much as trying to keep painful memories at bay.

"I'm sorry about your wife and baby." She shifted to face him better. She couldn't begin to imagine the loss. She'd dealt with plenty in her own life, but losing a child . . .

She'd witnessed the agony Gage had endured at the loss of his son. To think Jake had gone through that depth of pain—it physically made her heart ache.

Jake swallowed. "Thank you."

She had so many questions she wanted to ask, more cropping up each day. Right now the most prominent was whether he saw himself ever getting married again, but it seemed far too personal a question and way too inappropriate for the moment.

Besides, would his answer really make any difference one way or another? She was only fooling herself with hope. Yes, she had growing feelings for Jake. *Strong* feelings, but that didn't change the facts or her situation.

Laughter and yelling flooded out the open windows.

Jake smiled. "Sounds like some game."

McKenna games were hardly a spectator sport.

He inclined his head to the front path. "Want to take a walk?"

No. Say no. "Sure." *Sure? What are you doing?*

Jake moved down the front porch steps and paused, waiting for her to join him. She half wanted—okay, wholeheartedly yearned—for him to offer his hand the way he had last night when they'd danced, but he didn't. Instead he slipped his hands into his jean pockets.

Why did that make her so incredibly sad?

See. That was exactly why she refused to fall in love. Nothing good came of it. Unfortunately it appeared her heart hadn't gotten the message.

— 21 —

Rocktrex was crowded with every top line in use. Climbers waited on the blue mats for their turn, giving the usually open space a strongly congested feel. Kayden spotted Brody by the bouldering section and lifted her chin in greeting. He waved without an ounce of friendliness.

She blew a loose strand of hair from her face. *This ought to be fun.*

He held up a finger, indicating he'd be a moment.

She nodded and turned her attention to the small shop at the front of the gym. She scanned the racks while Jake surveyed the crowd. It mainly contained climbing clothing and gear, but Brody had also put in a natural remedies section, homemade products for climbers' ailments—lotions for rough, cracked skin; pumice stones for calluses; soaps for soothing tired hands. She picked up a bar. *Tate's Homemade Healers. Soothing sensations for cracked hands.*

She picked up another. *Moisturizing Madness for repairing wear and tear to climbers' hands.*

"Whatcha got there?" Jake asked so close behind her, she couldn't believe she hadn't heard him coming, even above the noise of the gym.

"Homemade products for climbers," she said, reading the label on Moisturizing Madness. "Didn't Booth say Dodecanol could be used as a moisturizer in soaps?"

"Yeah, he did." Jake smiled. "You think *Tate* is Patty Tate?"

"We can ask Brody."

"Shane told Patty another box of supplies arrived the first time we were at their house."

"Right, and she told him to put it in her workshop."

Brody had excused himself from his conversation and was moving their way.

Kayden held up the bar of soap. "Tate's Healers, as in Patty Tate?"

"One and the same," Brody said.

Kayden looked over at Jake with a smile.

Brody stopped and linked his arms across his chest, his feet in a military at-ease stance. "I assume you're not here to purchase soap?"

"Actually, I will take a bar," Kayden said.

"Okay," Brody said slowly.

"Can we ask you a couple more questions while I pay for this?" she asked.

"I imagine I don't have a choice." He led her

up to the register, where yet another teen was working.

"We believe Conrad was out somewhere between nine and ten thirty the night before his climb. Any chance he came back here for one more practice run?"

"Nah."

"Were you working that night?"

"Yes. Until close."

"So you would have seen him if he came in?"

"Absolutely."

Kayden paid the cashier for the soap and dropped it in her purse.

"We'd like to take another look at your logbook. Just to verify," Jake said.

"Whatever." He scoffed. "Kyle," he yelled to the kid behind the counter, "hand me the log-book."

Kyle complied, and Brody handed the book over to Jake.

He flipped to the day in question, and Kayden stepped alongside him to scan the record. Conrad had been in after leaving work, as everyone had said, but had never signed back in. Neither had Patty Tate.

Jake handed it back to Brody. "Thanks."

"Just get out of my gym."

Jake fought the urge to reach over and hold Kayden's hand as they walked over to Patty Tate's place. Ever since the dance, he'd been longing to hold her hand again, even if for the briefest of moments. The melody of the song still played through his mind whenever he saw her, the music bringing him right back to the moment and all the sensations wrapped up in it.

"Have you always enjoyed exercise?" he asked, trying to shift his mind off of that night.

"What?" Her nose crinkled. "Yeah, I suppose. I mean, we all grew up outdoors."

"Sure." He slipped his hands into his pockets —maybe that would lessen the temptation to reach for hers. "I mean *you,* though."

"What about me?"

He was trying to figure out what made her tick and why. Clearly he wasn't being direct enough.

"Do you like the outdoors because it's what your family does and that's how you grew up, or do *you* truly enjoy the outdoors?"

"I love being outdoors. Love running and climbing and kayaking." She studied him a moment. "What about you?"

"What about me?"

"I'm assuming you grew up in the city, in Boston. How'd a city boy get to be so at home in the outdoors?"

"Summers with my grandparents."

"Oh?"

"Yeah. They lived down on the western shore of Maryland, and I spent my summers with them."

"And your parents?"

"Would travel."

"Without you?"

"Yeah. They weren't much on having a kid—other than showing him off when it suited them."

"Oh." She kicked at the sand bordering the walk with her toe. "I'm sorry."

"It was what it was. They weren't horrible parents or anything—trust me, I've seen a *lot* worse." It was hard to explain. "They just weren't . . . involved."

She nodded.

He dipped his head, glancing up at her. "I wish I could have met your parents."

"Really? Why?"

"Because they must have been amazing."

"How could you know that? I mean, other than what we say about them, though I suppose that's enough."

"I know because they raised you." He smiled. "And Cole, Piper, Gage, and Reef."

"He's starting to change. Reef, I mean."

"I noticed that too." He'd also noticed the blush creeping up her cheeks when he'd said *you* and how she'd quickly moved on to a different topic.

"You must miss your folks."

She didn't look up. "Every day."

"I'm sorry." His parents were alive, but he hadn't seen them in years. They'd retired and moved up to Martha's Vineyard about the time he joined the force. They'd come into the city for his wedding and Becca's funeral, but no holidays, no weekend visits. And then, after the case was over, he'd left town without a word. . . .

"Thanks."

He let it go at that, not wanting to push, just thankful she'd shared as much as she had. They were making progress. Maybe he *could* hold a little hope in his heart. Was that so dangerous? Maybe one day . . .

His phone rang, cutting off that thought. He pulled it from his pocket and looked at the number. "Hey, Landon," he said, answering it. "What's up?"

"I just discovered that Conrad recently made a change to his life insurance policy."

"Oh?"

"Yeah. He added some beneficiaries."

"Okay?" Jake said, curiosity rattling through him.

"He added Patty Tate and her son, Shane."

"What?"

"Yep. The policy was to be split evenly between Vivienne and Patty, with each of their shares going to their children if anything should happen to them."

"I wonder if Vivienne knew."

"The change was just made last week. I'm waiting for a call back from Conrad's lawyer to see if a similar change was made to his will."

"Okay. Call us as soon as you hear."

"Will do."

"We're heading back over to Patty's to question her about the ingredients she uses in her hand-made soaps."

"Dodecanol on the list?"

"Here's hoping." Jake hung up, feeling like they were finally making progress.

"What was that all about?" Kayden asked, and he relayed the information.

"If that's the case, it would give Vivienne even more cause to be angry with Conrad."

"Absolutely. We'll have to follow up with her when we're done with Patty."

Kayden smiled. "Agreed."

— 22 —

"It'll be fun," Reef said, trying desperately to coax Anna into hiking with him. "We can take Rori. It'll be a blast."

How could he return home and not do any-thing active for his entire stay? He was itching to get out in the fresh air and move around. The only time they'd spent outside thus far was in his sisters' backyard and sightseeing downtown.

"Why don't we do some more sightseeing?"

He smiled. "There's only so much downtown in Yancey. You've seen it all. The rest of Tariuk is the outdoors. Believe me, it's gorgeous."

She ran her hand along the edge of the book she'd been reading.

Maybe Piper was right. Maybe he needed to be with someone who enjoyed adventure. Sitting around the house and shopping were not his idea of fun. But he genuinely liked Anna. She was so kind and sweet. If he could just get her a little bit active. It still baffled him how she could live surrounded by the beauty of Tahoe and couldn't care less about spending time in the outdoors.

"What do you say?" he asked, still hopeful.

She looked up at him with a smile. "We won't go for long?"

He sank down on the couch beside her. "Just a couple hours. I'd love to show you more of Tariuk. We'll take an easy hike. The views are amazing."

"Okay." She sat her book aside. "I'll give it a try."

"Great." He knew she'd love it once they were out there surrounded by lavender and fuchsia fields of fireweed, fresh air blowing through her hair, exertion warming her limbs. It'd be perfect.

Jake eyed the weathered wooden building that served as Patty Tate's workshop, a light emanating from inside.

Shane sat outside, working on his longboard—replacing the wheels. He eyed them but remained silent, sullen.

"Your mom in her workshop?" Kayden asked.

Shane nodded.

Jake looked at Kayden before rapping on the door, wondering what they were about to find.

"Come on in," Patty hollered. She stood with her back to them at a long, narrow wooden bench. Her shoulders were hunched as she stirred a creamy white liquid in a large steel bowl. One of her lotions, perhaps. She glanced over her shoulder and grimaced. "What do you want now?"

Jake scanned the countertops, Kayden doing the same, both looking for the murder weapon—a bottle of Dodecanol.

Kayden spotted it first, on a small shelf to Patty's right. Her eyes lit as she turned to Jake.

So this was it. He stepped forward. "Patty, I'm afraid I'm going to need you to come with me."

She looked up at them confused. "What? Why?"

"I think we just found the murder weapon." Jake slipped on his gloves and placed the Dodecanol in an evidence bag, sealing it.

"What are you talking about?"

"Conrad's killer mixed Dodecanol in with his chalk."

"But that would make his hands slippery rather than providing the friction he needed," she sputtered.

"Correct," Jake said, stepping toward her.

Patty stepped back, wiping her hands on a towel. "You got this all wrong. I didn't kill

Conrad. I use the Dodecanol in my soaps—it's a dry moisturizer."

Which is why it had worked in the chalk so well. Being a *dry* moisturizer hid the properties until it was too late.

"Come on, Patty. Game's up. We know Conrad added you and Shane to his life insurance policy last week. We know you had access to his chalk because he stopped over that night. And the murder weapon was sitting on your shelf."

Patty's brows pinched. "Conrad added us to his life insurance policy?" She looked genuinely perplexed.

"You're saying you didn't know?"

"No." Patty shook her head. "I had no idea. I can't believe he added us."

"So he added us to some dumb policy. Big whoop." They all turned to see Shane standing in the doorway.

Jake wondered how long the young man had been standing there and how much he'd overheard.

"He still treated you like a prostitute," Shane sputtered vehemently.

"Shane!" Patty's face turned bright red.

"What?" He shrugged. "It's true. He was never going to leave his prissy wife for you."

Patty walked to her son, smoothing his rumpled hair. "Where is this coming from?"

"Come on, Mom. You know it's true. You were always going to get his leftovers."

"You don't understand. Conrad loved us in his own way."

"Please," Shane huffed, and then turned to face Jake. "I'm the one that mixed Dodecanol in Conrad's chalk. Mom had nothing to do with it."

"Shane?" Patty stepped between Jake and her son. "What are you doing?"

"Sorry, Mom, but Dad was never going to come back when you were another man's whore."

She swatted him. "Don't call me that."

"Why? Everyone else in town does. Did you really think no one else in town noticed? I heard the gossip. All the juicy details. I saw you and Mrs. Humphries going at it in the square, and you know what, I'd had enough. When I heard Conrad say he loved you later that night, that he would take care of us but would never leave his precious Vivienne, I knew exactly where you stood with him, and I had to put an end to it."

"Shane, you don't understand."

"I understand plenty. I heard Conrad bragging about his upcoming climb, and I knew my opportunity had finally come. I did a little research, borrowed some of your stuff, and mixed it in with his chalk."

Jake pulled out his handcuffs, his heart heavy. "Shane Tate, you are under arrest for the murder of Conrad Humphries."

"No." Patty lunged for Jake. "Stop. You've got this all wrong."

— 23 —

Patty raged against Jake as he steered Shane toward his and Kayden's rental car. He opened the door and guided Shane into the backseat. Patty pushed past Kayden as she tried running interference.

"Get out of my way," Patty hollered, tossing in a few expletives at Kayden that curdled Jake's blood.

Shutting the car door, he turned to Patty. "Never speak to her that way again."

Patty got right in his face, belligerent. "I'll speak to your girlfriend any way I please."

"She's not my—"

"Let it be," Kayden said. "Our relationship is none of her business."

Our relationship? Had she . . . ? Was she . . . ? He tried not to stagger back.

"My son is very much my business, and you two are making a *huge* mistake." Patty dodged around them to the car window, rapping on the glass. "Shane, tell them you didn't do this. Now!"

Shane turned his head the other way.

She whirled around on Jake. "You can't take him. I won't allow it."

"I'm afraid you don't have a choice. He's now

in my custody, and I'm taking him back to the sheriff station in Yancey."

"Not without me, you aren't. You think you're so superior. Acting all cocky. Well, Shane's a minor, and I know our rights."

"You have the full right to get yourself to the station. I am under no obligation to allow you to accompany us there. If you have a lawyer, I'd give him or her a call."

"You're going to wish you were only dealing with my lawyer when I get through with you both."

"If you don't calm down, I'm going to have to lock you up," Thoreau said, dealing with the still-belligerent Patty Tate as Jake joined Landon in the interrogation room at Yancey's sheriff station. Kayden would be watching from the adjacent room, behind the two-way glass. It was hard to believe seven months earlier Reef had sat in the same interrogation room opposite Landon.

"Who are you?" Shane asked Landon.

"I'm Sheriff Grainger. I'd like you to tell me what you told Deputy Cavanagh."

"I killed Conrad Humphries."

He said it so coolly, so matter-of-factly, Jake wondered if he wasn't covering for his mom. No mother would let her son take the rap for her, but if Shane believed his mom had killed

Conrad, he could very well be acting on that even if she didn't do it.

Patty had insisted they wait to question her son until their lawyer arrived, but Shane waived his right to have a lawyer present. He was ready and eager to talk, but Jake and Landon decided not to question him until the lawyer arrived, just to make sure they did everything by the book.

"I don't want to make this any harder on my mom than it already is. There's no need to drag it out."

"Your mom has called Daniel Waters."

"And he is . . . ?"

"He *was* Conrad's lawyer."

"Great." Shane rolled his eyes. "She's still depending on him."

"Here." Landon slid a legal pad and pen to Shane. "Feel free to write down what you told Deputy Cavanagh while we wait for Mr. Waters to arrive."

Jake stepped with Landon into the hall, where Kayden met them.

"He's so cold, so detached," she said.

"He was too far removed from the actual crime," Jake explained.

She gaped at him. "He murdered a man. How can he possibly be removed from it?"

"All he did was compromise the chalk. He wasn't present for the results of his actions. Wasn't there to see Conrad die. It makes it easier to detach, to be more clinical." It didn't make it any less wrong. He'd still killed a man, but not being present left out a lot of the raw emotion he'd expect to see under different circumstances.

"Why do you think Conrad added Shane to his life insurance policy too?" Landon asked.

"If you love a woman, you love her child," Jake said. "He probably promised Patty that even though he'd never leave Vivienne, he'd still make sure she and Shane were taken care of."

"I wonder how Vivienne's going to react when she finds out—if she hasn't already."

"She won't react well. Not if her character holds true."

"How much money does Vivienne stand to lose because of the changes?"

"A lot," a man said behind them.

They all turned to find Daniel Waters standing there.

"How's it going, Daniel?" Jake asked. Daniel had taken several Last Frontier Adventure fly-fishing trips Jake had led.

"I'd be better if you hadn't talked to my underage client without legal representation."

Landon stepped forward. "Shane confessed to the murder of his own accord, with his mother present—and we haven't questioned him here at the station."

The cockiness faded from Daniel's scowl. "Where is he now?"

"Alone in the interrogation room. I've got a deputy posted on the other side of the two-way glass to make certain he doesn't try anything rash."

Daniel sighed. "All right. I'll need a few minutes to confer with my client in private."

"Of course. I'll pull the deputy from the observation room and cut the mic feed."

Daniel nodded as Landon reentered the observation room.

"Wait a sec," Kayden said. "What did you mean when you said Mrs. Humphries stood to lose a lot by Conrad changing his life insurance policy?"

Daniel frowned. "Life insurance policy? I was referring to Conrad's will. Are you saying he added Ms. Tate and her son to the life insurance policy as well?"

"Yes."

"Conrad didn't say anything about that to me the other night, but I suppose it makes sense."

"The other night?" Jake watched a spark ignite in Kayden's eyes. She was on the trail of something, and he was going to let her run with it.

"Yes. Conrad insisted he needed to change his will as soon as possible. My office hours are booked for weeks, but Conrad's an old friend, so I met him after hours the other night."

"Which night?"

Daniel sighed. "The night before he died."

"Around nine?" Kayden asked.

"Yes." He frowned. "How'd you know?"

She turned to Jake. "The missing hour."

He nodded and looked back at Daniel. "You said changing his life insurance policy makes sense. Makes sense, how?"

"Because of the circumstances. If you're going to change one, you might as well make the change on all estate assets. Though, if Shane is convicted of murder—and I'm not saying he will be; nor is that any indication of his guilt—but if murder is involved, that voids his share of the life insurance policy."

"Which was?"

"I don't know. You'd have to talk to his money manager or insurance agent for that, but I know that when he altered the will he left Vivienne and her boys fifty percent and Patty and Shane the other fifty percent."

"Wow," Kayden said. "That's really generous to Patty and her son."

Daniel adjusted his belt and looked around. "That's just it." He pushed his hand through his thinning hair. "Shane wasn't only Patty's son."

"What are you saying?"

"Shane was Patty and *Conrad's* son."

"How's that possible?" Kayden asked. "Patty said she'd just met Conrad a few years ago."

"Actually," Jake said, replaying the conversation back in his mind, "what she said was 'when Conrad first came *into the gym* a few years ago.' "

"So you think that wasn't the first time they

met? That the two had a relationship years ago resulting in Shane's birth and then decided to pick it back up years later?"

"Conrad first met Patty when they were both living in Anchorage," Daniel said. "He was an up-and-coming hedge-fund manager, and Patty was a student at U of A, Anchorage. They came from two different worlds, and Conrad was already engaged to Vivienne at the time. But he said he fell head over heels for Patty. He was going to break it off with Vivienne, but his father said if he didn't follow through on his commitment to Vivienne—whose parents were close personal friends—he'd cut him completely out of the family business, not to mention his will."

"So he left Patty pregnant?"

"According to Conrad, he never knew Patty was pregnant. She didn't find out until a month after they split, and by then Conrad and Vivienne were married, so Patty decided to raise Shane on her own."

Kayden frowned. "Then how . . . ?"

"Patty moved to Imnek to live with an aunt while pregnant, to have family near as she was adjusting to life as a single mom. Conrad and Vivienne had two boys of their own, and Patty married a guy named Steve Tate when Shane was still a baby. He raised Shane as his own, though he proved to be a lousy husband, according to Patty."

"Okay, so how did Conrad and his family end

up in Imnek? And, how did he discover Shane was his son?" Jake asked.

"Conrad saw an article in *Alaska* magazine about a climbing championship Patty had just won. There was a picture of Patty and Shane in the article."

"And that was enough?"

"Enough to make him curious. Shane has his eyes. He made a trip down to Imnek and confronted Patty. She told him Shane was his, but that she didn't want him in their lives."

"But Conrad didn't listen?" Kayden said.

"He made up some business excuse for why he and Vivienne had to relocate to Imnek and then started pursuing Patty."

"That's why he joined the gym and learned to climb."

Daniel nodded. "It got him time with Patty and the boy."

Kayden linked her arms across her chest. "I'll say he was determined if nothing else."

"Conrad was a bulldog when he set his mind to something."

The realization of the full depth of the situation kicked Jake in the gut. "Does Shane know?"

"As far as I know, Patty hasn't told him," Daniel said. "But you'd have to ask her."

Kayden looked to Jake. "Shane killed his own father. How do you live with something like that?"

— 24 —

"No," Patty seethed, swiping at her eyes with the back of her hand. "I never told Shane."

"Why not?" Jake asked.

"Because I wanted to protect him. He'd already lost one dad when Steven left—I didn't want him having to go through that again if Conrad decided to leave." She slumped into a chair, her hair frazzled, her clothes askew from nearly wrestling with Thoreau. "Maybe I should have."

She looked up at Jake, eyes full of venom. "Regardless, Shane didn't do this. He couldn't have."

"He confessed."

"To cover for me, no doubt."

"Are you saying you killed Conrad?"

"No. I'm saying Shane must have heard you stating the evidence against me and came to my rescue. We're all each other has. You can't do this."

"I don't have a choice."

Patty stood, her eyes narrowing, her sharp features taking on a hard edge. "We all have a choice. I suggest you make the correct one."

"That sounded like a threat."

Patty cocked her head. "I'm simply asking you to do the right thing."

"I am. Your son confessed."

Her jaw tightened. "I told you, you have the wrong person. I will not allow you to take my son from me—whatever it takes. Do you hear me?"

"That's enough, Patty," Daniel said from the doorway. "We need to talk."

Patty glared at Jake and Kayden before doing as the lawyer instructed.

Kayden rubbed her arms. "Was it just me, or did Patty suddenly go creepy on us?"

"Definitely nasty," Jake said.

"He is her only son. I imagine a mother will do just about anything to protect her child."

"I can't imagine how Shane's going to feel when he learns the truth."

"The shock of discovering you killed your own parent . . ." She couldn't imagine. Couldn't imagine the thought of wanting to kill someone in the first place. Plain scary how easily Shane had moved from anger to murder.

Kayden waited in Jake's office while he, Patty, and Daniel broke the news about his parentage to Shane. She was utterly grateful not to be present for that conversation.

She walked the perimeter of Jake's office, noting the lack of personal items. No pictures or mementos of any kind. She wondered what his office in Boston had been like. What kinds of pictures had decorated his walls?

She moved to his chair with his jacket draped over the back and sank into it. Swiveling around, she spun a couple times for decompression, then settled facing his desk.

Jake stood, leaning against the doorframe, a gentle smile on his handsome face.

She straightened. "Sorry, I was just—"

"You're fine. I'm glad you made yourself comfortable."

"How'd it go?"

Jake grimaced.

"That bad?"

"Let's just say poor Shane has a lot to deal with."

"Did he change his story any?"

"Nope, but Patty's become more volatile, insisting we have the wrong person and need to let Shane go."

"Or what? Did she actually threaten this time?"

"She didn't go that far, but was just short of it. Told me she wasn't going to let me take her only son from her."

"O . . . k . . . a . . . y."

"Moms are protective. She's just doing and saying what she feels she needs to, to keep her boy safe."

"What's going to happen to him?"

"Landon's booking him now. There'll be an arraignment tomorrow, where he'll be formally charged and a trial date set."

She pulled her hair over her shoulder, needing something to fidget with. She started braiding. "It's all so crazy. You think Shane left those messages?"

"I guess he was trying to make Brody look guilty."

"He was at the gym that day. He could have slipped out and left that note on our car."

Jake exhaled. "I just pray this is the end of it."

She narrowed her eyes, a sick feeling settling in her stomach. "What do you mean?"

"I've got a bad feeling this one isn't over yet."

Waiting was agony, but she couldn't rush this. She needed to wait for the right opportunity. Jake Cavanagh had taken someone she loved with his meddling. It was only fair that she repay the favor in kind. The perfect moment would present itself soon enough, and then she'd strike. No more beautiful Kayden McKenna.

Such a shame, but inevitably necessary.

— 25 —

"I still can't believe Shane killed his own father," Piper said, passing the salad.

Kayden took it and put some on her plate. She really wasn't feeling very hungry. "He didn't know Conrad was his dad."

Landon snagged a roll from the basket before Gage scooped them up. "Any way you look at it, murder is murder."

"I know." Piper drizzled Gage's raspberry vinaigrette dressing over her salad. "It just makes it all the more horrific realizing you killed your own father, I would think."

"Sadly, it happens more than you realize," Jake said, spearing a forkful of salad.

Piper shook her head. "I couldn't fathom hurting any human being, but your own family . . ." She shuddered.

"Goes all the way back to Cain and Abel," Landon said.

The day had been rough—seeing Shane's lack of remorse, his cold withdrawn stare, and Patty's belligerent threats. The urge to pray welled inside, and Kayden lowered her head while her siblings talked around her.

Please, Father, I love my family so much. I know I'm not the best at showing it, but please

let them know I love them. Please protect them.
And Jake too . . .

She glanced over at the man who had stolen her heart.

Please bring healing and renewal to his life. I so want to see him happy and at peace.

She bit down on the homemade dinner roll Darcy had made. It wasn't as good as Gage's, but she was learning quickly. The two had spent the day holed up in the kitchen preparing tonight's McKenna family feast—salad with homemade vinaigrette, fresh rolls, Gage's seven-layer lasagna, and for dessert, homemade cannoli.

She'd caught a glimpse of them, sprinkled with powdered sugar, with miniature chocolate chips mixed in the filling, and her stomach had done a flip. She had to remain good. She was a health nut—as her siblings labeled her—for a reason, and she couldn't deviate from it.

"How is it?" Darcy asked.

Kayden looked at Darcy's expectant eyes, then to the roll in her hand. "Delicious."

Darcy smiled.

"She's a fast learner," Gage said, clasping Darcy's hand and rubbing his thumb along her skin. The two were so in love. Who would have thought all of her siblings would find love, even Reef.

Speaking of Reef . . .

"Shouldn't Reef and Anna be back by now?"

According to Piper, the pair had taken the girls' husky, Rori, for a hike out on the south side of Tariuk.

"You know Reef." Gage slathered another roll with butter. It was a wonder he was as in shape and toned as he was, considering the way he ate. *Ridiculous.*

"The guy's an animal," Gage said. "He could hike all day." He bit into the roll, swallowing half of it in one bite.

A smile tugged at Kayden's lips. "He's not the only animal around here."

"What?" Gage smirked. "I'm a growing boy." He popped the rest of the roll in his mouth.

She laughed. "You're a mess."

Reef helped Anna over the rise. Perspiration dotted her brow and boredom her expression. How could she be surrounded by such beauty and not be enamored?

They'd gotten a later start to the day than he'd hoped. A much later start, but it was good. With only a few hours of daylight left, it'd help him keep his promise to Anna of only taking a short hike. And he could use all the help he could get. Once he was outside, it was so hard to curtail his time. He could go for days, but he'd honor his promise to Anna.

Rori whimpered on the leash at his side, looking as miserable as Anna.

He sighed. Piper had said to keep her on the leash, but they were in the middle of nowhere, with no one around. What harm could it do?

He let Rori off the leash, and she bounded through the fireweed like a young pup.

"Aren't the fields gorgeous?" Waves of fuchsia rolled along streams of green.

Anna swatted at a bug humming nearby. "Beautiful."

They crossed to the other side and headed for the hiking path that wound back down the mountainside to their car at the trailhead.

Reef whistled for Rori, and she returned, springing in front of them. Anna held tightly to Reef's hand, anxiety rather than enjoyment fixed on her sweet face.

"You aren't enjoying yourself, are you?" He'd hoped once they were outside that she'd come around, that she'd see the beauty of being enveloped by nature.

"I'm sorry. Walking around in the dirt just isn't my idea of fun. But . . ." She rubbed his hand in hers. "I'm happy to be sharing the time with you."

"Me too." He smiled. He just wished she were enjoying herself at least a little bit.

A half mile into their descent to the car, Rori's tail shot up, and she growled as she stalked to the edge of the ridge.

"What do you hear, girl?" He stepped toward

the husky, glancing over the ridge to the steeply declining drop-off below, trees and brambles clinging to the sharply angled hillside.

He didn't see or hear anything, but Rori clearly did.

She whimpered and then, before he could grab her collar, bolted over the edge.

"Rori, no!" he hollered, but it was too late. She was gone.

"Sure you don't want one?" Gage asked Kayden while dangling a cannoli in front of her.

"No. I'm fine."

"Okay. If you're sure." He took a bite, and then smiled. "More for me."

Kayden shook her head, but Jake could see she was eyeing the cannoli. She wanted one. But she never ate anything made with refined sugar or white flour or . . . The list went on. It was admirable that she wanted to eat so healthfully, but the rigidness of her diet coupled with her insane exercise regime made Jake wonder if she wasn't pushing it too hard.

Kayden settled back in the oversized armchair with a cup of green tea in hand. "Seven still good?" she asked Piper.

"Oh, I forgot to tell you. Thelma Jenkins has her root canal tomorrow. Her niece Susan was going to take her, but her son got sick. Thelma refuses to go alone, so I said I'd take her. I'm sorry."

"No worries. I'll just climb by myself."

"Kayden, you know that isn't smart or safe," Gage said. "I'd go with you, but I'm running the shop tomorrow."

"I'll go with you." The words were out of Jake's mouth before he considered their import. Of course he'd love to go climbing with Kayden, love to have more time with her, but where the two of them working alone on the case had been a necessity, this would be more like a . . . *date.* His heart hitched.

Kayden shrugged a shoulder. "Okay."

Shock rocketed through him. "Okay?" He blinked. Was he dreaming?

"I'll pick you up at seven."

He swallowed and sat back, thankful for the support of the chair beneath him. "Okay." He could feel everyone else's shocked gaze darting between him and Kayden, and he couldn't blame them one bit.

After helping clean up the dishes, Kayden headed to Nanook Haven. She pulled into the dirt parking lot and stepped from her car into the crisp night air.

Rex bellowed from the barn. He knew she was there.

She pulled her fleece on and headed for the blue barn, finding Kirra and Carol inside. The ladies were finishing up the nightly chores—

feeding the dogs dinner, cleaning their stalls, and giving them fresh water.

Rex pawed his stall door at the sight of her.

"Just a minute." She smiled.

"He's been pacing for the last half hour," Carol said. "Only wants you."

Kirra shut off the hose, lifting a bowl of water and carrying it to Rex's stall.

"It's because she's the only one who can keep up with him."

Rex ignored the water, his gaze fastened on Kayden.

"I'm going to drop by around six tomorrow morning instead of seven."

Kirra smiled. "Got plans?"

"Going climbing."

Carol shook her head. "I don't know how you get up the nerve for that. Seems so dangerous."

"It's all part of the fun."

"Danger is fun?" Kirra furrowed her delicate brow.

"I prefer to look at it as adventure." Kayden grabbed Rex's leash from the wall.

"A girl who likes danger," Carol said, wiping her hands on a towel. "That's kind of like playing with fire."

"Eventually you get burned," Kirra said with an unexpected heaviness.

"Have you gotten burned?" Kayden asked, sounding more like her overly curious sister than herself, but Kirra intrigued her. Something had happened while she was in vet school, something that changed her. Kirra never spoke about it, but she had come back from her final semester different.

Kirra smiled sadly, but otherwise ignored the question. She let Rex out of his stall, and he came bounding to Kayden's side. "You better get going. Rex is more than ready for his run."

"Sure." Kayden snapped his leash on. In the mornings she let him run free, but at night, back in the woods, it was important to stay on the path. "Sorry if I—"

Kirra held up a hand. "No worries. Have a nice run." She turned and headed for the barn office.

She'd pried where she shouldn't have. "Clearly I've been spending too much time around Piper."

"Her curious nature is wearing off on you?" Carol smiled.

"Did I mention she was curious?"

Carol laughed. "Only a dozen times."

"Well, I just stuck my nose where it didn't belong."

"Yeah." Carol glanced back at the small office Kirra had set up in the barn. "That one likes to keep things close to the chest."

"People say that about me."

"Really? I haven't found that to be true."

Probably because Carol was so easy to talk to— sort of like the aunt she'd never had.

Rex pawed the ground with a grunt.

"I hear you," Kayden said with a laugh. "See you later, Carol."

" 'Bye now." Carol waved as Kayden and Rex broke into a run, racing across the paddock and into the woods.

She loved to run. Had been at it ever since her dad's heart attack. It was her way to get away from it all. Just her and her heart hammering in her chest, her breath coming in short, even bursts. But then her mom had died, and her runs had shifted. She'd start out fine, but within minutes tears would fill her eyes, making the world around her hazy, which in a weird way felt right, because everything around her felt off-kilter . . . in upheaval. In the days and weeks after her precious mom's death, she'd run until her tears were so thick she could barely see.

Now she ran because it kept her fit, in control of her health, and still provided her some time alone, where she could allow herself to feel, to cry, to scream, or simply smile, as she was doing right now.

She'd said yes to Jake. Tomorrow, for the first time since he'd entered her life, the two of them would be alone just for the fun of it. She'd tried to make her response casual, like it was no big deal, but it was. It was huge. She shouldn't have said yes, but she couldn't help herself. She craved time with the man.

Forty minutes later, Rex broke through the tree line, and she followed—her heart racing, her pulse elevated, sweat clinging to her skin, her lungs pumping out air. She felt so alive.

"Good run?" Kirra asked, as a flash of light swished across Kayden's eyes.

That added an extra little jump to her heart.

"Sorry." Kirra stood less than ten feet away. "Didn't mean to startle you. Carol mentioned a loose board out here, and I wanted to check it out before I forgot."

"No problem." Kayden paced back and forth, giving her heart time to slow down. "Hey, about earlier. I—"

"Don't mention it." Kirra hammered in the nail.

She nodded, wishing she'd kept her mouth shut. "You need any help with that?"

"Nope." Kirra slid the hammer into her belt loop. "All done."

She moved in step with Kayden as they followed Rex back to the barn. The husky's pace was more a lope than the usual gallop.

"Looks like you may actually have worn Rex out."

Kayden laughed. "I think it's the other way around."

"Kayden!" a male voice hollered.

She squinted toward the parking lot. "Reef?"

— 26 —

Reef rushed toward the barn. Was that Rori in his arms?

"What's wrong, Reef?" She raced toward them, Kirra at her side. "What happened?"

"We were hiking. Rori latched on to something and took off."

"You didn't have her on her leash?"

"Piper said your vet was here?"

"I'm the vet," Kirra said. "Let's get her into an exam room."

"Unless we're on our property and she's used to the smells, Rori always has to be on the leash," Kayden said as they moved for the vet clinic doors. "Piper should have told you that."

"She did, but Rori looked miserable."

"She wasn't miserable. She was just pouting. You ignore her and she gets over it."

"I'm so sorry."

She just prayed Rori was okay. It was too dark to see the extent of her injuries.

"In here." Kirra unlocked the office building, switching on the lights as she led them back to an exam room.

Rori was bleeding, a lot. Kayden couldn't tell if it was her leg or paw. She whimpered as Reef laid her on the exam table.

She fought the urge to call Reef irresponsible,

because it was plain from his pained expression that he already felt awful.

Kirra bent over, examining Rori.

"What's wrong with her, Kirra?" Kayden asked impatiently.

She looked up at Reef, her frustration and displeasure evident.

Reef's eyes narrowed. "Kirra . . . Jacobs?"

"Hello, Reef. I see you haven't changed. Still your irresponsible, reckless self."

Kirra had loved and cared for Rori since she was a pup. It was no surprise her hackles had risen at Reef, but what she didn't understand was how much Reef had changed and was changing still.

"I could say the same about you," he countered. "Still judgmental, I see."

She opened her mouth to argue.

"Seriously?" Kayden said, needing to nip their spat in the bud.

"Reef?"

Kayden turned to find Anna—no more than five foot tall, slender, and blond—standing in the doorway, her T-shirt splattered with Rori's blood. "Is she okay?"

"She will be," Kirra responded.

Anna rubbed her arms. "Can we go back to the house now?" she asked.

"I'd like to stay until Rori's fixed up."

"Typical Reef." Kirra shook her head. "Always expecting an easy fix."

Reef's shoulders tightened. "We haven't seen each other in, what . . . like seven years. I'm not the same person I used to be."

"Uh-huh." Kirra used gauze to soak up the blood oozing from Rori's paw. "The evidence would suggest otherwise."

"Reef?" Anna said, more whine in her tone this time.

"Here, take my car." He handed her the keys. "Make a right out of the driveway, and it's a straight shot back to the house."

"Are you sure?"

"Positive. It's been a long day. Head on back. Get a hot shower and something to eat."

"We saved some lasagna for you,"Kayden said.

"I'll be back as soon as we're done here," he promised.

"Okay." She pressed a kiss to his cheek and turned to leave without another word.

For the next half hour Kirra worked on Rori with love and expertise, cleansing, suturing, and bandaging her torn paw and then setting her leg. "I think it'd be best if you left Rori with me for a couple days. Just to help keep her comfortable and her leg immobile."

"Piper will—"

"Hate the idea," she said from the doorway.

Kayden spun around. "Piper, what are you doing here?"

"I'm here for Rori." She stepped to the table,

tears in her eyes. "Is she going to be okay?"

Kirra rested a reassuring hand on Piper's shoulder. "She's going to be just fine."

Though loath to do so, Reef had to admit Kirra Jacobs was impressive.

She had taken great pleasure in torturing him through grade school, middle school, and even on into high school. She was a goody-goody and so judgmental. Clearly not much had changed—other than losing her knobby knees and braces and growing into a beautiful woman.

Kayden was talking with Piper in the hall, leaving him and Kirra alone in the exam room.

He felt horrendous for not listening to Piper and then seeing Rori get hurt because of his stupid mistake. He was surprised Kayden had not reamed him out, even though he deserved it. Kirra had, of course, leapt at the chance—but he was thankful for her skill. "You did good," he said, the words surprisingly not that hard to say.

"Thanks." Kirra turned off the faucet and dried her hands. "Look, Reef, I'm sorry if I was—"

"Harsh?"

She smiled. "Yes, harsh, but I hate seeing an injured animal, and if the injury was preventable, it's extremely frustrating."

"I didn't mean for Rori to get hurt."

"Of course you didn't, but if you'd listened to Piper . . ."

"Believe me, I know."

Her eyes narrowed.

"What?"

"Nothing."

"No. What?" She clearly had something to say. Kirra Jacobs *always* had something to say.

"It's just, when you'd get caught at something at school, you were quick to apologize, but . . ."

"But?"

"You lacked sincerity and follow-through."

"So you're trying to figure out if I'm really sorry or if I'm just feeding you a line."

Kirra didn't say anything. She didn't have to. That was exactly what she thought.

Jake tossed on his bunk in the trawler's master cabin. He'd called the old boat home for close to a year now, and it was his haven. The water in the harbor was calm tonight, just a gentle lulling. If only he felt as calm on the inside. His heart hadn't stopped hammering since Kayden said yes to his offer to accompany her on her climb.

It wasn't an official date, but it was the two of them alone for the first time just for fun—no work and no case. Just them.

His palms were already clammy, and he still had six hours before Kayden picked him up, but all he could think of was her.

— 27 —

After a quick stop at Nanook Haven to check on a recovering Rori and help with morning chores, Kayden pulled up to the harbor for Jake a little after seven. He stood waiting for her with a cooler in hand at the end of the pier, the sun rising in the sky behind him. It was full and orange and promised a beautiful day. She needed a beautiful day—one free of killers and creepy messages. Shane Tate was behind bars, and their investigation had concluded, so why didn't she feel more at ease?

She stopped her SUV, leaned over, and opened the passenger door for Jake. "What's that?" She gestured to the cooler.

He lifted it up with a smile. "I packed us some food."

"That was thoughtful." All she'd brought was bottled water and a protein bar.

"I figured we'll need to eat at some point." He shrugged a shoulder, much as she had last night when he'd offered to accompany her on the climb. "Thought I'd carry it in my pack and we could eat at the summit."

"Like a picnic?" She'd seen Piper go on several romantic picnics and had secretly yearned to be taken on one. It was silly and a tad cliché, but it was something she'd always wanted to do. However, the few men she'd dated had been far too practical for picnics. Practical she liked, but lack of imagination, not so much.

"If you'd prefer to eat in the truck, we can," he said at her prolonged silence.

She waited while he climbed in the 4Runner beside her, placing the cooler in the backseat. "No, a picnic sounds nice."

"Yeah?" he said with a hint of surprise.

"Yeah."

The temperature was only going to make it up into the low sixties, which made for a perfect climbing day. The sky was clear, and though there was a chance of rain showers in the evening, they'd come through long after the climb was done. They were headed for the far side of the mountain range to an isolated area she enjoyed. While she wasn't positive that isolation was a good thing, she refused to care. She was going to enjoy the day in Jake's company and let everything else fade away for a few hours. It was frighteningly freeing.

"So how does it feel to have solved your first case back in the saddle?" she asked as they hiked from the trailhead to the base of the climb.

Back in the saddle? Was he really back? He'd told Landon it was one case and one case only, but he had to admit it felt good being in law enforcement. Felt exhilarating and right doing what he'd been born to do. And it felt even better with Kayden at his side. Could he really start fresh? Become a cop again? Pursue a relationship with the woman his heart beat for?

God redeemed, renewed—he'd seen it, witnessed it in Gage in particular—so maybe the same hope awaited him, but the possibility seemed too good to be true.

The sun was warm on his skin, the air fresh. So far they hadn't passed anyone and no other vehicles had been parked in the lot. Maybe they'd have the climb to themselves today. The thought thrilled him. Kayden, of course, would be free-climbing, but for this 5.7 route, he'd be on belay. New as he was, safety had to come first. Kayden had been training and climbing for years. He couldn't just jump in at her level. In fact, he'd probably never reach her level, but he liked sharing in something she loved so ardently. It made him more a part of her world, and he treasured that.

They reached the cliff base in under an hour and found they had it all to themselves.

Kayden fitted her harness around her waist. "I'll climb up first and belay you from the top."

He nodded. He had no complaints about getting to sit back and watch her climb. She was amazing—an exquisite combination of strength, agility, and grace. She took his breath away.

She coiled the rope she'd use to top-belay him, secured it to her harness, and smiled at him, sending warmth through his limbs. "See you at the top."

"Have a good climb." He winked and sat back to watch.

Finding her first foothold, she pushed up, grabbing a notch in the rock and moving swiftly from foothold to foothold, using her arm strength only when necessary. She reached an overhang, and he temporarily lost sight of her.

He waited, his eyes fixed on the granite face, and when she appeared atop the overhang, the anxiety in his chest loosened momentarily, until a rumble sounded overhead. His chest seized, his eyes widening in horror at the rockslide headed straight for Kayden. He screamed her name, scrambling up the rocks.

She disappeared beneath the rocks as they bounced on the ledge. A few plunged toward him, but he avoided them.

Please keep her on the ledge. The hundred-foot drop would kill her for certain.

He scrambled up the face, twenty feet to the right of Kayden's climb route, to find a less difficult ascent. He prayed the rocks hadn't crushed her, prayed he would make it up to help her.

Father, I know even this route is beyond me. Please intervene and give me the ability to climb it. Please let me reach Kayden. Don't leave her alone on that ledge.

He worked to push off his feet, letting his legs do most of the work, as Kayden had taught him, scrambling up the cliff as quickly as possible—the worst scenarios racing through his mind and heart.

Please let me reach her in time. Please let her be okay.

He couldn't fail another woman he loved, couldn't lose Kayden.

His breath came in powerful bursts, his muscles hot with exertion. He finally crested the ledge and saw her—a crumpled heap. Her right leg was pinned beneath a small boulder, her forehead bleeding, her chest . . .

He held his breath, watching for hers to lift.

After a terrifying second, he saw it—her chest rising and falling. She was breathing. *Praise God.*

She moaned and he raced to her side. "I'm here, honey. I'm here. I'm going to get you out of this. I promise."

Reef knocked on his old bedroom door. Anna had not left the room all morning.

"Come in," she called.

He stepped inside to find her packing her suitcase. "What are you doing?"

She slipped a folded pile of shirts inside. "Going home."

"What? Why? We aren't supposed to leave until the end of the week. Are you sick?" Maybe that's why she hadn't come down to breakfast.

"No."

"Then why are you packing?" He couldn't say *leaving*. She couldn't be leaving. Things were going so well. Okay, to be honest, things were going adequately, but that was all right. Relationships took work, took commitment. Isn't that what Pastor Braden had said at Cole and Bailey's wedding?

Anna released a long breath and turned to face him. "I just don't see any point in prolonging the inevitable."

Reef leaned against the doorframe, crossing his arms. He recognized the certainty in her manner, in her tone—because he'd been the one to do the leaving more times than he could count. But this was different. Anna was different. He didn't think good Christian girls just up and walked away. "What's inevitable?"

"You and I are not going to work out." She shut her suitcase.

"Why?" Because he wasn't good enough? She had to have known that all along, so why now? What changed her mind?

Anna strode toward him, her eyes brimming with kindness. "You're wonderful . . ."

"But?"

"But being here this week with your family,

with your siblings and their significant others, has shown me that we're trying to force something that never was."

"It's only been a couple months. Don't you think it's a little too soon to throw in the towel? Relationships take work."

She glanced down. "The truth is, I've been using our relationship as an excuse."

"An excuse? For what?" To make her pastor father mad? Anna wasn't that kind of girl.

"For not following the path God's calling me to."

"Huh?" He hadn't seen that coming.

"For the last six months, God's been calling me to the mission field in Cambodia, but I was too scared to give up my comfortable lifestyle. When we met and hit it off, I thought . . ."

"I could be your mission project?" He prayed not.

"No. Of course not. I just thought meeting you, forming a friendship, developing feelings were all signs that I was wrong about where God was calling me to be. But I see now that, while we were meant to have a friendship, it's not meant to go beyond that. God has other plans for me, and it's time I started listening."

She was the first woman he'd brought home to meet his family, and they all thought she was great. Now she was leaving.

"I'd truly like to remain friends, to stay in touch," she said, hopefully.

How many times had he uttered those words and never followed through?

She grasped the handle of her suitcase. "Besides, I think it's pretty clear this is where you need to be."

"What do you mean? I am here."

"Not just for weddings, Reef. I think you've been running too—from your family, from where God wants you. I've always had an ache in my heart for orphans. I hear an ache in your voice, a longing, whenever you talk about your family. Stay here, spend some time with them."

"For how long?" If they stayed in touch, maybe there would be a chance for them down the road. He could make a life in Tahoe, and when she returned—

"Move back to Yancey, Reef. This is where your heart is. I can see it all over your face. You belong here. Just like I belong in that orphanage in Cambodia. We can only run from God's plans for so long. Embrace what He has for you."

He stepped closer and stroked her face. "I thought I was." He'd thought that, for once, he was doing the right thing—dating the right girl, even if the feelings, the sparks, weren't there. He liked Anna, he really did, but if he was being perfectly honest, though there was an attraction, he didn't have deep romantic feelings for her.

"I'm sorry, Reef. I hope you understand."

"Why don't you stay until the end of the

week?" They could leave together as planned, and maybe they would work through some things.

"No, I've put this off long enough."

A car horn honked.

"My cab's here." She pressed a chaste kiss on his cheek. "Take care, Reef."

He sunk onto his childhood bed as she closed the bedroom door behind her. *What do I do now?*

It didn't take long for the patter of Piper's bare feet to echo up the back stairwell. At least Cole and Bailey were on their honeymoon so he wouldn't have to face letting down his big brother again in person. At least not yet.

Piper rounded the corner, sank down on the bed, and put an arm around him, as she'd done so many times in their youth.

"You two are as thick as pea soup" their mom had always said about their special bond.

Perhaps it was because they were the youngest two in the family, or perhaps because they were similar on a heart level. He'd suppressed, or at least miserably attempted to harden, his weakness—his "tender heart," as his mom had called it—for more than a decade.

Losing his dad had been painful, but losing his mom had been excruciating. Why had God taken them *both?* Why so close together? Just when he needed them most? It had been impossible to continue the daily routine, as his siblings somehow had. Oh, he knew they'd mourned the loss, but the depth of grief wresting inside him, of anger beating relentlessly through him, had pounded hurt into insolence and pushed his reckless streak to the limit.

He'd burst through every boundary he could think of, taunting God to take him too with every limit passed. He'd longed to feel a surge of life in all its reckless chaos, and to numb his heart to the point of never feeling pain again.

He'd been selfish, immature, unable to look past his own feelings to even care about the needs of others. He'd been a self-absorbed mess, but that had changed.

Piper nudged his shoulder at the silence. "You wanna talk about it?"

He shrugged. "Not much to say."

"Reef." She angled his chin so he was facing her. "It's me. You don't have to pretend." Piper had always "gotten" him, and shockingly, always loved him—no matter what. And she'd demonstrated that in a tangible and irrefutable way when she'd stood by his side during Karli Davis's murder investigation.

He exhaled. "I thought I finally made a good choice."

"You did."

"But it didn't work."

"And?"

"I finally picked a good girl, and she said the relationship was forced."

Piper shifted, bending her leg and pulling it beneath her. "Did it feel forced?"

"Yeah, sometimes." *All the time.* "But relationships take work." And he'd been committed, for the first time in his life, to making it work.

"Yes, but just because she was a good girl doesn't mean she was the right one."

Of course Piper would hit the nail directly on the head.

She bumped his shoulder with hers. "You still staying the rest of the week?"

The easy way would be to take off, but it was time for him to stop taking the easy way out. Be there for others, not just himself. "Yes, I'm staying. I promised I would."

Relief swept over Piper's face, and the fact that his staying meant that much to her filled him with joy—joy that he could finally bring her happiness after so many years of bringing her pain. Maybe Anna was right. Maybe this was where he needed to be, where God was calling him.

Footsteps thundered up the back stairs, and Gage burst into the room. "We've got to go. Kayden was caught in a rockslide."

"What?" Piper's eyes widened. "Is she okay?"

"Jake said she's pretty battered."

Piper swallowed. "I'll call Landon."

"He knows. I just got off the phone with him. He said he called your cell, but you didn't pick up. Had a momentary panic attack thinking maybe you'd decided to join Kayden on the climb after all."

Piper patted her pocket. "I must have left it in the Jeep again."

"I assured him you were fine. He said he'd meet us at the hospital."

Reef clutched Piper's hand, giving it a gentle squeeze. He was so thankful he could be there for her, that he could be there for his whole family. "She'll be okay. Kayden's a fighter."

— 28 —

Jake's pulse whooshed in his ears as the paramedics handed Kayden off to the hospital staff waiting on the helicopter pad.

The rotary blades were silent, but he still felt their pounding in his chest.

They loaded Kayden onto a gurney, the severity of her injuries hitting him anew. Her leg was swollen. Her head was crusted with dried blood and quickly bruising.

Please, Father, I beg you. Let her live.

As he followed them into the hospital, harsh fluorescent lighting replaced the bright sunlight. The doctor and techs wheeled Kayden down the corridor, the doctor assessing during transport, calling out orders as the freshly painted taupe walls blurred by.

They wheeled through a set of automatic doors, and the McKennas—Piper, Reef, Gage, and Darcy—and Landon rushed forward, their frantic expressions echoing the fear churning inside him.

"Is she going to be okay?" Piper asked, her eyes full of tears.

"Her right leg is broken and she's sustained a head injury, but the paramedics don't know how severe the injuries are."

Landon engulfed Piper in his arms as tears rolled down her face.

"That's far enough." Peggy Wilson met them at the second set of double doors. "I need you all to wait out here."

Jake knew it was useless to argue with the RN. They all did. Having worked search and rescue, they knew the rules. No family past the second set of doors. The doctors needed space to work.

"What happened?" Gage asked.

"Rockslide. It came out of nowhere."

"Thank God you were there." Gage clamped him on the shoulder.

He'd called for help, stopped Kayden's head wound from bleeding, and set her leg by the time the copter arrived. It was ironic, though. Usually Kayden flew the rescue copter. This time she was the victim.

And now he felt utterly useless. He had to move, had to get air. "If you'll excuse me." He bolted for the exterior door and rushed outside, feeling as if he'd been drowning and was finally bursting above the water's surface. He gulped in fresh air.

"You all right?" Landon asked, having followed him.

"Yeah." He paced. "Just needed some air."

He took a few more steadying breaths, and the earth stopped spinning. "This was Patty Tate's doing."

"What?" Landon asked.

"Patty Tate. She was livid we put her son away. She's an expert climber. She could have easily staged a rockslide."

"You really think she'd do that?"

"Yeah, I do."

"Okay." Landon nodded. "I'll get Thoreau on it."

Jake paced the hall. It seemed the waiting would never end. He stared at the clock above the nurses' station, watching the second hand progress around the dial. How long did it take to cast a leg and bandage a head wound?

His chest tightened, knowing more was involved. She'd taken a hard hit to the noggin.

Please, Father, let her be okay.

Hunger for justice seethed inside. Landon clearly hadn't been convinced Patty Tate had caused the rockslide, but thankfully he was acting on Jake's claim nonetheless.

Jake paced past the nurses' station for what

seemed the hundredth time. What had happened to Kayden was no accident. He could feel it in his bones.

Patty Tate would pay for what she'd done. He would see her brought to justice, put behind bars where she belonged. She wasn't getting away with this.

After what seemed an eternity, Dr. Graham stepped into the waiting room.

The group stood, and Jake wondered if they were all struggling to catch their breath, as he was.

"She's going to be fine. She's one tough lady."

The pressure squeezing Jake's chest lightened.

"She has a broken leg—which Jake, here, set perfectly, I might add."

"And her head?" Piper asked.

"She took a pretty good knock and will have a grand headache for a while, but all scans have come back clean. She's awake and surprisingly alert."

"Can we see her?" Piper asked.

"Give us a few minutes to get her settled in her room, and then, yes, you can see her. We'll keep her overnight, as a precaution, but she's fine."

Jake breathed a sigh of relief, and the McKennas formed a group hug.

"She'll be in room—" Dr. Graham glanced at his clipboard—"203. Give the nurses ten minutes and you can head up."

"Thank you, Dr. Graham." Piper turned from her siblings to hug him.

"You're welcome." He pulled back, looking Piper in the eye. "Maybe this will finally convince you to stop climbing."

Kayden and Piper stop climbing? *Fat chance.* Besides, they could step off the curb and get hit by a car. Risk existed everywhere. Giving up adventure wasn't the answer. Not for them. You trained well and followed all the safety precautions, but you didn't stop living. Besides, the rockslide had not been an accident. It was a direct assault by a vengeful woman. Jake was positive of that.

"You coming?" Gage asked as they headed for Kayden's room.

"I'll meet you up there," he said, needing to do something.

Gage arched a brow. "Okay."

Jake walked in the opposite direction of the McKennas, moving for the hospital's chapel.

He entered, finding it empty. The chapel was small with brown pews and stained-glass windows. He stepped to the front and knelt before the altar, a spiritual release of anxiety washing out of him. He lowered his head.

Thank you, Jesus, for sparing her.

Losing Becca had been devastating; losing Kayden would have destroyed him.

— 29 —

Jake opened the door to Kayden's room, his heart in his throat. Why was he suddenly so anxious again? Doc Graham had assured them she'd be just fine. No, these nerves were coming from an entirely different place. He was excited to see the woman he loved, and the fireballs rumbling through his gut proved it.

"There he is," Gage said, catching sight of him first.

Kayden sat up in the bed, a white bandage fastened across her forehead, a cast on her right leg. She looked battered, but beautiful, as always.

"Hey," she said, a soft smile curling on her lips.

Man, what that smile did to his insides. "Hey." He tried to ignore the fact that everyone in the room was fixated on their interaction. "How you holding up?"

She shifted and winced. "I've been better, but it could have been way worse if you hadn't been there."

"I didn't do much." Other than fear the woman he loved was about to be ripped from his life and regret that he'd never even told her how he felt. Though he suspected she knew. He glanced around the room at everyone watching them. They all knew.

"We both know that's not true."

"If you weren't there, who knows how long it would have taken someone to find her," Reef said. "She could have . . ." He stopped and shook his head. "It could have been really bad. Thank you." He shook Jake's hand, and all the McKennas and their loved ones thanked him in turn. But none melted his heart like Kayden's thank-you. Two simple words and a world of meaning.

"Anything for you."

Color infused her pale cheeks. Had he actually said that out loud? Heat rushed his cheeks.

He caught Gage grinning, but to his shock, Gage left it at that.

"Well, I should, um . . ." He cleared his throat. "Let you get some rest." She needed rest.

She nodded, the slight smile still hovering on the curve of her supple lips.

He backed up, straight into something solid. *Gage*.

"You all right there?" Gage grinned.

"Fine." He tried to look and sound as fierce as possible, but Gage wasn't buying any of it.

"Can I talk to you?" Landon asked as Jake stepped past Gage.

"Absolutely."

"Let's go outside."

"All right." He followed Landon down the flight of stairs and back out to the parking lot where they'd stood several hours earlier.

"What was that all about?" Landon asked with a gigantic grin.

Not him too. "Nothing."

" 'Anything for you' doesn't sound like nothing." Landon folded a piece of gum into his mouth, the scent of spearmint wafting in the air. "I saw the way you two looked at each other."

Two? As in Kayden was looking back at him the same way? No way. He knew she was intrigued by him now that she knew his past, but looking at him with love . . . ? No way.

"I know you don't see it, but she's as into you as you are into her."

"Yeah, right."

"Trust me."

The thought engulfed him with audacious hope.

"Want a piece?" Landon offered him a stick of gum.

"Thanks." He took a piece and popped it into his mouth, realizing it was the first food he'd eaten since breakfast, if gum counted as food.

He turned to toss the wrapper in the trash can, and a woman caught his eye. She was leaning against the grill of a car, her legs crossed genteelly. Her dark-brown hair was pulled back in a twist. She wore a navy-and-white polka-dot blouse, tan A-line skirt with matching heels, and tortoiseshell sunglasses.

She slid the sunglasses down her nose momentarily and smiled when he caught her eye.

"Jake, you okay?" Landon asked.

"Yeah." He looked back at his friend, his mind racing. "She just looked familiar."

"Who?" Landon scanned the parking lot.

"That woman by . . ." He looked back to where she'd been standing, but she was gone. "Never mind. That's not important. Any news on Patty Tate?"

"Yeah." Landon rubbed the back of his neck. "I'm sorry, man, but Patty Tate has a solid alibi for the rockslide."

"What?"

"She's been at the station all day long. Thoreau said she's been sitting around, refusing to leave. Visiting with Shane during the approved hours and harassing my deputies to let him go the rest of the time."

"Then she staged it ahead of time."

"Shane's defense lawyer said he was with her all day yesterday, going over Shane's defense. She took him around to every witness he wanted to interview. He bunked in her guest room last night. Besides, even if she'd set it up ahead of time, she would have to have been there to trigger it just as Kayden reached the ledge. She couldn't have done it."

"No. There's got to be some mistake."

"It could have just been a freak rockslide. These things happen."

"There's more to it. I can feel it."

"Then let's head back out there and see if we can find any evidence of staging. We've got a handful of hours of daylight left."

"All right." He nodded, needing to do something. Needing to get whoever did this to Kayden. "Let's go."

Jake approached the scene of the rockslide, trying to be objective but knowing, when it came to Kayden, objective was the last thing he could truly be.

"Check this out," Landon said, indicating an area just above the ledge.

"Looks like rocks might have been stacked here." In a conveniently placed pile.

They both turned, looking for something that could have been used for a lever.

"Here," Landon said, slipping on gloves and lifting a long stick, two inches in diameter. "This could have easily done the trick. We can hope for fingerprints, though with the rough surface and public nature of the area, chances we'd get anything are slim."

"But you agree it's obvious the rockslide was staged."

"Sure looks that way."

"Rocks don't stack themselves at the top of a rise. This was Patty's doing."

"It couldn't have been Patty. She's got an ironclad alibi."

"Then she got one of her climbing pals to do it for her. Or she hired someone to do it. I'm telling you, Patty's the only person who makes sense." Who else would want to hurt Kayden? The thought left a hollow ache in his gut.

— 30 —

Jake heard scraping. No, that wasn't quite right. It was the sound of . . . shoveling, of dirt being tossed onto a pile.

Why was someone digging so late at night? The moon was barely a slit in the sky, leaving little to see by.

The ground was moist beneath his bare feet. It had rained recently. He could smell it in the air.

A flashlight lay on the ground, illuminating a hole—a large hole. The shovel appeared at the top, and a shovelful of muddy earth flung onto the pile nearby.

Who was in the hole?

He stepped toward it, making out Angela Markum standing over what he realized was a grave.

Her husband crawled from it, and they rolled

something in—someone wrapped in a blue tarp.

They didn't acknowledge his presence, just kept at work, now refilling the hole, flinging the heavy earth on top of the body.

He rushed forward, needing to see Candace Banner's face before they sealed it away forever.

He raced to the edge, pulling up fast to avoid slipping in.

The harsh glare of the LED flashlight illuminated the woman's face, and bile rose in his throat. *Becca?*

He stumbled for purchase. They'd killed Becca. He'd known it wasn't a random hit-and-run, and this proved it. They'd murdered Becca and their precious baby.

Composing himself, he leaned over again, wanting one last look at his wife, but horror engulfed him at the sight of Kayden. Her exquisite face pale in death, earth quickly covering it with every shovelful tossed in. Her eyes were no longer visible, her nose going next, now her lips. Nothing was left to see of her face—only damp, dark earth burying the woman he loved.

"Kayden!" He shot up in bed, a cold sweat piercing his heated skin.

Angela Markum. Wife of the college president who'd killed the young co-ed, Becca, and their baby. Her hair was darker, her sunglasses hiding her eyes except for the briefest of moments, but that's who the woman in the parking lot reminded him of.

But it couldn't be her. Angela Markum was still in prison, serving a ten-year sentence for perjury, obstruction of justice, and helping her husband dispose of the co-ed's body.

He threw off the covers and climbed from his bunk. The waters were choppier tonight, and he stumbled as he moved for the galley to pour himself a cup of cold water.

Bracing his free hand against the counter, he took a long draught, letting the cold water quench the heat burning inside.

It couldn't be her.

His heart still racing, he lay back down, staring at the cracked-open hatch overhead, a gentle summer breeze wafting through the slit.

Seeing Kayden injured had brought memories of Becca dead on the road flooding back, which obviously was bringing the Markum case back to mind—that was all. Not to mention his certainty that Patty was responsible but being unable to prove it—just as with Becca's hit-and-run death. He'd been certain Joel Markum was responsible for his wife and daughter's deaths but had been unable to prove it. The similarities were there, enough to tug at his subconscious. He needed to settle down. He was overreacting. Angela Markum was still in prison.

He lay for hours, tossing, turning, trying to force himself to sleep, but to no avail.

Angela Markum had vowed revenge on him for his part in destroying her perfect life, as she sickly saw it. What if she'd escaped? What if . . . ?

Enough. He grabbed his cell off the nightstand. There was an easy way to put this to rest. He'd call his old partner and confirm that Angela Markum was still behind bars. The day was already in full swing in Boston.

Sam answered on the third ring. "Barnett."

"Hey, Sam. It's Jake."

"Jake? Where on earth have you been?"

"Here and there." It had been easier to leave his old life behind when no one in it knew where he was.

"You doing okay? It's been too long, man."

"I know, and I'm sorry. I just needed some space and time to clear my head."

"A reporter from California called about you last winter. She told me she had met you and that you were okay, but she didn't seem to know where you were—or at least wasn't willing to tell me. I gave her some information about the Markum case . . . and about you. I hope that's okay."

"Sure, no problem. It worked out all right. In fact, that's why I'm calling."

"Oh?"

"Angela Markum. Please tell me she's still in prison?"

Silence.

"Sam?"

"I'm sorry, man. She got out about six months back."

"She had a ten-year sentence. It's only been four."

"What can I say . . . good behavior."

"She gave her husband a false alibi and helped him bury the poor girl's body. She helped her sicko husband cover up murder." Not to mention helping him cover up the hit-and-run on Becca. Again, she'd provided an alibi and no doubt covered for him.

"She was a model prisoner. And without you at the parole hearing to speak against her . . ."

"Surely Candace's parents were there." The co-ed's folks had been vehement about Angela's culpability in it all.

"Yes. The mom was. Apparently the Banners have split up, and Fred's living somewhere out west. Regardless, the judge ruled that Ms. Markum had served enough time and was no longer a threat to society."

"No longer a threat? Then what's she doing out here in Alaska?"

"Alaska? Is that where you are?"

"What's important is that Angela's here, too, and I think she's already begun enacting the revenge she swore she'd get."

"What happened?"

"It's a long story. I better go, Sam, but I'll be in touch." He needed to inform Landon and all the McKennas. If Angela Markum was in Yancey, no one close to him was safe.

He should have paid closer attention to Angela's status. Why had he stayed in one place for so long? He knew exactly why. She was lying in a hospital bed.

He exhaled. How far was Angela prepared to go? "Wait. Do me a favor?"

"Yeah?"

"Send me copies of my case files."

"Sure. What for?"

"I need to remind myself exactly who Angela Markum is and what she's capable of."

After giving Sam delivery details and promising again that he would stay in touch, Jake threw on some clothes and raced outside. But he stopped short at the fist-sized rock perched on the hood of his truck. Swallowing, he stepped closer. Pulling a handkerchief from his pocket, he lifted it and read *Nice to see you again* scrolled across the surface in black paint.

Angela had caused the rockslide and probably had been the one leaving the creepy messages all along.

How long had she been watching, plotting out her revenge? Fear racked through him.

Please, Father, not again.

— 31 —

"Knock, knock," Kirra said at the door to Kayden's hospital room. Carol stood beside her with a beautiful bouquet of cypress flowers in hand.

Kayden smiled. "Hey, guys, what are you doing here?"

"We heard about your accident," Kirra said. "You know how fast news travels in Yancey."

"Yes, I do."

Carol set the bouquet of vibrant red flowers on Kayden's bedside table. "We wanted to make sure you were okay."

"Reef." Kirra nodded at Kayden's brother in the chair.

He stood. "Kirra. How are you?"

"Better than your sister."

"Here." He gestured to the seat he'd just vacated. "Please."

"Thanks, but I'll stand."

"So what happened?" Carol asked, gesturing to Kayden's leg. "We heard you were climbing. . . ."

Kayden shook her head and then winced slightly. She had to remember to make slow movements or the dizzy spells returned, and then Doc Graham would never agree to let her go home this afternoon, like she was hoping. "Rockslide."

Kirra took a sharp intake of breath. "Oh, Kayden, that could have been serious."

"Thankfully Jake was there, or who knows how long I'd have been out on that ledge beneath a pile of rocks."

"Yes. You are a fortunate young lady," Carol said, arranging the flowers.

Jake raced into the hospital, needing to make certain Kayden was safe. Well, as safe as someone with a broken leg and head wound could be.

He rushed past Peggy Wilson, waving at her in greeting but not bothering to stop. He pushed into Kayden's room to find Reef sitting in the chair beside Kayden's empty bed.

Panic surged through him.

"Where is she?" He nearly ripped Reef from the chair.

"In the bathroom." Reef's eyes widened. "What's wrong?"

How did he explain? "She's okay? She's safe?"

"She's fine. A little cranky because she's ready to go home, but otherwise fine."

The pent-up tension released, the adrenaline dissipating with a surge. *Thank you, Lord.*

Kayden stepped from the bathroom, somehow managing to look radiant in a hospital gown. "Hey."

"Hey, yourself. How are you feeling?"

"Ready to go home."

Reef looked at him with a smirk.

"So I heard." She was so stubborn. Though Doc Graham was a pretty formidable opponent, she'd no doubt get her way. "Let me help you get back in bed."

"I've got it." She hobbled over on her crutch and shifted to sit, struggling a bit.

"Stop being so stubborn and let the man help," Reef said.

"I've got it." She plopped on the bed and leaned the crutch against her bedside table.

Jake's heart stopped at the sight of the flowers. "Where did you get those?"

"Kirra and Carol brought them in."

"When?"

"About twenty minutes ago."

"Kirra's from the area, right?"

"Yes . . ." she answered slowly, clearly trying to figure out where he was headed.

"Like, born here?"

"I don't think so."

"How long has she lived here?" He'd met Kirra. She wasn't Angela Markum, but perhaps she had some tie to her.

"Long enough to hound me every year of school since kindergarten," Reef said.

"And Carol?"

Kayden clumsily adjusted her blankets. "What about her?"

"How long has she lived here?"

"A few months."

"Give me your laptop," he said as panic flared through him.

"Okay." Reef handed it over. "What's going on? Is everything okay?"

Jake pulled up an old news article on the Markum case. He found a picture of Angela standing beside her husband. He turned the screen to face Kayden, his gut sinking. "Is this Carol?" *Please say no.*

"What?"

"Is this woman Carol?" He tapped the screen.

Kayden studied the photo. "Her hair's lighter, and she looks a bit younger, but, yes, it looks like Carol."

Bile rose again in Jake's throat. "What's Carol's last name?"

"Jones." She was looking at him as if he had lost his mind.

He turned to Reef. "Call Kirra and see if Carol's still with her. If she is, make up some excuse why you want to talk to her—we don't want to put Kirra in danger—and if not, see if Kirra knows where she is."

"Okay." Reef stepped from the room with his cell in hand.

"What's going on?" Kayden asked. "She looks like Carol." She studied the screen again. "But it can't be. It says here her name is Angela Markum. Wait . . . Markum?" Realization dawned, the color draining from her face. "As in the last case you worked in Boston?"

Jake nodded, too choked to speak.

"Kirra, it's Reef."

"Yes?" she said, slowly.

"Is Carol with you? Kayden has a question for her."

"Carol?"

"Yes. Is she with you?"

"No. I dropped her off at her place about fifteen minutes ago. If Kayden—"

Reef covered the phone with his hand. "She just dropped her off at her place," he said to Jake, who'd joined him in the hall.

"Ask where home is," Jake said.

"Where does she live?"

"Carol?" Kirra asked, confusion filling her tone.

"Yes."

"Why the sudden interest in Carol?"

"It's a long story."

"I don't exactly feel comfortable giving out volunteers' addresses."

"Carol isn't who she says she is. Landon and Jake need her address."

"Is she in some sort of trouble?"

"Yes. Big trouble."

"Oh . . . She's renting a place on Sterling Road, next door to Ralph and Mabel Barnes."

"Gotcha. Thanks." He relayed the information

to Jake, who headed out the hospital door before he'd even finished the sentence.

"Hello?" Kirra said, still on the line. "You can't just leave me hanging like this. Explain."

"I will as soon as I have the go-ahead from Jake. In the meantime, just know she's dangerous. If she shows up at the kennel, avoid her without being obvious and call me right away."

— 32 —

Jake picked up Landon at the station, where he was waiting with a warrant. Luckily Judge Morrell had been at the station on business when Jake's call came in, and Landon pounced.

Carol's rental home sat on the corner of Sterling and Thomas Run Road. A small one-story cabin next to the home of Yancey's fire marshal, of all people.

The cabin looked quiet, too quiet.

Landon signaled he'd cover the back as Jake stepped to the front door with Thoreau.

He knocked. "Sheriff's Department. Open up."

Nothing.

Signaling Thoreau to cover him as he entered, Jake kicked in the door.

The front room was dim, the shades closed. Jake scanned the space. A light shone from beneath a door at the end of the hall.

He signaled Thoreau to move as Landon entered from the rear.

They cleared each room they passed en route to the one at the end of the hall.

Jake leaned against the wall and tapped. "Sheriff's Department. Open up."

Nothing but the soft sound of . . . *music?*

Landon nodded, and Jake opened the door. The three men moved in . . . and stopped short.

"What on earth?" Thoreau hitched. "She's one sick puppy."

The wall ahead was a shrine to Jake—newspaper articles covering the Markum case, pictures, and a U.S. map with red circles around towns he'd spent time in before landing in Yancey. Not all of them, but a fair number. Had Angela hired someone to track him? How long had she been planning her revenge? Close to four years stewing in a cell was more than enough time to fixate on someone and to lose sight of anything else.

Articles on Becca's death, Joel Markum's suicide, and Angela's imprisonment—they were all there, along with surveillance photos of the McKennas, each going about their daily life. She'd been studying them for weeks. She was here to exact revenge.

In the center of the twisted collage, and most disturbing of all, was a picture of Jake and Kayden dancing at Cole and Bailey's wedding, a red target around their heads. What had been one of the most perfect moments of his life . . . and *she'd* been there, watching them. It made his skin crawl.

"What's up with the music?" Thoreau said, disconnecting the iPod.

"It was the song Kayden and I danced to at Cole and Bailey's wedding." He stepped over and tapped the picture. "The night this was taken."

"So she's clearly after you and Kayden," Landon said.

"Why is she after Kayden?" Thoreau asked.

"She just is," Landon said, kindly sparing Jake the need to express his love for Kayden for the first time publicly, to Thoreau, of all people. If he was going to express his love, it would be to her.

"Are you sure she's not just trying to goad you? Trying to make you emotional, so you're not thinking clearly?" Landon asked.

"I'm sure that's part of it, but she's already attacked Kayden and left me several blatantly clear messages."

Landon arched a brow.

Jake explained the rock left on his truck and the cypress flowers left in Kayden's room. The same flowers had been left on Becca's body. "They symbolize death."

Angela watched from her vantage point with a smile and set her binoculars down. So, he'd found her little presents and the groundwork for her masterpiece. Excellent. The game was in full swing.

251

Jake studied the wall display, following Angela's tracking, her thought process frighteningly displayed for them, while Landon ran a full crime-scene analysis of the house. It would take the rest of the day but hopefully would produce something of help in catching her.

Landon looked up from lifting fingerprints off the iPod. Thankfully Thoreau had been smart enough to put on gloves before turning it off. "What do you think her next move is?"

Jake pointed to the picture of him and Kayden dancing, the bull's-eye on them. "To pick up where her husband left off. To hurt me by hurting the people I love. But I won't let that happen. I'll stop her—one way or another."

Jake rapped on the fire chief's door. Strange that Angela would choose a property right next door to someone with close connections to the police. Maybe she hadn't known, or maybe she'd hoped Ralph was a talker—which both he and his wife, Mabel, were—and she could get some juicy information out of him.

Ralph answered the door. Mabel stood in the hall not five feet behind him.

"Afternoon, Jake."

"Ask him what's going on," Mabel said.

"Shh, Mabel. He'll get around to it."

Mabel crossed her arms over her chest with a huff.

"I assume you noticed the activity next door. I need to ask you some questions about the woman who rents there."

"Carol? Sure. Nice lady."

So she had them all fooled. But he knew the depth of her evil, prayed he'd already seen the worst of it. "What can you tell me about her?"

"Pleasant sort."

Mabel pushed past her husband, propping open the screen door. "She is an absolute doll."

A *doll* who had nearly killed Kayden.

He would eventually explain the truth of who Carol was to Ralph and Mabel, but he wanted to get their unbiased impression of her first.

"When did she move in?"

"Oh, I'd say at least five months back," Ralph said, rubbing his chin.

"Yes. Arrived in Yancey just after New Year's," Mabel added.

New Year's. She'd been spying on him and the McKennas that long?

"Did she say where she moved from?"

"Anchorage," Mabel answered before Ralph could.

"Did you ever see her with anybody? Did she have any repeat visitors?"

Mabel twirled a strand of hair around her finger. "Can't say that I ever noticed anyone."

And Mabel, being the busybody she was, would have noticed.

"What about you, Ralph?"

"No. Can't say that I did. Wait. I did see Kirra Jacobs over there once. She didn't stay long. Looked like she was dropping something off or picking something up."

"Carol volunteered over at Kirra's shelter," Mabel said.

"Yes. I'm aware." Angela had used the shelter as a way to get closer to Kayden.

"What else can you tell me?"

"What else do you want to know?" Ralph asked.

"Anything. Everything."

Mabel's eyes narrowed. "Why the interest in Carol?"

Jake exhaled. Time to explain.

Ralph was clearly shocked and Mabel seemed as if she half didn't believe Jake, like it was all some sort of mix-up. Carol was too kind to be a killer's wife.

Jake knew better. He knew the cold heart that beat inside Angela Markum, and there was nothing kind about it.

"Ma'am, you can't go in there," Deputy Earl Hansen said outside Kayden's hospital room.

Reef stood, moving for the door. He needed to

254

protect his sister at all costs. Had Carol been foolish enough to return? Reef shook his head. *Angela.* Carol Jones was Angela Markum. How bizarre. And he'd thought this trip home would be a calm one.

"I'd feel a whole lot better with my rifle," Kayden said, propping herself up straighter in bed.

Taking a deep breath, Reef opened the door to find Kirra arguing with Earl.

Of course she'd barge in demanding answers.

He half considered letting Earl haul her away.

"Reef, tell him it's okay for me to come in."

Earl looked to him.

"Reef!" She huffed at his hesitation.

"She's fine," he finally said.

Earl narrowed his eyes. "You sure?"

Reef nodded, and Earl stepped aside, letting Kirra pass.

"Thanks," she said, pushing past him into Kayden's room.

"You're welcome." Could she be more abrasive?

"Hey, Kayden."

"Kirra," Kayden said with a smile, clearly anticipating what was about to go down.

Kirra whirled around on Reef, hands firmly planted on her hips. "Explain yourself?"

"Still bossy, I see."

"I think I deserve an answer."

Of course she thought she was deserving. Always had.

"You call me out of the blue and tell me one of my volunteers is in trouble and wanted by the law, and you think you can just leave it at that. No way! I want an explanation. What do you think Carol did?"

"First of all, her name isn't Carol Jones. It's Angela Markum."

Kirra frowned. "What?"

Reef looked over at his sister, dark splotches under her eyes, and then back to Kirra. "Let's take this outside." His sister needed her rest.

Kirra looked at Kayden and nodded at Reef. "Fine."

They stepped from the room.

"All right. Time to explain."

"Why do you think I owe you anything? Maybe it's none of your business." Okay, he was being rude, but she had a way of getting under his skin.

"None of my business? Carol volunteered at my shelter for months, was a trusted volunteer, and now you're claiming she's someone else? Trust me, if someone's not who they appear to be, it is so my business."

Nothing had changed. Kirra still assumed everyone else's business was her own. Just like in grade school, when she'd caught him and his buddies playing an innocent prank and she busted them to their teacher. He'd spent more hours in time-out and detention because of Kirra Jacobs. The woman may be beautiful but she was still Killjoy Kirra.

Relief and worry wrestled inside Jake as Gage helped Kayden, or attempted to help Kayden, back into her house. Doc Graham had given her the all clear, but Jake feared it was too soon. He preferred she stay in the hospital with a deputy posted at her door. At home, out in the open, he feared what Angela had planned.

She swatted at her brother as they crossed the front porch. "I got it."

Gage lifted his hands. "Suit yourself."

She hobbled on her crutch. With her right leg broken and casted and her left shoulder swollen from the fall, it made an awkward combination for moving, but Kayden, as always, insisted on doing everything herself, despite the pain. All Jake wanted to do was jump up and help her, but he resisted the urge, knowing she'd only shoo him away.

A wonderful aroma greeted them as they stepped inside. Piper and Gage had spent the day making a delicious meal for Kayden's home-coming.

Fettuccine Alfredo with shrimp, along with lemon-steamed broccoli, homemade seven-grain bread, and organic cobbler for dessert—it was made with sugar in the raw and steel-cut oats, all the healthy things Kayden loved and the rest of them tolerated, but tonight was for her. If Jake had his way, the rest of his life would be for her. Now Angela was threatening any fledgling hope he had of him and Kayden one day building a life together.

He hadn't realized how much hope he'd actually had of it really being a possibility, of it really happening, until Angela threatened it.

"I still can't believe Carol was a total fake," Kirra said, settling in Piper and Kayden's family room after the meal. "How could I not see that?"

"You had no reason to doubt what she claimed," Gage said. "Stop beating yourself up."

She sighed. "It's just that, since everyone who works at the kennel is a volunteer, there's no reason to fill out employment records or tax forms. I've never even asked to see an ID. I guess that's pretty naïve."

Reef shifted in his seat. "I'd say."

Piper gave her brother a stern look before turning to Kirra. "No it's not. We live in a small, close-knit community. It's only natural to be trusting."

Kirra swallowed, painful memories nipping at her. "It's never wise to be too trusting."

Reef arched a brow.

"Is there anything you can think of, anything

Angela said or did that seemed odd to you?" Jake asked.

She started to say no, but then . . . "Well, there was this one time she said something about having to ship her good face cream all the way across the country, that she couldn't find good stuff way out here."

"So?"

"So she said she was from Anchorage. That's hardly across the country."

"What else?" Jake asked.

"That was it." Kirra shrugged.

"No. I mean what other conversations did you two have?" Jake scooted forward.

"Mostly basic stuff. The weather, the dogs . . . Kayden."

His eyes widened. "You two discussed Kayden?"

Kayden frowned. "What about me?"

"Well, she asked about all of you at one point or another, but I guess she just showed more interest in you. Not weird, at least it didn't seem so at the time. Just casual conversation."

"Like what?" Jake pressed.

"I'm trying to remember. We've talked a lot over the past few months."

"Take your time," Jake said. "Anything you can think of. You never know what might be helpful."

"I guess she seemed interested in how Kayden spent her time when she wasn't at the shelter."

"And what did you tell her?" Kayden asked.

"That you enjoyed rock climbing and spending time with your family. I'm sorry. I was just making conversation."

"Don't worry about it. I told her as much myself," Kayden said.

Angela had worked at the shelter for months, interacting with her and Kayden on a daily basis. Kirra shuddered to think how much Angela had learned about the McKennas during that time. It was staggering.

— 34 —

Kayden hobbled down the pier, frustration searing inside. She hated being on crutches, hated feeling weak and dependent on anything or anyone.

It was chilly and starting to get dark, and Jake's home—a forty-two-foot converted trawler—sat moored at the end of the dock, a light shining inside.

She tried to tell herself she was there because she was interested in the case, and she was, but that wasn't the real reason she was approaching his houseboat at ten thirty on a Thursday night. It was *him*. She missed him, and it'd only been a day. *Pathetic*.

As she hobbled down the gangplank, her foot caught on a raised board and she went tumbling, her jaw colliding with the wood. Heat and embarrassment flushed through her. She scrambled for her crutch and pulled somewhat to her feet as Jake came running out.

"Kayden?" He squinted in the dim light. "Is that you?"

She blew the hair from her eye, horrified by how she must look. "Hi."

"What are you . . . ?" He stepped toward her. "Are you all right? I heard a thump."

"Yeah." She ignored the stinging along her right arm. "I'm fine. Just tripped." Embarrassing as it was.

He inspected her more closely, and she tried not to revel in the warmth of his intent gaze.

His eyes filled with worry. "You're bleeding."

"What?" She gingerly touched her bandaged head wound.

"Your chin."

"My . . . ?" Her fingers skimmed it. *Ow.* It must have busted open on the planks.

"Come on, I've got a first-aid kit inside." He moved to help her.

She instinctively pulled back. "I've got it."

"I'm resanding and revarnishing the planks, and I'm only halfway done. The surface is uneven. I'm sorry."

"I'll be okay." The last thing she wanted was Jake viewing her as helpless.

He lifted his hands in surrender but watched

with a tense jaw as she made her way inside. Her jerky movements would never be deemed graceful, but at least she'd made it on her own.

The inside of his houseboat was warm and welcoming. White paneling covered the walls instead of the traditional darker wood.

"Here." He moved some files off a futon couch. "Take a seat. I'll grab the first-aid kit."

She lowered herself onto the futon, amazed at how plush and comfy it was. What appeared to be case files were strewn out on the old trunk serving as a coffee table in front of her.

She leaned forward, lifting a picture of Joel and Angela Markum. Their clothes were fancy, and they appeared to be at some sort of high-society event. She never would have pegged the man as a murderer.

"It was taken at a dinner to benefit the college where Markum was president," Jake said, returning with the first-aid kit that looked like it'd seen its share of wear. "I first interviewed him that night. Not as a potential suspect, but as the college president."

She shook her head. "I'd never guess he was a killer." He was dapper with a rather charming smile.

"I don't think Joel intended to kill her—Candace Banner, the co-ed."

Kayden shifted as Jake sat beside her. "What do you mean?"

"I mean, he liked things rough in the . . ." Jake cleared his throat.

"Oh."

"I think things got out of hand with Candace and she ended up dead."

"It doesn't make it any less horrible."

"No, it doesn't." He shifted to face her. "Let me take a look at that chin."

"It's okay. I can take care of it. Just need a mirror."

He rested his hand on hers. "Stop being so stubborn. Let me wipe up the blood."

Before she could argue, his hand was on her chin, wiping delicately at the blood with an antiseptic towelette. "This might sting."

It did, but it was nothing compared to the overwhelming tingling jostling inside her at Jake's tender touch.

He took great care cleaning out the wound and then applying antibacterial cream, his fingers firm yet gentle.

She studied him as he worked, his strong jaw and soulful green eyes. She'd always considered him handsome, but she'd never let herself take pleasure in viewing him—to really see *him*. He was gorgeous, masculine, and kind.

"There," he said, topping off her wound with a Band-Aid. "All good."

She sat back with a jolt. Had she just let someone, let *Jake,* take care of her? What was wrong with her?

She stiffened. That couldn't happen again.

Jake put everything back in the kit and shut it. "I'm glad you came by."

"Oh. Yeah. I just thought I'd see how everything's coming with the case."

He smiled, seeing right through her. As always. It was so annoying.

"You're really hooked, aren't you?"

She cleared her throat uncomfortably. "I beg your pardon?"

"On the case. It's got a hold of you." He set the kit up on a shelf.

Something had gotten ahold of her, all right.

He stepped back toward her. "Do you want to stay awhile and . . . ?"

"I . . ."

He stepped closer still. ". . . work through the case files with me?"

She swallowed and nodded. "Yeah, that'd be good."

"Great. Would you like something to drink? Juice? Ice tea?"

"Ice tea, if it's unsweetened."

"You got it."

She settled back in, wondering what she'd gotten herself into.

Angela stood on the dock, watching. Weren't they sweet, huddled over her husband's case files.

This was going to be even better than Jake's

wife and unborn child. He'd been too young then to truly realize what he had.

Now . . .

She shifted the binoculars to rest on Kayden's face. He'd soon know the depths of what he'd lost, and it would be exquisitely painful.

Jake refilled Kayden's ice tea, pretty sure he'd never been happier in his life. The time alone with her had been amazing, even if the time had been spent looking through files of the case that had nearly broken him.

Was this God's way of giving him a second chance? Was catching Angela this time going to finally lay his demons to rest? Could he rise from the ashes and begin again with Kayden? It seemed too good to be true, and until it actually happened, he wouldn't dare believe it.

"So how did you know she was involved?" Kayden asked, lifting Angela Markum's photo.

"I didn't, at first." Jake sat back, resting his hands behind his head. "Not until Joel Markum killed himself."

"How did that change things?"

"It showed us that someone else with strength and ingenuity was involved. If Markum was too cowardly to stand trial, I questioned whether he had been in it alone."

Kayden stretched beside him. Her neck was stiff, hurting, tired from bending over case files for the past two hours. He could tell by her tentative movements.

"Here." He gently placed his hand on her neck, praying she didn't bolt. He started rubbing as she started to protest, and she fell silent after a moment, leaning into his massage.

Jake focused on taking care of her and the tightness in her neck, not on the sensations or emotions racing through him.

"You were saying?" she asked.

"Right." He tried to refocus his thoughts. "Angela Markum. I took some time away from the case after Becca's . . . death. And when I returned, we were close to proving the alibis Angela had provided for Joel for both the night of Candace's murder and Becca's hit-and-run were false. Joel must have learned we were closing in and decided to take his own life rather than face the consequences.

"When we arrived to arrest him and found him . . . let's just say the maid showed more distress than Angela. Her lack of compassion and emotion led us to reconsider whether Joel would have been solely behind the ingenious burial location and the strategic moves that followed the murder—and suddenly it all pointed to her. Luckily the evidence did too."

"How'd she react when you arrested her?"

"She was cold and calculated. Very calmly swore she'd get revenge."

Kayden shifted to face him. "And now she's back."

He scooted back. "Yeah."

"And this time?"

"She wants to take away everyone I love."

Kayden swallowed. "Because she blames you for her husband's suicide?"

"Maybe. But more likely, because she thinks I destroyed her perfect life, she's bent on destroying mine."

And Kayden, whether she knew it or not, had become his life.

He looked at the clock. "It's late. I'd better get you home." He needed to keep her safe.

"Piper dropped me off. I'll call her to pick me up."

"No need. I can take you." Jake grabbed his keys.

"It's no problem." Kayden reached for her cell.

"No problem for me to take you." He jangled his keys.

She relented. "Okay. Thanks."

Jake watched with frustration and pride as Kayden made it to his truck by herself and climbed inside.

He drove her the ten miles home and escorted her to the door.

"I had fun tonight," she said, clearly without thinking. "I mean, going over the case files was interesting."

He exhaled. "Right."

"I can tell you were a really good detective. Still are."

"I don't know about that." Back then he'd been arrogant and cocky, and his job had gotten his wife and child killed.

"The way you caught Joel Markum and his wife. That was brilliant."

Had Kayden just complimented him twice? He slipped his hands into his pockets, fighting the urge to reach out to her. Now that he'd held her during the dance at Cole and Bailey's wedding, held her in his arms, he never wanted to stop. The urge to pull her into an embrace was always there. "You better get some sleep. It's been a rough week."

"I'm—"

"Fine." He smirked. "Trust me, I know."

A smile tugged at the corners of her full lips, but she held it in check. "Good night, Jake."

" 'Night."

She shut the front door and he moved back to his truck, every fiber of his being alive and tingling.

"You two kids have fun?"

Jake whirled around with gun drawn to find Gage standing ten feet away.

Gage lifted his hands. "Easy there, cowboy."

Jake holstered his weapon. "You shouldn't sneak up on someone like that." Especially not him.

"I assumed you heard me coming. You always hear me coming."

"I was . . ."

"Distracted." Gage grinned.

"What are you doing here?"

"I'm staying at Cole's while he and Bay are on their honeymoon. With everything going on, I felt better staying closer to the girls."

"Good idea." Cole's cabin sat on the other side of the tree line, only a few hundred feet away from the girls' place.

"Piper said she dropped Kayden off at your place hours ago." Gage leaned against the grill of Jake's truck, his grin still beaming. "That's gotta be a first."

He and Kayden had been experiencing a lot of firsts lately. "Yeah. She came over to go through the case files with me."

"Uh-huh. I saw the way you two were looking at each other on the porch, all googly-eyed."

That was the second time Gage had said "looking at *each other*." Was there a chance Kayden really was interested in him? Might she love him the way he loved her? It would be too good to be true. But the last time he'd been in that position, he'd lost everything.

"So?" Piper met Kayden at her bedroom door.

Great. "So?" She stepped inside her room and dropped her purse on the bed.

"How'd it go with Jake?"

"Fine. We went over his old case files."

Piper followed her in. "And?"

"And they were very interesting."

Piper smiled. "Must have been for you to have stayed so late." Her eyes narrowed. "What happened to your chin?"

Kayden fingered the Band-Aid Jake had applied, remembering his assertiveness and tenderness, the combination a reminder of the amazing strength and gentleness her dad had displayed when it came to those he loved.

Kayden leaned her stupid crutch against the dresser and pulled out her PJs.

Piper plopped on the bed. "Earth to Kayden. What happened to your chin?"

"Oh. I tripped. No big deal."

Piper shook her head. "If you wouldn't be so stubborn."

"If you wouldn't be so smothering."

"It's called compassion."

"It's concern, and in this case it's unwarranted. I'm fine."

"Well, that's a first," Piper mocked.

If they were still kids, now's right about when she'd pummel her sister with a pillow. "Well, thanks for the chat, but it's late."

Piper crossed her legs Indian-style. "We both know I'm not going anywhere until you give up the deets on Jake."

Kayden set her PJs on the dresser with a shake of her head. "You're impossible."

"I prefer *persistent*."

Kayden sighed and moved to sit beside her sister on the bed. "What do you want to know?"

"Everything."

Kayden laughed. "Fat chance. I'll answer one question. One," she reiterated before Piper could argue, "but then you have to let me get some sleep."

Piper mulled it over a minute. "Fine. One question." Her smile returned.

Kayden braced herself.

"Are you in love with him?"

Of course Piper would go for the big one.

"Well?"

They both looked over to find Gage leaning against the doorframe.

"Gage!" Piper scowled. "She's never going to answer now."

"Please . . ." He stepped from the doorframe into the room. "She wasn't going to answer you."

"What are you doing here?" Kayden asked, thankful for the reprieve.

"Jake said you took a spill earlier. Just wanted to make sure you were okay."

"I'm fine."

"Of course you are."

"Okay. Enough. Both of you out." She stood and scooted Piper with her crutch toward the door.

"Not until you answer my question," Piper said, stalling against her forward motion.

"Good night, you two." She gently shoved Piper into Gage and both of them into the hall, closing the door behind her with a huff.

"Gage, your timing stinks," Piper said from the other side of the door.

"Oh please, like she'd ever answer that question," Gage retorted. "Besides, she didn't have to. Her face said it all."

Kayden let the door support her weight. Great. Now her siblings knew. Did Jake know too? Could he read it on her face? He had an uncanny knack for reading her.

A mix of embarrassment and excitement drilled through her as she flopped onto the bed. This, as Gage liked to say, was ungood.

Jake walked down the pier, the stars overhead big and beautiful against the black night.

It was cool, the breeze off the water chilling his heated skin. Something akin to happiness soared inside, but he tried to temper it. Angela Markum was out there somewhere, but so far no trace of her had been found—no car registered to her name or her assumed name, no credit-card usage, no one in town having seen her since they raided her place. It was like she'd just vanished, but he knew that was too good to be true.

He moved down the gangway, feeling horrible

that Kayden had tripped. The woman was so incredibly stubborn. Half of him admired her for it, but the other half . . .

He paused at the sight of his glass door cracked open. Pulling his gun, he entered and found a bouquet of cypress flowers wrapped with black ribbon and a note on top of his case files.

Angela had been in his home. There was no sense looking for her. She was long gone.

He lifted the note.

You've got a lot of catching up to do.

He fought the urge to crumple the note, knowing he'd need to admit it into evidence. She'd spent the last four years fixated on him while he'd gone out of his way to forget her. He made himself a cup of coffee and sat back down with his files. She was right. He did have a lot of catching up to do if he was going to snare his prey.

— 35 —

"Still no word on her whereabouts?" Jake asked Landon, who had his deputies canvassing Yancey.

Landon set his coffee mug down with a sigh. "None, I'm afraid."

Jake laid the latest note on Landon's desk. "She's still here. Somewhere."

Landon lifted the note, reading it. "Don't worry. We'll find her."

"Before she strikes again?" Jake asked, the image of Kayden beneath the rocks flashing through his mind.

"We're all taking precautions. She's on our turf this time."

"For only being here a few months, she's studied it well." As the surveillance photos demonstrated.

"Any new insight from the case files?"

"Only regarding the level of her involvement, the fact that she was the one running things."

"I thought you already knew that."

"I knew she was helping her husband, and that the burial spot chosen for Candace Banner's body was too rational to be chosen by the panicking Joel Markum, but at the time I saw her simply as a society wife determined to maintain her lifestyle by any means necessary.

"But now, as I reread our interviews with Joel and Angela, as well as the interviews with the people who worked with them and knew them, a different picture emerged. The fact that Joel took his own life proved his weakness, his desperation. The decisions made about burying Candace's body, disposing of the evidence, covering their tracks—they were all undertaken by a shrewd and calculating person, one with no remorse or emotional attachment."

"You think Joel Markum regretted killing Candace?"

"We'll never know if he regretted killing her or simply regretted getting caught, but the murder appeared to be a crime of passion and emotion. Everything that happened after the murder was cold and calculated. Those decisions were made by a different person."

Landon sat back, his chair creaking. "Angela."

Jake nodded. "Which makes me more concerned than if we were dealing with Joel. She's smart and she's clearly invested the time in whatever she's got planned. We need to find her before she makes her next move."

Kayden sat on a chair in the middle of Angela Markum's war room, studying the labyrinth of photos, articles, and plans laid out on the wall in front of them.

Jake had wheeled in a large whiteboard, making notes and setting up a timeline to track Angela's whereabouts and focus. The only way to catch the woman was to get inside her head—twisted and vengeful as it may be.

"That picture"—Kayden pointed to one of her climbing Jagger's Peak—"was taken about a week after we returned from the *Bering*."

"Are you sure?"

Kayden nodded. She always remembered her climbs. It was unnerving to realize the woman had been watching her then, making her plans.

How many times had she talked with Carol about her upcoming climbs? How much had she told her, period? Her mind raced back through their conversations. She'd never considered Carol overly pushy or intrusive. All their chats had been comfortable, and it was frightening to imagine all the information she'd passed on unwittingly. Tidbits about her siblings, about their interests, even some of their routines and schedules. It had all been casual—casual but calculated on Angela's part.

Jake rested a warm hand on her shoulder. "You okay?"

"Yeah. Just regretting ever speaking to her."

"There was no way for you to know."

"I know, but it's frustrating. She was so friendly and laid back and . . ."

"She's good at fooling people. When I first met her, I thought she was the proper president's wife—dutiful, elegant. I had no idea the heart of a killer resided inside."

"Killer?"

"I doubt she was just trying to wound you with the rockslide."

Kayden took that in, really thinking about it for the first time. "What do you think her next move will be?"

"Another attempt."

"On me?"

"My gut says yes, but she's clearly been following all of you." He gestured to all the McKennas' photos, along with Landon and Darcy. "She likes to toy with people. She might make a smaller move."

"Or?"

"Go straight for the kill."

It wasn't Jake's intent to scare Kayden, but he wanted her to understand the depth of Angela's depravity. Her need for revenge fueled her, propelled her on. She wouldn't stop until he lost those he loved again—unless he stopped her first, which was exactly what he intended to do.

They'd checked with the landlords of every rental property in Yancey and now were spreading out to cover the outlying cabins on Tariuk. So far no one recognized Angela's photo or Kayden's police sketch of "Carol."

The cabins rented to women were few, and it didn't take long to rule them out—most going to younger women in their twenties, transplants, divorcees, or migrant workers in town for the salmon season. No one matched Angela's description. They'd also ruled out the B and Bs and lodges; Jake's frustration grew with each dead end.

He studied Kayden, her eyes tracking Angela's postings on the board and then switching to follow Jake's notes. He'd written down everything they knew about Angela Markum. Both of her early-morning messages to Kayden had come at 5:11. The same time Becca had been pronounced dead, albeit p.m. Angela was leaving a very clear message. Kayden was next.

Jake stood and stretched.

They'd been surrounded by Angela's madness for hours, and it was getting to him. He needed a break. He glanced at his watch. They'd completely bypassed lunch.

"Let's grab some dinner."

"Dinner?" Kayden looked up at him.

"It's already six."

Kayden blinked. "Wow. I didn't realize we'd been here that long."

"Occupational hazard." Jake smiled. "Cases have a way of sucking you in."

"Dinner sounds good. I'm sure Piper has something going at the house."

"I was thinking Chinese."

"Oh?"

"I've been craving General Tso's, and I know you love the Imperial Garden."

She hesitated a moment. Was she trying to figure out if he was suggesting a date? Whatever they called it, he was simply thrilled to continue spending time with her.

"Okay. I could go for some Hunan beef."

"Great." He moved to help her up.

"I got it."

He backed off. She was so incredibly stubborn.

It took her a few minutes, but she hefted herself out of the chair and stabilized herself, for the most part, on her crutch.

"After you."

The Imperial Garden was packed—families, couples, even a few singles, crowded the red vinyl booths and black lacquer tables.

The waitress showed them to one of the booths near the front entrance, not far from the rice-paper screen dividing the takeout counter from the dining area. The restaurant was louder and a lot less intimate than he'd hoped, but he wasn't complaining. He was eating out with the woman he loved.

After perusing the menu to make sure neither had changed their mind, they ordered, and then Kayden excused herself, hobbling to her feet. "I'll be right back."

"Let me help you." The thought of her weaving her way through the crowded restaurant made him beyond nervous.

She smiled. "I think I can handle the ladies' room on my own."

His face heated. "Of course. I just meant I'd help you back there." The restrooms were on the opposite side of the restaurant.

"I'll be fine. But don't eat all the noodles while I'm gone." She lifted her bruised chin, indicating the crunchy noodles they both loved.

Jake caught himself holding his breath as she

worked her way around tables, waitresses, and a little kid's train that had fallen from his booster seat onto the floor. He sighed with relief when she finally reached the back hall leading to the restrooms.

Kayden made it to the ladies' room, her shoulder sore from the crutch, her body taxed from the uneven gait. She couldn't wait until the stupid cast came off and she could walk easily again. She used the facilities and stepped to the sink to wash her hands, propping her crutch beside her and her weight against the marble sink. A mother with two small children left the restroom just as a stall door opened behind her.

She switched on the water, pumped soap onto her palms, and began to lather. A man appeared behind her—short and slight.

She turned as something sharp pierced her neck. "What on earth?"

Her eyes fixed on the man's, and she recognized the smile. "Ange—" Everything faded away.

— 36 —

Jake pushed the bowl of crunchy noodles away before he ate them all. What was taking Kayden so long? Yes, she was on crutches, and yes, it would obviously take her longer, but . . .

He glanced at his watch. It'd already been twelve minutes. What if the floor was slippery and she'd fallen in the ladies' room?

He moved to stand and then sat back down. If he barged in on her, if he even knocked on the door and she was fine, she'd be ticked. Better to wait. He watched the numbers on his digital watch tick by. Thirteen minutes. Fourteen. At fifteen he stood. She could be mad at him if she wanted, but he had to be certain she was okay.

He moved across the restaurant toward the back hall, his chest tightening.

He passed the men's room and paused at the door to the ladies' room. Bracing himself for the backlash, he knocked.

No answer.

"Kayden." He knocked a second time.

No answer.

He pushed the door open a crack. "Kayden, just making sure you're all right." The sinks were empty.

"Excuse me?" A woman said impatiently behind him.

He turned to find a short blonde.

"Sorry. My friend went in there fifteen minutes ago and hasn't come back out. I'm worried something's wrong."

"Maybe she ditched you." The woman pointed to the back door not five feet away.

Fear grasped Jake by the throat. *Please, no.* He rushed into the bathroom.

"Hey!" the woman yelled.

"Kayden." He searched under stalls. *Empty.* She wasn't there. He raced past the blonde and out the back door. The alley was narrow but wide enough for a vehicle. Had Angela . . . ?

Terror choked the breath from his lungs.

Kayden woke to the sound of an engine and road noise. She opened her eyes, but darkness engulfed her. She was lying on her back on what felt like a hard metal floor—a pickup?—and something hard was poking beneath her shoulder blade.

She shifted, her hands bound, her legs too. It didn't feel like rope against her skin. It was sticky and tight. Duct tape, perhaps. It covered her mouth as well.

She turned her head to her right and saw two slits of red equal distance apart. Taillights. She shifted to move her feet closer to one of the lights. Whatever was poking her back dug in deeper. Leading with her casted foot, she kicked at the red light, trying to bust it out. It took several kicks until it shattered. Hopefully it would draw a cop's attention.

She kicked at the pickup's hard top, trying to pop it open, trying to keep most of the force on her uninjured leg, but pain radiating down her leg was all she got for her trouble. She settled back, knowing the next best thing she could do was listen for any markers that might help her identify where Angela was taking her.

Jake burst into Landon's office. "She's taken Kayden."

"Angela? Are you certain?"

"Kayden went into the bathroom at the Imperial Garden and never came back. I checked the bathroom and it was empty. The rear door is only a few feet away. And there's space in the alleyway for a vehicle."

"You think Angela followed you there and then sat in wait?"

"That's exactly what I think."

"Did you try calling Kayden's cell?"

"It was in her purse, at the table with me." He dropped it on Landon's desk.

Landon picked up his phone. "Let me call Piper and make sure Kayden didn't bolt . . . for some reason."

"Like what?"

"Maybe she realized you two were on a date and—"

"She just took off without her purse, cell phone, or a means of transportation?"

"I know it's farfetched. I just need to confirm." He moved his hand off the mouthpiece. "Hey, babe. Is Kayden with you?" His expression hardened. "When's the last time you heard from her? Jake's here." He went on to explain, trying to calm Piper down in the process. "Let me get on this, and I'll call you back. You don't have to . . . Okay. See you soon."

"She's on her way over?"

"I imagine they all will be."

"That's good. The more people we have to track Kayden, the better." They were going to need all the help they could get. They had no leads on Angela's whereabouts. *Wait a minute* . . . "Kirra. I'm such a fool."

"What about her?"

"When we checked with the DMV and didn't get a hit on anything registered to Carol Jones or Angela Markum, we let it go, decided we'd hit a dead end, but Kirra must at least know what her car looks like. We can put out an APB on the description."

"You really think she's stupid enough to drive the same car she did when posing as Carol?"

"It's a long shot, but right now it's the only lead we have to go on."

Landon lifted the phone. "I'll call Kirra."

Within twenty minutes all the McKennas, Darcy, and Kirra had descended on the station.

"We should call Cole," Gage said.

Jake hated to bother him on his honeymoon, but if he had a sister who'd been kidnapped, he'd want to know ASAP.

Kirra provided a description of the car Angela

had used when posing as Carol—a Nissan Altima. Silver. Four-door sedan.

"Any chance you caught some of her license plate?" Jake asked.

Kirra grimaced. "Sorry. I don't notice things like that."

"Was that the only car Angela ever drove?"

"Yes . . . Well, there was one day she showed up in a truck. She said it was a loaner while her car was in the shop."

"Can you describe it?"

"It was an older model Toyota Tacoma. Midnight blue. Still looked to be in good shape."

"Did she say which shop she went to?"

"No, but I asked. Told her Lenny's was the best in town."

"And she'd gone to . . . ?"

"William Rogers' place."

Jake nodded. "On it."

Jake entered William Rogers' garage. William was in his sixties, and both of his sons ran the shop. "Hey, Will," he greeted the junior William—he was working late; it was almost eight.

"Hey, Jake. Don't tell me your truck's acting up again."

"No. I'm here for an entirely different reason." He took a moment to give Will the details.

"Yeah. I remember the Altima. Needed a new timing belt."

"Did you happen to note the license plate number by any chance?"

"Yeah, actually. We record the license plates of all the cars we service."

Thank you, God.

Jake anxiously paced while Will retrieved Angela's records.

"Here you go, man."

"Can I take this, or do you need me to make a copy?"

"I'll copy it for you. It'll only take a sec."

"Thanks." Now they had a way to track her, possibly, if she hadn't changed vehicles. "Oh, Kirra Jacobs said Angela drove a loaner truck while you repaired her car."

"She might have, but I don't recall seeing it."

"You didn't loan her the truck?"

"Nah. We don't have the resources for that sort of thing."

"So, if she got a loaner . . . ?"

"You should talk to Nadine over at the rental-car company. Only place I know she'd get one, but they don't usually rent out trucks. They get too much wear on the four-wheel-drive vehicles."

"Thanks. Heading over there now."

Jake made the quick walk two blocks down the street, praying the rental company wouldn't close before he reached it. The night air was cool on his heated skin. He rounded the last corner and found Nadine locking up for the night. "Hey, Nadine."

"Hey, Jake." Nadine's close-cropped hair was a deep shade of red, though dark roots crowning her part said the color wasn't natural. "What's going on?"

He explained, showing her Angela's photo.

"I'm sorry. I didn't rent anything to her. And I don't have any trucks that fit that description. We try not to rent out four-wheel-drive vehicles, because people use them to go off-roading and bring them back all muddy and busted up."

So Angela Markum had kept a second car. Very smart, but thankfully they had a description of the vehicle from Kirra. It'd be better if they had a license plate to go with it, but at least they had someplace to start.

The truck pulled to a stop with a jerk, and Kayden readied herself to kick out as soon as Angela opened the truck-bed cover.

The cover lifted and she kicked, but Angela stood, still dressed as a man, a safe distance away.

"I suggest you settle down or I'll have to make you."

No way she'd comply willingly. She'd never go down without a fight.

"I expected as much. I see we're going to have to do this the hard way." Angela lifted a pole and jammed it at Kayden, sending jolts of electricity through her.

— 37 —

Landon put out an APB on both known vehicles of Angela Markum, praying they'd get a hit, but so far, no luck.

The Altima was registered to Carol *Willis,* which meant not only had she adopted the persona of Carol Jones that she used when meeting people in Yancey, she'd also used a second false name to establish fake documentation. Two layers of disguise. Angela had thought of everything—and that terrified Jake.

Unfortunately the Altima was the only vehicle registered in Carol Willis's name, so chances were she'd stolen the secondary vehicle or paid cash for it to someone desperate enough to sell it without going through official channels.

"I'm going to go talk with Ralph Barnes, find out if he remembers seeing Carol driving the truck," Thoreau said. "He might have had a reason to observe the license plate."

"Good idea," Landon said. "All of Yancey's search and rescue have been called in. Gage is coordinating search parties now."

If Kayden was still on Tariuk, they'd find her. Jake's fear was that Angela had gone off the island with her, and that would greatly extend their search parameters.

Gage paired up the search teams. Kirra was frustrated when she ended up with Reef, but she didn't want to make waves by asking for another partner. Kayden's life was on the line. Surely she and Reef could work past their differences for his sister's sake.

"Let's run by and pick up Rex before we start our grid," she said, heading for the door.

"Why?" He followed her out of the station into the cool evening air. "We have our grid. We should get started."

"Rex is Kayden's favorite, and he adores her. Using him will greatly aid our search."

Reef stood, leg twitching. He always wanted to race straight to action. And to be honest, his way of approaching things—act first, think later—was part of what made him so attractive to her . . . and what most annoyed her about him.

"Trust me," she said.

"Fine, if you really believe it will help, but let's hurry. That's my sister out there."

"I know."

The ride back to her place took fifteen minutes, and Reef's leg never stopped bouncing. She fought the burning urge to reach over and clamp her hand on his knee just to make the constant motion stop.

She pulled up outside the barn and raced inside. They'd been assigned the grid surrounding

Northface, along a line of hunting and fishing cabins, but they would follow where Rex led.

She grabbed the sweatshirt Kayden had left hanging on the hook inside the barn and let Rex out of his kennel. "Here, boy." She let him sniff the sweatshirt. "Let's find Kayden."

Kirra drove while Rex rode in the back. "Where's the last place Kayden was seen?"

"The Imperial Garden. She went to use the bathroom and never came back."

Kirra stepped on the gas. "The Imperial Garden it is."

"But we're supposed to cover Northface."

"And we will, but Kayden's scent will be strongest where she was last seen. Rex can even track which direction she was taken."

Reef looked back at the husky. "Really?"

"Yes. He's a trained search-and-rescue scent dog."

"Who trained him?"

"I did."

"I didn't realize you knew how to do that."

"I do. I run Yancey's canine search-and-rescue unit."

"Kayden mentioned that. I just didn't realize you did the training too."

"I've been doing it for years, along with my dad, until my parents moved away." Dogs were so much more faithful than people, at least in her experience.

"Interesting," he said with a smile.

She shifted to study him better. Reef McKenna found something *she* did to be interesting? Well, that was a first.

For the rest of the drive to the Imperial Garden, she tried to keep her mind focused on the task of finding Kayden and not on how very handsome Reef McKenna was sitting beside her—tall, sculpted body, curly blond hair, deep blue eyes. The man was breathtaking. *Just like William.*

Agony pricked her afresh. It'd been weeks since she'd thought about . . . since her last nightmare. More than a year had passed, and she still had nightmares. When would they stop?

After Reef notified the owners, Kirra led Rex through the front of the Imperial Garden, had him smell Kayden's sweatshirt. He immediately picked up her scent and followed her path from the front table to the ladies' room and on to the back door. Kirra opened it, and they stepped outside, the alley nearly dark. Rex sniffed, signaling east.

"She left from here, heading east in a vehicle."

"He can tell that?"

"Yes."

"What's your best guess of their destination?"

"The docks."

Jake hung up, trying not to chuck his phone against the wall. *The ferry.* He should have known, but how did Angela get Kayden on the ferry and keep her subdued during transport?

No doubt she'd knocked Kayden unconscious or drugged her, and what . . . ? Hid her in her truck? Kirra had said it had a hard-shell cover over the bed. Angela had clearly put a lot of thought into her plans. It was downright frightening, and he feared what else she had in store before their nightmare was over.

His stomach clenched. If Kayden had been at full strength, there was no way Angela could have overcome her. But being nearly immobile, Kayden . . .

He had to focus. *The ferry.* From Yancey there were only two direct options—Imnek and Kodiak. That helped narrow their scope, but only if Angela remained on one of those islands. If she took another ferry from there . . . He rushed to the ferry station. Reef had said he would call everyone else.

During the summer, the ferry ran every three hours. The ride to Imnek only took an hour and a half. The ride to Kodiak took about three hours. Jake looked at his watch. "Call the ferry stations. Have them watch for Angela arriving," he said to Landon. He prayed she was headed for Kodiak and they'd still have time to intercept —but she was probably too smart to give them that much time to figure out she had taken the ferry. And if she'd gone directly to Imnek, they were probably too late.

Once Landon was on his cell with the ferry station in Imnek and Gage on the phone with the Kodiak station, Jake stepped inside Yancey's terminal office. "Hey, Cal," he greeted the man working the desk, "any chance you remember this lady buying a ticket in the last three hours?" He held out Angela's photo.

Cal studied the photo. "Can't say that I do, but the boys were working the line." During tourist season, the guys stood outside by the vehicle line and sold tickets directly to the drivers, helping avoid a backup.

"Are they still on shift?"

Cal raised an eyebrow. "Yeah. I'll call them."

Jed and Russ met Jake by the pier. Jed was young, early twenties, with light blond hair; Russ was older, midthirties, with the weathered skin of a mariner.

Jake showed them Angela's picture. Both inspected it, and Jed tapped the photograph. "That looks a lot like Carol. I've seen her plenty of times, but not today."

"Oh?"

"Yeah, a real hottie for an older lady."

Jake supposed a woman in her midforties would look *older* to a twenty-year-old.

"Why do you remember her?" There had to be some reason she stuck in his mind.

Jed shrugged with a smile. "Because she was nice. We chatted during her trips. Maybe even flirted a little."

"Trips?"

"Yeah she made weekly trips to Imnek and back."

"For how long?"

"Past couple months."

So she'd been preparing for this all along. "What did you two chat about?"

"I don't know." Jed leaned against the rail. "Nothing in particular."

"Did she say why she was going to Imnek so frequently?"

"Nah. I think I asked once, but she just changed the subject. You know how folks around here are about their privacy."

"Yeah." People in Yancey, in most of Alaska, prided themselves on the privacy that living in such a rugged land, away from crowded cities and the need to always be in your neighbor's business, afforded them.

"And you're positive you haven't seen her tonight?"

"Positive . . . but I saw her truck. Some dude was driving it."

"A man?"

"Yeah."

"And you're sure it was her truck?" He pointed to Angela's picture.

"I'm sure. Had the cool Brembo calipers that kick-started our first conversation. Thought it was pretty cool a chick like her was driving a truck with red Brembo brake calipers."

"Which ferry did the man with her truck take? Imnek or Kodiak?"

Jed thought a moment. "Imnek."

"Has it docked there already?" Unfortunately, Jake already knew the answer. He just wished it were different.

Jed looked at his watch. "Twenty minutes ago."

Jake exhaled, frustration searing through him.

"Can you describe the man?" Landon asked, coming up behind him.

Jed raked a hand through his close-cropped hair. "He was kind of short for a dude."

"How short?"

"Maybe five-six or five-seven."

"What else?"

"He had short dark hair and a goatee."

"Have you ever seen him before?"

"Nope." Jed shook his head. "Not that I recall."

"Never with Angela?"

"Angela?" Jed squinted.

"*Angela* is Carol's real name."

"Oh, right. No, I never saw them together."

"Did you talk to him at all?"

"The man?"

"Yeah."

"Nah. Just saw him pull up in Carol's truck. I thought it was kind of odd, but I just figured he was a friend of hers."

"Was anyone else with him?"

"Not that I saw." He looked at his co-worker, who to this point had remained silent but interested. "You, Russ?"

Russ shook his head. "Sorry, I don't know who you're talking about. And I don't remember the truck either."

Landon glanced over at Jake. "You think she has an accomplice?"

"It's possible. Or it could be Angela, wearing a disguise." He lifted his chin at Jed. "Could you describe her truck, besides the brake calipers?" Though that detail alone was extremely helpful. "Make? Model? Any chance you saw the license plate?"

"It was an older Toyota Tacoma. Dark blue."

Jake nodded. "When you say older . . . how old are you talking?"

Jed exhaled. "Oh, I'd probably say an '03 or '04."

"Any chance you saw her license plate?"

"It wasn't a vanity plate. Just a regular Alaskan plate. Three letters. Three numbers." He draped his arms along the rails, his fingers tapping the wood as he thought.

"Any guesses?"

"I have no clue about the letters." Jed rubbed

his chin. The faint shadow of blond whiskers dappled his sun-tanned skin.

"Any idea on the numbers?"

"That was 122."

"You're sure?" Seemed an odd thing to remember.

"Positive. I do a thing with license plate numbers and football stats. Keeps things interesting. Anyway, 122 . . . Staubach was number twelve and he won two Super Bowls. The man's a legend—and I'm telling you, that lady looked like she could have been a Dallas Cowboy cheerleader back in her prime." He blushed a bit. "Well, that's how I made the connection."

"Thanks, Jed." Jake clamped him on the shoulder and then pulled a card from his pocket with his cell number scrolled across the back. "If you think of anything else—anything at all— you give me a call."

Jed nodded.

Landon ran the partial he supplied through the database while Jake called Ned at the Imnek ferry station to let him know they were looking for a truck that had arrived on the last ferry.

Nobody had noticed Angela's truck unloading on Imnek, but Ned said they would comb the parking lot for it, just in case Angela was waiting to take another ferry out from there.

"I've got two possible truck matches to the

partial on Tariuk," Landon said. "A 2004 Toyota belonging to a Paul Freeman, and a 2003 that last belonged to a Roger Harris."

"Last belonged?"

"Tags haven't been renewed in three years."

"You think he just had it sitting on his property?" He'd seen it before. Unable to afford the vehicle expenses, the owner let it sit, collecting dust.

"That'd be my guess. Somehow Angela connected with him and paid cash to take it off his hands. Smart on her part. It keeps her name off of everything and leaves no paper trail." She was one shrewd woman.

"I'll send Thoreau to talk to Mr. Harris, and then I'll call the Imnek Sheriff's Department and inform them of what's going on," Landon said. "Get an APB out on the plates."

"All right. I'm heading for Imnek," Jake said, his first instinct to ask Kayden to fly him there.

"We don't know that they're still on Imnek."

"We know they aren't here. Imnek is the last point of reference. I need to be there."

"We'll come with you," Gage said behind him.

He wasn't going to argue. The more people he trusted looking for Kayden, the better. "Okay. Grab anything you need and meet at the airport. We have no idea how long we'll be gone or where we may end up." He looked to Piper. "Call

Chuck Lassiter to see if he'll fly us over. He's got a ten-seat Cessna."

Piper nodded and stepped from the room.

"I'll call my volunteers so they can arrange to watch the dogs while I'm away," Kirra said.

Jake checked his watch. "We need to be airborne in thirty."

— 38 —

Chuck graciously complied with their request, and they landed on Imnek mere minutes past the hour mark. They disembarked into darkness, and Jake headed for the ferry station with Reef, Kirra, and Rex, while Landon and the rest of the crew headed for the sheriff's station and the local SAR headquarters. Without Cole present—he and Bailey were on a flight back, but weren't due to arrive until tomorrow evening—Gage ranked highest in Yancey search and rescue and regional command, with Imnek local Rodney Neary second in regional command. The only problem before their search began in earnest was determining if Angela had stayed on Imnek or used it as a launching point. He prayed she was still on the island and that they were closing in.

Jake followed Kirra and Rex up onto the ferry still docked in port, and the dog traced her scent to the vehicle deck. She'd been on the ferry.

If only he'd been quicker. Jake glanced to his left with a sigh and walked through the boat's cafeteria. He squinted at a piece of paper wedged in the frame of the window. He knew what it was before he reached it. The woman was taunting him.

Anger flaring, he snatched the note free of the frame and unfolded it.

I see you haven't lost your touch. That will make this all the more enjoyable. See you when I'm ready.

Jake slammed his fist into his palm, crushing the paper—smashing his fear and frustration into her lethal words.

"See you when I'm ready."

She was in control of the playing field, and she knew it.

He rushed up to the wheelhouse, where he found the captain ready to off-load for the night. "Are there any cameras on this ship?"

"Only one. In the cafeteria. Sometimes we're short staffed and kids think it's a license to steal snacks or to mess with the vending machines, but we catch it all on camera."

"Can I see the footage from the last run?"

"Sure."

Landon stood beside Jake as they scrolled through the footage.

"There." Jake pointed.

The captain hit Pause.

It was Angela sipping her drink, staring straight up at the camera with a smile.

"She's bold," Landon said.

"And extremely dangerous." And she had the woman he loved.

They spread out in search teams from the west end of the parking lot, where Kayden's scent went cold, trying to cover as much ground as possible. They alerted the airport—though getting a subdued Kayden on a plane without someone noticing and asking questions seemed unlikely—and continued to comb the remaining marinas.

"You holding up okay?" Reef asked Jake.

Jake shook his head. How could he have been so stupid? He should have insisted on walking Kayden back to the ladies' room despite her protests, but who would have thought Angela would be so bold, kidnapping Kayden from a public place? Wearing a disguise. Assuming a new identity. Dual vehicles. The woman was devious, and she'd done her planning.

Question was, where would she take Kayden? A remote cabin? If so, she'd choose someplace with high ground. A boat, perhaps? It would provide maneuverability. With her disguises, she could try to hide in town, but he doubted it. She'd have a canvas laid out, a playing surface for the dangerous game she'd arranged.

"I'm sorry, Jake," Sheriff Jacob Marshall said. "So far, there's been no sign of them."

Angela was smart. It'd been late when she'd landed in Imnek. Most people would have been at home, not walking around town. She'd slipped right in or through without drawing much attention.

"Why choose a truck for a second vehicle?" he asked.

"It's what was available?" Kirra suggested.

"No. Everything Angela's done up to this point has been deliberate. She needed a truck because . . ." Jake posed.

"She needed four-wheel drive," Gage said.

Jake snapped. "Yes! Which means off road."

"She could have also needed hauling capabilities," Reef said as his eyes widened. "I mean for supplies."

And Kayden. The thought of what she might be going through twisted Jake's gut. When he found Angela Markum, it was going to take God's strength to stop him from killing her.

Kayden woke. The vehicle was bouncing over bumpy roads, knocking her about the truck bed with force.

It was dark. No daylight shone through the busted taillight.

The temperature had dropped, and a damp mustiness engulfed her. Where was Angela taking her, and how far behind was Jake?

Sheriff Marshall allowed them to set up a command center within his station. Jake found a rolling whiteboard and was outlining what they knew. He'd brought his working file with him, and soon his case board was in place. But what was he missing? Something was off. Angela wanted to be found. It was part of her twisted game, so what clue was he overlooking?

"Here." Landon handed him a cup of joe.

"Thanks." He gulped it down, ignoring the burn, needing the recharge the caffeine would supply.

"We need a topographical map of the island, need to pinpoint abandoned areas Angela may have taken Kayden to."

"*If* she settles somewhere, and *if* she's still on Imnek," Landon said. "I'm not trying to be negative, but we have to consider the possibility that Angela's moved Kayden off the island."

Jake looked at Gage, who was co-leading the search-and-rescue teams with Rodney Neary. "Any sign of Angela's truck?"

"I'm afraid not. We've canvassed the airport and all the marina parking lots and surrounding areas."

"Then she's still here."

"How do you figure that?" Landon asked.

"Because she didn't take a ferry out. She couldn't haul an unconscious Kayden onto a plane, and there's no way Kayden would go willingly. If Angela had taken a boat, her truck would be found at a marina or nearby. She's still on Imnek. I can feel it."

Landon took a sip of his coffee. "I pray you're right."

Jake took a deep breath.

Please, Father, guide me to Kayden before it's too late.

He couldn't even think about, couldn't fathom, not finding her.

Landon clamped a hand on his shoulder. "You okay, man?"

"As okay as I can be."

"You just got real pale and looked like you were going to hurl."

"I'll be fine. I just need to stay focused on the task at hand." On rescuing Kayden. He couldn't allow the doubts to creep in or they would paralyze him. He would find her, and she would be okay.

"One of Marshall's deputies is pulling the topographical map as we speak."

Jake nodded, thankful Landon had such a good relationship with Jacob Marshall. The sheriff was going above and beyond, and Jake would be forever grateful, but time was slipping away. Every hour, every minute that passed took Kayden one step farther from him.

He studied the board in front of him, wondering what he was missing.

Gage stood beside him. "You've been staring at that board for an awful long while," he said as his team prepared to head back out and widen the search as soon as the first glimmers of dawn appeared.

"I'm just trying to figure out the clue I missed." Angela's MO was to leave "clever" messages. Back in Boston it'd been the cypress flowers. In Yancey it'd been the rock, the flowers, the notes. What message was he missing now?

Gage frowned. "Why do you think you missed something?"

"Because Angela's been leaving me messages. She expected Rex would lead us in the direction of the ferry station and knew I'd search the video. She wants me to find her, so what am I missing?"

"See you when I'm ready."

Maybe she hadn't left the next message, the next clue. Did she want time with Kayden to—Jake cut off the thought with a hard swallow. The silence was torture. He needed the next move, and now.

"You think Angela is reeling you in?" Gage asked, concern thick in his tone.

"Absolutely."

"Doesn't she realize the rest of us will be coming with you? That she'll be caught?"

"No. She's got something planned. Something that'll separate us, that will draw me in alone."

"And then?"

Then she'd kill Kayden before his eyes, if she hadn't already.

Becca's death flashed through his mind. Joel Markum had mistimed it. Three minutes later and Jake would have witnessed the horrific event. Instead, he'd rounded the corner to find his wife lying dead on the pavement, a handful of cypress flowers bunched on her belly. They'd taken Becca to the ER, tried to save the baby still alive inside her belly, but they were too late. His daughter died too. His little girl, no bigger than the palm of his hand, had died at the hands of Joel Markum. Whether Joel did the actual driving or hired someone to do the heartless deed for him, he was to blame. Now his wife was picking up where he'd left off, ready to rip Kayden from his life.

Please, God, not again. Not Kayden.

— 39 —

The truck stopped and Kayden held her breath, bracing for what was coming next. The front door opened and then shut. Footsteps moved toward the rear of the vehicle.

Painfully, she scooted down to the tailgate,

ready to kick out as it opened. Instead the bed cover lifted, and Kayden kicked, but Angela wisely stood off center and out of range.

"I can see we're still going to have to do this the hard way." She lifted the pole and jammed it at Kayden, once again sending jolts of electricity coursing through her.

Kirra walked beside Reef as they explored the last marina on Imnek. It was on Imnek's south side—completely across the island from Spruce Harbor—but Jake had decided all marinas and modes of transport to get off the island needed to be checked before they moved on to the hunting and fishing cabins. It was still dark, and a chill hovered in the predawn air.

"Are you cold?" Reef asked.

Yes. "I'm okay."

"Here." He slid off his jacket—"Take this"— and draped it across her shoulders.

She wanted to say no. She should say no, but she was freezing. "Are you sure?"

"Positive."

"You won't get cold?" she asked.

"I'm a boarder. I'm most at home in the cold." He smiled.

She slid her arms into the sleeves, grateful for the warmth but careful to keep a fair amount of distance between her and Reef. "When we were growing up, you seemed most at home in the water," she said, feeling more at ease while the conversation kept going. It was the silence that bothered her.

Reef slid his hands into his cargo-pant pockets. "I love the water," he said. "I love the mountains. Pretty much as long as I'm outdoors, I'm thrilled."

She'd always thought he'd follow in his mom's footsteps and become a professional swimmer, but he'd gone with snowboarding and surfing instead.

Seeing him on the beach growing up, his tanned skin, the sun glistening off his blond curls, his toned body . . .

She shook off the image. This was Reef McKenna. They had nothing in common, he had a girlfriend, and more importantly, she was done with men, so there was no point in thinking about his tanned anything. "Where's your girlfriend?" Why couldn't he have been paired with her? "You didn't want her helping search?" It was her best guess. The lady hardly looked the outdoor type.

Reef's step faltered, and then he cleared his throat. "Actually, Anna and I are no longer together."

"Oh. Sorry."

He glanced at her sideways. "I know what you're thinking."

She doubted it. "What's that?"

"That either Anna came to her senses and realized I wasn't good enough for her or that I screwed up again."

"I wasn't thinking either." She was thinking how vastly different they had appeared. Kayden had been going on and on about how Reef had changed. Perhaps it was true, as unlikely as it seemed.

"I know what you think of me. Though based on my past behavior, I suppose it's understandable."

For once she kept her mouth shut, but her mind *still* raced. Had reckless Reef really changed?

Kayden woke, her body in severe pain, her neck stiff. It was dark, except for a small battery-operated lantern set up on a table about fifty feet to her left. She turned, her arms catching with the movement. She yanked, finding herself handcuffed and chained to a wall.

Fear rippled through her.

Where was she? And what did Angela have planned?

"We got it," Landon said, spreading the topographical map across the table.

"Okay," Jake said. "We could use Marshall's help."

"Right here."

He turned to find the sheriff already standing behind him. Marshall nodded. "Whatever you need, Jake."

"What are the likely places Angela might hide

out? Hunters' cabins, ski lodges closed for the summer months, even cave systems—though I doubt that's Angela's style. The ferry employee said she'd taken the ferry to Imnek once a week for the past couple months. She could have been searching out a spot and supplying it."

Marshall set to work circling areas in red. "Can't say I know every hunting cabin, but most are in these two regions." He boxed them in red. "We've got two ski lodges, but both areas are pretty heavily hiked and mountain biked during the off-season. We've got a number of wilderness emergency shelters and ranger stations that can all be empty at any given time. An abandoned mine out on the south face of the Eagle Mountain and, of course, a handful of abandoned military bunkers."

"Bunkers?" Jake asked.

"Left over from World War II and the Cold War."

"Like Fort Greely on Kodiak?" Gage asked.

"Yes, but like the majority on Kodiak, they haven't been designated as historical landmarks. They're just abandoned facilities. You'll get groups of teens or vandals partying out there, and the occasional group of eager explorers or history buffs, but for the most part they are just a reminder of Imnek's pivotal location during World War II and the Cold War."

Few people realized the role Alaska played in World War II or how close to American soil the threat had come anywhere other than Pearl Harbor.

"Okay," Jake said, quickly formulating a plan. "Let's split up. I'll call Reef and Kirra, tell them to go ahead with the blocks of hunting cabins. Landon, you and Piper take the old mine and shelters. Gage and Darcy, you'll be with me on the bunkers." He couldn't explain why, but deep down he was certain Angela had Kayden in one of the bunkers. Even so, they had to spread out the searchers. He couldn't take the chance he was wrong.

"And Rodney has organized the search-and-rescue volunteers—they'll head out at dawn, if not before," Sheriff Marshall said.

Gage nodded. "Yes, they're ready to roll."

"We've got to assume Angela's armed and dangerous," Landon said, "so if anyone locates her, call it in immediately. And remember to keep an eye out for her truck. She'll be keeping it close by."

"For a quick getaway?" Reef asked.

"That, and she had to transport Kayden from the truck to wherever she's holding her. With her broken leg, Kayden couldn't walk too far, especially out in the wilderness."

Please, Father, don't let Angela hurt her.

"We meet back here at the end of the day?" Kirra asked.

"Yes, unless you want to take supplies and camp out. It would save a lot of time not having to make the trek back to town each night."

"That's a great idea," Gage said. "Except we don't have our camping gear with us."

"We can get you what you need," Marshall said. "Just give us a list."

"We can also call Natalie Adams over at Imnek Adventures," Gage added. "She rents out equipment. I'm sure she'll be happy to help."

Jake wasn't so sure, but it didn't hurt to ask. "Let's do this quickly, people," he said, urgency nipping at him. "I'd like us deployed ASAP." Angela already had way too big of a head start.

Forty minutes later, the teams were packed and ready to go.

Reef and Kirra headed for the first grid of hunting cabins, their camping gear stowed in their packs.

Rex was thrilled to be outside, but the fact that the search was extending into a second day had him antsy.

The sun had risen, signaling the beginning of a gorgeous day, but all Reef could think about was his sister in some madwoman's clutches.

He was so thankful he'd been home to help. He couldn't imagine the agony Cole must be going through while trying to make it back.

"Are you familiar with Imnek?" Reef asked.

Kirra shook her head. "We aided in a SAR rescue here last year, but no, I don't know it like I do Tariuk."

"You think that's why Angela brought Kayden here, because it's not as familiar to us?"

"Absolutely." She kicked at a pebble in their path with tremendous force. "I still can't believe she totally fooled me."

That really seemed to bug her. "You weren't the only one she fooled. Kayden thought she was a sweet lady." He hated to imagine what that "sweet" lady might be doing to his sister.

"I know, but the thought that a maniac worked at my shelter, at *my* home, with my dogs. . . . It creeps me out."

"I can only imagine."

Kirra pointed at the hunter's cabin ahead.

Reef pulled his gun, thankful his dad had taught them all to shoot from a young age, taught them respect for the weapon and for life, but also the importance of self-defense and self-protection.

He focused on the cabin before them.

"I'll head around back while you knock on the front door," Kirra said, "but Rex isn't signaling he smells her."

Reef nodded and knocked on the cabin door, his rifle tight in hand. No one answered. He knocked a second time, then jiggled the handle and found it unlocked. He stepped inside the one-room cabin and waved at Kirra peering in from the back window. *Empty.* One down, who knew how many more to go. Rex wasn't the only antsy one.

Where are you, Kayden?

— 40 —

The bunkers Marshall had labeled on Jake's map were spread across the island at strategic military points, and it would take them days to reach and explore them all. Jake prayed the rest of the teams were having better luck, moving quickly through their search grids. Unfortunately no one had called in yet, which meant Angela and Kayden were still missing.

It took much longer than he'd hoped for Jake to get to the second bunker on his list. It was more than a simple bunker, as the first had been—it was a military outpost. A large five-story tower loomed over him, and he had no way of telling how deep or wide the underground complex ran, or how long it'd take him to thoroughly search it. Frustration seared through him. Where was the next clue? Why was it taking him so long to find it, and what was Angela doing to Kayden in the meantime?

He surveyed the grounds and found no sign of Angela's truck, though he supposed it was possible she'd stashed it farther away after getting Kayden inside. As he turned a corner, he saw a pair of fresh tire tracks leading up to the east side of the bunker and then off into the woods.

Hope tugged at him. Someone had been there recently, most likely last night.

Pulling his Sig, he approached the ground-level opening—it was nothing more than a jagged hole in the crumbling concrete. Judging by the structural damage, he was betting the damage had occurred as a result of the '64 earthquake.

He left his pack outside, carrying only his gun, sat phone, and flashlight. It was best to travel light and be able to move quickly.

Kayden's wrists were chafed nearly raw from the cuffs and her fighting to get out of them. The concrete floor was cold and damp beneath her. She leaned against the wall, trying to make out details in the dim interior.

She still couldn't figure out where she was, and it was maddening. If she hadn't been knocked out, she'd have a better feel for the length of their journey.

She didn't recognize the building—an old run-down factory, perhaps. She'd considered the few abandoned buildings she knew of on Tariuk, but a match hadn't come. Had she been moved off Tariuk? It would have been smart on Angela's part—removing those searching for her from their well-known surroundings, creating a more level playing field. The only ways off Tariuk were by plane, by boat, or by ferry, and of those, the ferry seemed most likely.

The ferry only had two direct destinations out of Tariuk—Imnek and Kodiak.

Kodiak was the bigger of the two, but Imnek had more remote areas once outside the town of Spruce Harbor.

Her bet was on Imnek, but where? She didn't know the island like she did Tariuk, particularly not the buildings. What she did know were the climbing and camping spots.

She swallowed, the movement painful with her dry mouth. How long was Angela going to keep her chained? And where was Angela? Setting a trap for Jake, no doubt. The woman was bent on revenge and appeared to be lacking the normal compunctions of conscience sane human beings had.

Wrestling against her bonds, Kayden yet again found herself fully restricted.

"I admire your persistence." Angela stood in the doorway with a plate of food. "But you might as well accept that you aren't going anywhere." She set the plate on the rusted metal table and pulled a chair up to it. "At least not until your boyfriend arrives."

She fought against the restraints, pain radiating from her wrists up along her weary arms. "He's not my boyfriend." Though she wished he was and planned to tell him exactly that if she escaped this madwoman's clutches.

Angela popped a chip into her mouth.

"Formalities matter not. He's clearly desperately in love with you, and that's all that matters."

In her heart she knew her words were true, but nobody had said it out loud before. Jake loved her—*desperately*. And she loved him, but she'd been too stubborn, prideful, and plain scared to ever let him or anyone else see. What if it was too late? "How do you know he'll come?"

"Please. He's been scrambling to find you since the moment he realized you were gone."

"What if he doesn't find us?"

"Don't worry, he's a great detective. Far too capable for his own good. Trust me, he'll find you."

"But what if he doesn't?"

"Don't worry, pet. I've left him messages he can't ignore."

She hated to imagine what that might mean.

"And when he comes?"

Angela smiled coldly. "Payback."

"Payback for what? Putting you behind bars, where you belong?"

Angela dropped the chip she was holding and brushed off her hands. She stood and moved to Kayden, kneeling on her haunches just out of kicking range. "Payback for ruining my life. For taking my husband from me."

"No one *took* him from you. Your husband made his own choices. He killed himself. Not to mention Candace Banner, and Jake's wife and child."

"Is that what you think?" She stood with a sinister smile. "Well, this is going to be a whole lot more fun than I anticipated."

Kayden squirmed, fighting in vain to break free.

"Enough! You're ruining my dinner."

Angela stood with the pole in hand and zapped her again. Before Kayden could brace herself, her world went dark.

Frustration searing through him, Jake left the empty bunker—empty, except for the taunting note he'd found on a broken-down table in what was left of the bunker's mess hall.

You've chosen poorly. Now I get more time alone with your lady. What a shame for her.

Bile rose in Jake's throat. She wasn't leaving him clues, only messages to cut deep at his heart.

He crumpled the note into his pocket and headed for his truck. Unfortunately the tire tracks had only been evidence of teens who had partied inside and left a mess of beer cans and Cheetos bags behind.

The sun was lowering in the sky, and he knew he should make camp for the night—eat, rest, recoup for tomorrow's search—but there was no way he'd sit still while Angela had Kayden. He'd press on through the night, through the days

318

ahead, if necessary. He wouldn't stop until he found her and she was safe in his arms.

He studied his map. The closest bunker was nearly fifty miles away, but on roads long abandoned, it would take him several hours to reach it.

Please, Lord, lead me to her.

He checked in with the others, but unfortunately no one had found Kayden, only an equally taunting note in one of the two bunkers Gage and Darcy had searched. He felt like a rat in a maze of Angela's design, and he hated it.

Please, Lord, don't let me fail.

He climbed in his truck and headed for the next bunker.

"We should find a camping spot before nightfall," Kirra said as she and Reef crossed yet another cabin off their grid.

"I don't want to stop. Not until my sister is found."

She rested her hand on his arm and pulled back quickly at the surprising tingling. "Uh . . ." She cleared her throat, trying to focus. The last time she'd gotten sidetracked by physical attraction it had nearly destroyed her.

This is Reef, Kirra. What was she doing being attracted to him, anyway? Instead of decreasing with the more time she spent with him, her attraction had increased. That had to stop *immediately*.

"Look, I understand wanting to press on. But once night falls, we could walk within twenty feet of a cabin and not see it. We don't want to miss anything on our grid."

"You're right." Reef sighed. "But I don't like it. It doesn't feel right."

"If I'm remembering correctly, there should be a decent spot up beyond that ridge. It has level ground and a freshwater stream nearby. Plus it'll be a good starting point for finishing this grid bright and early tomorrow."

"We start at sunup?"

"Absolutely. As soon as we can see." She had no desire to linger.

Reef reluctantly agreed. She understood his concern—she had a few of her own—but they had to be wise, professional, and that meant waiting until daybreak to continue the search. All that aside, Rex needed to rest. He'd never let on, but she knew the husky had to be tiring.

Within a half hour they located the spot she'd been thinking of—the spot where she and her dad had camped numerous times before he and her mom moved to Juneau.

"Nice pick," Reef said, dropping his pack. "I'll get a fire going."

Even in the summer months, the temperatures in the mountains dropped into the low forties. They'd need a fire for cooking and warmth until they settled into their sleeping bags.

Kirra set to work on the tents while he got the fire started.

"You got those up quick," he remarked as she finished.

"Been camping as far back as I can remember."

"Huh."

She narrowed her eyes. "What was that *huh* for?"

"Nothing." He tossed the last of the kindling into the fire pit and lit it. "I know you do SAR and all that, because of the dogs, but I didn't picture you as the outdoorsy type."

She wasn't sure she wanted to know, but her curiosity won out. "What did you picture me as?"

"I don't know . . ." He shrugged. "A reader?"

She couldn't wait to hear where he was going with this one. "And readers aren't outdoor people?"

"No. You can be both. Piper and Kayden are both serious readers."

"But?"

"I just always thought you spent all your time studying."

"Because I got good grades?"

"Yeah." He stoked the emerging fire. "And you always had your homework done, showed up to class on time, got the highest score on tests—which totally obliterated the curve, by the way."

"And yet I still managed to have a life." Or, at least, she had until . . . Now it had been permanently altered, fractured.

"Of course, I didn't mean . . ."

So she'd been right all along. Reef had her pegged as a goody-two-shoes, stay-at-home-studying-Saturday-night bookworm. He'd had no idea she loved camping, glacier surfing, working with sled dogs, volunteering with SAR, watching action flicks, and gardening.

He glanced up at her from the fire. "Look, you have to admit you pegged me a certain way too."

She had, and if she was being totally honest, she still did.

Something cracked in the woods behind them and Rex shot up. She quickly signaled for him to heel.

Reef put a finger to his mouth to silence her and lifted his shotgun from the ground. He stood with his back to the fire, facing the woods, where the sound emanated from.

Rex growled, and Kirra pulled him close, holding his collar tight.

She watched the woods and spotted movement in the trees. "Is that a bear?"

Reef looked back at the hot dogs cooking in foil in the embers.

A huge black bear paced back and forth along the tree line. Piper would describe it as adorable if in pictures, but out here in the wilderness it was nothing but dangerous.

Reef grabbed a nearby stick and stuck the end in the flames, and once it caught fire, he stepped toward the bear, waving the torch. "Go on. Get out of here."

The bear reared up and released a growl that tremored through Kirra. Even though she'd lived in Alaska her whole life, she was still afraid of bears.

"Go on." Reef waved the flaming stick again. "Don't make me shoot you."

A lot of guys she knew would have been raring to bag a bear, but Reef was trying to scare it off, and it worked. After a few minutes of a standoff, the bear dropped back down on all fours and lumbered off.

Kirra stood and moved to Reef's side as he threw the stick back in the fire.

"What if he comes back tonight?"

"I doubt he will. The rest of the food is tied up between the trees. There'll be nothing left for him to eat."

"Unless he decides we look good."

"We'll move our tents side by side. Rex will let us know if anything approaches. I'll keep my gun with me, and I'll use it if need be."

She nodded, praying it wouldn't be needed and praying for Kayden. As scared as Kirra had been as they faced the bear, she couldn't imagine how frightened Kayden must be or what terror she might be enduring.

Please, Lord, protect her in the midst of danger.

It was something only He could do. It defied

logic, but she knew it was possible. She'd been there.

Kayden came to, a burnt taste in her mouth. She'd been electrocuted again. If that woman tried to poke her with that pole one more time, she'd break it over her head—even if she had to break her hands to get free of the cuffs.

Angela rolled out a sleeping bag on top of an air mattress on the table, with the lantern at her head.

Kayden followed the lantern light up to the ceiling, where water was dripping in. *Great.* That explained the constant damp feeling.

"I'm going to sleep," Angela said. "If you wake me up with any of your shenanigans, I'll jolt you yet again."

"You do and you'll regret it."

Angela arched a brow. "Ah, so you've got some of your fight back. That's good to see. Makes it all the more enjoyable knocking it back out of you."

— 41 —

Jake drove along what may at one time have qualified as a road but certainly didn't now.

From what he could tell from his regular study of the map and his GPS coordinates, the bunker lay five miles due east, on the edge of a bluff.

According to Marshall, it also had a tower, and over the year some kids had made an extreme-sports snowboarding course out of the debris, even filmed a video—jumping down five stories from the tower and across the concrete ramps. It probably didn't see much activity in the summer, so it could still be a potential option for Angela, though he doubted she'd choose something that had been visited so recently—the snow sometimes not melting this high up until mid-May.

He finally cleared the last rise, his headlights illuminating the tower, stopped his truck, and walked the last couple hundred yards. Gun in hand, he let the moon light his way. Using a flashlight across the clearing would make him a sitting duck.

He skirted the edge of the perimeter, eyeing each open "window" up along the tower. No signs of anyone present, at least not from this vantage point, but he needed to get closer.

He approached the building, keeping his back flush with the concrete. Except for the low hum of insects, silence surrounded him.

Debris littered the grounds—no doubt part of the snowboarding course when snow-packed.

Clicking on his flashlight, he entered the tower and cleared the first floor before moving on to the second, third, fourth, and finally the fifth and final level.

"What's your problem, dude?" A teen shielded

his eyes from Jake's flashlight. A girl, no more than sixteen, sat beside him on a cruddy blanket.

"Are you the only ones here?"

"Yeah, that I know of. What's your problem?"

"My problem"—Jake flashed his badge—"is that you're trespassing. Now, I'm going to count to ten, and I want you out of here before I finish. One, two, three . . ."

The kid scrambled, grabbing the blanket and darting down the steps, leaving the girl to follow.

"And take her straight home—you hear?"

The boy was too busy running to respond.

Jake shook his head. Three bunkers, and still no Kayden.

He swung his flashlight across the windowsill and paused at the military action figurine glued to it, a wilted cypress flower tucked under its bent arm.

He leaned out the window, shining his flashlight at the kid darting across the grounds, the girl a dozen feet behind.

"Hey, kid. Freeze!"

Both kids stopped in their tracks. Illuminated by a dim circle of light, the boy turned, hands lifted.

"Is this action figure on the sill yours?"

"What am I, four?"

"So that's a no?"

"Uh. Yeah."

"Was it there when you arrived?"

"Yeah."

"Have you seen it before?"

"It showed up a couple days ago."

"Did you see who brought it?"

"Nah. Just saw it last time Jasmine and I were up there."

"Thanks."

"Can I go now?"

"Yeah. Go on. And I'm serious—take her home."

The kid nodded and the two disappeared into the woods. Their vehicle was no doubt parked farther on down the pass.

Jake inspected the toy. It was army.

He pulled out the sat phone and dialed Marshall.

Reef settled into his sleeping bag, feeling awful for letting go of the search while his sister was out there, but Kirra was right. It was the smart thing to do, the best way to make sure they properly covered their grid, but he didn't have to like it.

He shifted, his shotgun within hand's reach.

Kirra had been adorable when the bear showed up—always putting on the brave, self-reliant front, it was nice to see a gentler side of her. He hoped she felt safe and protected knowing he was right next door.

He shook his head. Who would have thought he and Kirra Jacobs would be camping together under any circumstances and, even more surprisingly, that he'd have such a strong desire to protect her.

He could hear Rex's rhythmic breathing through the tent walls. With the light on in the other tent, he could see the husky's shadow against the yellow fabric—and Kirra's too.

She lay in her bag but wasn't sleeping. It looked like she was reading.

He rolled over, resting his head on his hand, studying her silhouette, watching her flip pages.

Maybe all these years he had pegged her wrong.

Images of her ratting him out over and over again during his school years flashed through his mind. Okay, so maybe he'd pegged her *a little* wrong, about *some* things.

Kayden worked to slip her wrists from the hand-cuffs. They were tight, but her left wrist felt looser. Maybe if she crumpled her hand enough . . .

Angela shifted, and Kayden stilled. She waited until Angela settled down and tried again. If she could just get one hand free, maybe she could reach one of the metal scraps on the floor and work the other cuff open. She was suddenly very thankful that, much to Gage and Landon's chagrin, Darcy had taught her how to pick locks.

She pressed her hand as small as she could make it and, positioning her back to the wall for leverage, pulled.

Pain burned through her as the metal grated along her chafed skin.

She bit back her cry, determined not to wake Angela.

If she could just grasp a piece of metal debris, one of the many nails lying just out of reach on the floor . . .

It came to her as she sat struggling. She'd seen it done on a crime show. She grimaced. Dislocating her thumb was the only way to break free.

Positioning her right thumb atop her left thumb's ball-and-socket joint, she placed her right fingers into her palm and pressed as hard as she could with her right thumb. The socket popped and slid out of place, and her hand was free. She bit back the cry of pain threatening to rip loose. Fighting the dizziness swirling over her, she reached for one of the nails lying in the debris pile to her left, now able to reach them without the left cuff pinning her to the chain.

Grasping with her fingers—her thumb utterly useless and throbbing—she clasped hold of one and shuffled back to a sitting position. As she worked to free her other hand, she quickly realized it would be nearly impossible without a working thumb. So using the same method in reverse, she set it back in place, again swallowing the holler of pain. Her thumb was swollen and in excruciating pain, but at least now she had a modicum of function with it.

Working as quietly as possible, she popped the other cuff open.

Angela rolled over with a groggy mumble, and Kayden waited stock-still until she heard Angela's rhythmic snoring resume. Then she rolled onto all fours and, careful not to put pressure on her thumb, crawled in the opposite direction of Angela, until she reached the pitch-dark doorway she'd seen her go through time and again.

The only light source was the lantern next to Angela's head, and trying to retrieve it wasn't worth the risk of waking her. So now she was headed blind into an unknown maze.

Using the doorframe for support, Kayden pulled herself to her feet, moved her hands ahead of her for guidance, and began feeling her way down the passage.

She had no idea which way was out, only the direction Angela came and went. Kayden prayed it would lead her outside, but then what? If she didn't put some serious distance between her and Angela before Angela woke, she'd never outrun her with a broken leg.

She stumbled blindly down the corridor, praying for God's protection, for His guidance.

Father, I know the darkness is as light to you. Please guide me through this. I can't do this on my own.

Feeling with her hands, her fingers brushed some cold metal. She scrambled to grasp a handle or knob, but found nothing other than solid wall. She hit one dead end after another.

She continued moving along the cold surface, feeling for a door, praying for a door. She bumped into something hard, and pain ricocheted up her legs, but she managed to remain standing. Too much leftover debris littered the building. If she moved too fast, the next collision might incapacitate her. But what choice did she have?

She prayed she wasn't making too much noise, that Angela was far enough away that she couldn't hear her clattering about.

The wall indented, and hope sprung in her chest as she quickly followed it down and found a handle. She lifted, but it remained stuck.

"Come on." She tried again, using only her right hand, her left thumb swollen and throbbing.

She needed more leverage.

Taking a deep, steadying breath, she clasped her left hand on the handle as well, biting the inside of her cheek to keep from crying out as she hefted it up. A horrible squeak sounded, echoing through the room.

She stilled, listening for any sound of movement on Angela's part.

Hearing nothing, she proceeded forward, nearly tripping over the raised doorframe. Water sloshed around her feet, a horrific musty smell assailing her nostrils.

Please lead me out.

If water was dripping in, it made sense it was

coming from somewhere outside. If she could find the entrance point, maybe she could find her way out. She followed the sound of dripping, sloshing unceremoniously through the murky water.

She fought the tears stinging her eyes. She *would* get out of this. This wasn't going to be her end. Not before she had the chance to tell those she loved how she really felt—her family and, God help her, Jake too.

He deserved to know she loved him, deserved to know what an amazing man she believed him to be.

She'd always thought protecting her feelings and guarding her heart was best, but now the thought of dying without ever saying the words, without truly expressing her deep and abiding love for them all, left her feeling helpless.

Her casted foot caught on something and sent her flailing forward. She landed on the ground, her hands breaking her fall, her thumb breaking in the process. A cry of pain escaped her lips, but the water covering her head swallowed it.

She pushed to her knees, spitting out the disgusting sedentary liquid and gulped in air. She needed to find another light source, or she could end up walking in circles and harming herself more in the process. Getting to her feet, she sloshed forward, shivering. Thankfulness soared through her as she found a second door. She lifted the handle, prying it open, and a light flashed on.

Angela? With a bat?

The wood flew at her face, and she heard a crack—

— 42 —

Marshall said there were only two army bunkers on Imnek—the others being a combination of navy and coast guard. Jake was roughly twenty miles away from the first one, and the second was on the other side of the island, across a mountain from Gage and Darcy's search area. It was Angela's way of making sure the search party was split.

Please, Father, let her be at the closer one. Let me find her now.

He couldn't let a Markum rip another woman he loved away from him. Couldn't let anything happen to Kayden. Though knowing Angela's vindictive nature, he feared she may already have started inflicting pain.

She and Joel sure made a pair. Evidence had proved he liked to torture women. Jake only prayed his wife wasn't following suit.

His throat constricted at the thought of Kayden being at the woman's mercy, fearing Angela possessed none.

But this was Kayden. She was the strongest woman he'd ever met. If anyone could stand up to

Angela, it'd be her . . . and that's what worried him. Angela would want complete domination, and Kayden wouldn't comply.

Climbing back in his truck, he punched the closer army bunker's coordinates into his GPS and flew back down the rutted road.

Please, Father, let her be here. Let her be okay.

Fifty miles an hour wasn't fast enough, but he couldn't go any faster on the dirt roads leading toward the bunker. Truth be told, he should be going a lot slower, but he couldn't. He had to reach Kayden before it was too late.

Kayden came to with a throbbing headache. Had the woman seriously hit her with a bat?

She looked up in dismay to find herself cuffed once again. This time her shackled hands were mounted on a hook on the wall over her head, and not far from her an empty pair of shackles hung on a second hook. *Jake.* She swallowed. How sick was this woman?

"I should have known you'd be trouble." Angela sat in a chair with a gun leveled at Kayden's head. "You're nothing like the last one."

Kayden frowned. "The last one?"

"Jake's wife, Rebecca."

Kayden blinked to clear her vision. "What about her?"

"She was very different from you. Docile, submissive. Just stood there frozen as I hit her."

Shock roiled through Kayden. "*You* hit Becca?"

"Yes. I warned Jake to back off, but he wouldn't listen, so I had to teach him a lesson."

"I thought your husband . . ."

"Joel." She laughed. "Please, he got physically sick when he realized he'd killed that girl. Called me in tears, the weakling."

"So you stepped in?"

"I had to. It's not like Joel had the strength to take care of his own mess. He just wanted to ball up and cry." She shook her head. "Pathetic."

"So you helped him cover up the crime."

"There was no way I was going to let some trampy co-ed ruin my life."

"So you helped him bury her?"

"No. He helped me. Lots of help he was, though. Kept getting sick. Such a pansy."

"And when Jake discovered the body?"

"Jake," she snapped. "He couldn't just let things rest. Had to keep hammering, keep digging until he discovered Joel's connection to the girl."

"And then?"

"And then Joel, coward that he was, was planning to confess, to turn himself in."

"But I thought . . ."

"That he killed himself?" She laughed. "That was my plan. Racked by guilt, my husband takes his own life, leaving me alone—the poor, innocent, grieving widow."

"You killed your own husband?"

"It wasn't hard. He'd been drinking. I played on his insecurities, got him to hold the gun to his head, and . . ."

"You pulled the trigger."

"Over his finger, of course." She smiled. "The perfect crime."

"Not so perfect. Jake figured out your role in the aftermath of Candace Banner's murder. He knew you helped cover up evidence and helped hide the body."

"That was unfortunate, yes. I thought taking his wife would distract him enough that he'd quit digging, but no, he just kept coming until he had me behind bars. He didn't figure out the rest of it, though, did he?" She stared—cold and heartless. "He didn't figure out enough to keep me there for longer than a few years." She leaned forward, hatred welling in her dark eyes. "Do you have any idea what prison is like?" She glanced at Kayden's shackles. "Well, you and Jake are about to learn."

"Please . . ."

Angela checked her watch. "I'm sure he'll be here soon. He's very good at following clues."

The woman was mad.

Please, Father, don't let Jake walk into her trap. I know he'll do it just to try to save me, but don't let him sacrifice himself in the process.

Jake cut his engine a mile out from the bunker, not wanting to announce his arrival. Dawn approached, the last wisps of night air cold and crisp. He trekked in on foot, following the tire marks to Angela's truck hidden behind an overgrowth of bushes.

He called the confirmed location in to Marshall, knowing he'd in turn alert the others, though it would take them the better part of the morning to arrive—spread out as they were in their search quadrants, and with Gage and Darcy headed to the other side of the island.

He walked the perimeter of the bunker, assessing the entrance and exit options, and only found two—the main entrance and a small door at the rear of the bunker.

Going in the front was no doubt a trap, but going in the rear could take too long to locate Kayden. As Marshall had explained and as he was quickly learning for himself, these bunkers were underground mazes. However he approached, she'd no doubt see him coming. Angela Markum was clearly crazy, but she was not a fool. She'd no doubt planned out every detail.

Unwilling to leave Kayden alone with Angela any longer, he entered through the front door. The bunker was dark and dank. Old barrels and spare mechanical parts littered the floor. It was the perfect place to hold Kayden with her broken leg and wounded shoulder. It would be a nightmare to try to escape in the dark.

There were only two ways he could get Kayden

out safely—be lucky enough to kill Angela off the bat or convince Angela to take him in place of her. He was more than willing to do either. Whatever it took to keep Kayden safe.

— 43 —

Angela hurried along the side corridor, moving to intercept Jake with a good old-fashioned jolt. Soon she'd have her revenge, and it would be glorious. By her calculations she still had a good while before the others showed, spread out as they would be in an island-wide search. She'd left some surprises for the future guests, but she should be long gone by the time they arrived.

She slowed as she approached the spot, following Jake on the camera feed. The four years in prison had given her time to formulate an undefeatable plan—with contingencies for every deviation. Jake no doubt saw the *Bering* article she'd left for him on the board along with particularly timed surveillance photos, so he'd think that's how she'd found him, but in truth the PI she'd hired—well, the third PI she'd hired—had located him nearly six months before her release.

She'd sat back and watched, learned their routines, seen the way Jake looked at Kayden, seen the sickening look of love in his eyes.

And now to begin the final phase of her plan.

She stood ready, weapon in hand. Jake paused before reaching the door, his gun shifting in her direction, as if sensing where she stood.

Frustration seared inside. The man was good, but she was better. She pulled the trigger from her pocket and flipped the switch. A small explosive went off to Jake's right. When he moved to shield himself from the blast, she reached out and tased him.

Within seconds, he was writhing on the floor at her feet and then went still.

Perfection.

Kayden waited, her heart in her throat. What had Angela done to Jake? What had caused the explosion? Surely Jake hadn't come alone. Was one of her siblings hurt?

Angela reentered the room, pushing Jake strapped with bungee cords on a red metal dolly. She wondered if that was how Angela had moved her.

"I think we're going to need a little more light for this," she said, her voice sending a chill down Kayden's spine.

She opened a trunk and pulled out a series of battery-operated lanterns, setting them up around the room. "I want to be certain Jake can see you clearly."

She removed the bungee cords, letting Jake fall to the floor.

Kayden once again bit back a cry.

Angela pulled him by the legs to the shackles beside her.

Fear reverberated through Kayden. What did the evil woman have planned?

Reef woke to the ringing of his cell phone. "Yeah?"

Please let it be good news, Lord.

"Jake's found Angela's hideout," Sheriff Marshall said. "The old army bunker up on the north bluff. It's marked on your topo map. If you and Kirra cut across the ridge rather than going around, you should be able to reach them in under a couple hours."

"Okay, I'll wake Kirra now and we'll head straight out. Have you alerted the rest of the teams?"

"I have my deputies on it as we speak."

Good. The more, the better.

"Be careful."

"Will do."

Unzipping his tent, he moved to Kirra's. "Kirra?"

Rex moved, his collar jingling.

Reef unzipped her tent. She was sound asleep, Rex sitting at the ready beside her.

He growled.

"It's okay, Rex. It's just me. We need to wake Kirra up."

Man, she was a sound sleeper.

"Kirra," he said louder, and she stirred, shifting her arms over her head. Her blond hair was disheveled about her.

"Kirra!"

Her eyes shot open—beautiful crystal blue staring back at him, full of . . . *fear?* "What?"

"Jake found them. We need to move."

"Oh." She shook off the lingering sleep and whatever had her fearful. "Give me five."

He nodded and set to dismantling his tent.

A few minutes later Kirra emerged from hers—dressed for the day, Rex bounding out beside her. "Just give me a minute to get my pack set and we can go."

Reef nodded, amazed by how vibrant and beautiful she looked just minutes after waking. *Whoa!* He had to stop thinking of Kirra that way. The elevation must be going to his head.

He exhaled. Who was he kidding? He lived at this elevation all snowboarding season.

He rolled his tent and sleeping bag, putting both in his pack while Kirra did the same.

"Where are they?"

"The old army bunker out at the north bluff. Marshall said if we cut across the ridge we can make it in under two hours."

Kirra studied the topographical map they'd brought. "He's right. It's a strenuous hike, no truck access through a good portion of it, but it's a lot faster than hiking back to the truck and taking the road all the way around."

Reef cinched his pack on his back. "Let's do it."

"Did Jake say how Kayden was?"

"Marshall just said he'd located Angela's truck, not that he had eyes on Kayden yet."

"I just pray she's okay, that they both are."

Reef appreciated her sincerity. "I do too."

"Would you like me to say a quick prayer?"

"That'd be nice." God would no doubt be more likely to listen to her prayers. She was the ultimate good girl.

She bowed her head and Reef did the same.

"Father, only you know what's happening with Jake, Kayden, and Angela now. We pray for protection for Jake and Kayden and that justice would be done. Please lead us to them quickly, and may we all be home secure in our own beds tonight. In Jesus' name we pray. Amen."

"Amen," he said. "Thank you."

"You're welcome."

"Not just for the prayer, but for caring about my family." Being away so long, it was good to know his siblings had such good friends standing by them and looking out for them. He wanted his siblings to know he'd stand by them too. Maybe Anna was right. Maybe this was where God wanted him.

"They're good people," she said, shifting her

pack and the topic, a hint of longing in her voice. "Have Cole and Bailey landed?"

"Marshall said they have, and they're en route now."

"Jake."

It was Kayden's voice.

"Jake." Chains rattled nearby. "Can you hear me?"

He forced his eyes open. Lights glowed in the dimness around him.

"Are you okay?" she asked, her voice weaker than he'd ever heard it.

He turned to see her shackled beside him, dried blood in her hair, bruises on her face . . .

His heart lurched.

"Kayden." He reached for her, his shackles pinning him tight to the wall overhead.

"I'm okay."

She clearly wasn't.

"Angela's crazy."

"I figured that one out."

"She killed her husband."

"What?"

"She made it look like a suicide. And Becca . . ."

"What about Becca?"

"Oh, now you've gone and ruined the surprise," Angela said as she reentered the room.

"You!" He struggled against his shackles. "You killed Becca and our daughter?"

"I didn't know she was pregnant." A cool smile spread on Angela's lips. "Not that it would have made any difference. In fact, it made it all the better revenge-wise."

Jake wrestled against his bonds, determined to get out of them, even if it meant breaking his own hands.

"This time you get to *watch* the woman you love die."

Jake looked at Kayden. He prayed she knew he truly loved her, even if Angela was the first to actually say the words.

She looked over at him, such sweetness and sincerity brimming in her eyes despite the dark circumstances. "I love you too."

"What?" The breath left his lungs. She loved him? He'd been praying he'd been right about her starting to care for him, but she *loved* him?

"I'm sorry I didn't tell you earlier." She wept. "Sorry I kept you at arm's length."

"It doesn't matter. You've just made me the happiest man alive."

Angela lifted her gun. "Not for long."

An explosion rocked the south wall. Angela glanced over. "Looks like we've got company." She moved to the camera feed.

Jake took the opportunity to dislocate his thumbs and slide his hands free of the cuffs. He signaled Kayden to be quiet while he grabbed the Taser.

He moved behind Angela. She must have caught his reflection in the monitor because she turned and shot.

He stumbled back with the force of the bullet, with the heat searing down his arm.

"No!" Kayden screamed.

Rex burst into the room, followed by Reef and Kirra.

Angela took off with Rex at her heels.

"Jake." Kayden wrestled to break free.

"Kayden." Reef's gaze landed on her with alarm.

"Jake's been shot."

Reef and Kirra's attention shifted to Jake. Kirra moved to assess.

"It's just a shoulder wound. He'll be fine." She grabbed the blanket off the air mattress and began tearing it into strips long enough to bind his wound.

Reef moved to help Kayden.

"Angela has the keys, but there are some nails on the floor."

"How are nails going to help?"

"Here." Jake moved before Kirra could finish bandaging his shoulder, popping his thumbs back in place with an agonizing grunt. He pulled a pick from his pocket, surprised Angela hadn't patted him down while he was out. She'd taken his gun and knife but hadn't bothered checking his pockets. Sloppy.

He bent and picked Kayden's handcuffs until they both opened. She lunged forward and hugged him.

He winced as she collided with his gunshot wound.

She pulled back. "Oh, I'm sorry."

"I'm not." He cupped her face gingerly and brought her lips to his, kissing her with all the loving fervor he'd been storing up for years.

She kissed him back, just as passionately, and he never wanted to let her go.

But Gage and Darcy barged in.

"Well, it's about time," Gage said before Darcy elbowed him.

"What?" he said. "Everyone else is thinking it."

At the distant sound of Rex's bay, Jake pulled back. "Which way did she go?" He needed to keep Kayden safe, and that meant finding Angela and getting her back behind bars, where she belonged.

Kayden pointed. "She took off down that corridor. Rex should distract her for a bit."

Jake focused on Rex's barking. "It sounds as if he's chased her into the underground maze at the rear of the bunker. I've explored three of these already, and from my experience, it might be a while before she makes her way out.

"Gage and I will go out the front and wait at her truck. Reef, you and Kirra go after Rex and flush her out."

"She's got booby traps set up," Reef said. "Luckily Kirra spotted the trip wire or we would have been toast, or at the very least, seriously maimed."

Jake smiled at Kirra. "Nice work."

"Thanks. As a vet I deal with the effects of far too many poacher traps. I've learned to watch for them whenever I'm in the wilderness."

Jake turned to Kayden. "Please stay here. There's no way Angela will work her way back. Please. I need to know you are safe."

Clearly too exhausted to argue, she nodded and sat down at the rusty table as he and the others raced out of the room.

Relief filled Jake when he and Gage reached the brush and found Angela's truck still there. After disconnecting her spark plugs, they hid behind the nearby copse of trees.

It didn't take long for Angela to burst out a hidden door to the east, Rex's howls not far behind her.

She climbed into her truck and tried starting it. Jake watched realization dawn on her face as Gage came up on her passenger's side with a gun leveled at her head, and he did the same on the driver's side.

She looked at him with a smug smile, lifted a grenade, and pulled the pin.

"Down," Jake roared, lunging away from the vehicle. Birds flew from the trees as the cab of the truck exploded.

Jake covered his head until it settled. "Gage?"

He coughed. "Yeah?"

"You okay?"

"Yeah."

Reef, Kirra, and Rex burst out the same door Angela had moments before.

Kirra took a look at what remained of Angela and turned green.

Reef pulled her into his arms and turned her away from the sight.

Within the hour Piper and Landon reached the site. Cole and Bailey were still several hours away. Now that they were safe, Jake had told them they'd meet up at the local hospital instead.

A pair of EMTs loaded Jake and Kayden into the rescue helicopter resting at the edge of the bluff.

"We'll meet you at the hospital," Gage said, shutting the door, but by the time they actually made it down the mountain, he and Kayden would hopefully have already been released.

He glanced over at her—his brave, wounded warrior, so fierce and lovely—and linked his fingers with hers.

— 44 —

Kayden tapped on Jake's sliding door.

He smiled through the glass and moved to open it.

"Hey there." He stepped back, welcoming her inside.

"Hey." She moved past him.

"How you feeling?"

She gingerly brushed her hair back from her bruised face. "Better."

Jake moved some papers off the couch. "Take a seat."

"Probably better if I stand for this."

Uh-oh. Now that they were out of danger, would she retract her declaration of love? Would she put her guard back in place?

"There's something I need to say."

He braced himself. "Okay."

She swallowed. "I meant what I said, back at the bunker."

He blinked. Had he just heard her correctly?

She leaned against the half wall separating the galley from the living space. "I didn't want you to think I only said it because of the situation we were in."

"That's amazing to hear."

"But . . ."

Somehow he'd known there was going to be a *but*.

"But just because I told you the truth and we kissed . . ." She shifted, looking down.

Was Kayden McKenna actually embarrassed?

She cleared her throat. "It doesn't mean it's going to be easy with me. I'm far from perfect, hard to get along with, and . . ." She looked up at him. "Well, I'm giving you the chance to walk away."

He smiled. Like that was even possible. He was hers come what may.

He reached for her hand and led her to the couch. *"You are perfect for me."*

She took a deep breath and exhaled. "There's one more thing." She sat beside him. "I know this is way jumping the gun, but I feel I need to be totally up front before . . . before *we* go any further."

"Okay." He clasped her hand.

"I can't have kids."

He hadn't seen that coming. As healthy as she was . . . "The doctors found something wrong?"

"No, but they might."

"What? I'm confused."

"I could end up with rheumatoid arthritis like my mom. I saw what it did to her. It doesn't affect everyone with the same intensity it did my mom, but it destroyed her health and her body. If that happens, I don't want you taking care of me, watching me fade away physically."

"Why not?"

"I don't want you to see me that way, and I don't want to be dependent on anyone."

"Did you mind taking care of your mom?"

"Of course not. I loved her."

"Then why wouldn't you want me taking care of you, and what does any of that have to do with your having children?"

She looked down. "You don't understand. My mom was a strong, beautiful, athletic, vibrant woman until the disease ravaged her. I want people to remember me as being strong."

"Honey, you don't even know if you're going to get RA."

"There's a high risk when you have a family member with it. And I look just like my mom. Everyone said how alike we were. If anyone's going to get it, it'll be me."

"You can't live your life differently because of something that may or may not happen."

"But how can I have kids knowing I might pass it on to them?"

He cupped her chin in his hand. "Sweetheart, is that what you're worried about?"

She nodded.

"Are you angry at your mom for having you?"

"Of course not. But she had me before she knew she'd get RA."

"And would you not want to have been born if she had?"

"Of course not."

"Then how's this any different?"

She shrugged.

"I know this is hard for you to hear, but you're not in control. God is. Living your life in fear isn't the answer."

"No, I'm being strong. I'm making a hard decision."

"No. Choosing to live your life to its fullest every day is the hard decision. I bet your mom displayed amazing grace through it all."

She narrowed her eyes. "How did you know?"

"Because God doesn't promise the way will be easy—far from it—but He promises to carry us through, to give us the courage and grace we need when we need it. He most often doesn't change the circumstances; He changes us."

He exhaled and tipped her chin up gently. "I love you, and I want to be with you through the good and the bad, in sickness and in health. Through it all."

"Whoa!" She scooted back. "What are you saying?"

"That you are stuck with me, Kayden McKenna. I'm not going anywhere."

Tears welled in her eyes. "You promise?"

He lowered his mouth to hers. "With all my heart."

— Epilogue —

Kayden stood beneath the evergreen tress surrounding Landon's cabin, watching her sister pledge her life to the man she loved. Six months ago Kayden would have never imagined herself in such a place someday, but as she watched Jake standing between her brothers at Landon's side, she envisioned a future with him.

Pastor Braden asked Piper and Landon to exchange rings following their declaration of the vows they'd written. Kayden couldn't get over how amazing everything looked—the pine archway Landon had handcrafted for him and Piper to stand under, the full moon and blanket of stars overhead, lanterns lighting the rest of the forest around them.

A nighttime wedding in the woods they loved. It was so Piper and Landon.

"You may now kiss the bride." Landon took Pastor Braden's instruction to heart, grasping his wife in his arms and dipping her down as he pressed his lips fully to hers.

"Hey, she's still our baby sister, dude," Gage grumbled.

"Yes." Landon wrapped a hand snugly about Piper's waist. "But she's my wife."

"Good thing, after that kiss." Gage smirked

and lightly punched his fist into his cupped hand.

The photographs took under an hour, and soon everyone was seated on their picnic blankets beneath the stars with their baskets of homemade food. Piper had outdone herself—gourmet sandwiches and fried chicken, homemade potato salad (their grandmother's recipe), fresh fruits and veggies, cheese and crackers, and Black Forest wedding cake complemented with dark chocolate.

As people started their dessert, Jesse, the leader of their church worship band, called the happy couple onto the dance floor.

Kayden's heart drummed in her chest, anticipation dancing through her at what was coming next.

Piper and Landon finished their first dance as man and wife, and invited the rest of the bridal party onto the dance floor—a circular clearing they'd made in the forest.

She didn't even have time to look for Jake before he was at her side, his hands extended to help her to her feet. Her cast had been removed just days before, and she was still a bit unsteady.

Her skin humming from her fingertips to the tips of her toes, she placed her hand in his and let him lead her onto the dance floor.

The music started slowly and pleasure curled on her lips as "Collide" by Howie Day played.

Jake smiled at her.

This would be their song, and it couldn't be more fitting. They'd collided and were becoming one. It was only a matter of time before they followed in her married siblings' footsteps.

She rested her head on Jake's strong chest, and he cradled it tenderly for a moment before pressing a kiss to her brow. "I love you, Kayden Beatrice McKenna."

She nestled deeper into his embrace. "I love you, too, Jacob Westin Cavanagh." And she did—fully, passionately, and irrevocably.

— Acknowledgments —

Dr. Tiffany Geirsach and Tylynn Miner: For sharing your wonderful chemical expertise.

Janet: Our first official book together. It's a joy working with you. I look forward to many wonderful books and years ahead.

Kayla: For still reading every single draft of every single manuscript with a smile and enthusiasm.

Mike: I love you more each day.

Joe: For your friendship, support, encouragement, and prayers.

My BHP family: It is a privilege and a blessing to work with each and every one of you.

To Jesus: Without You there would be no stories, no beauty or fullness of life. I'm so grateful You are my Savior.

In loving memory of Pamela Pressman. It was a blessing knowing you.

— About the Author —

Dani Pettrey is a wife, home-schooling mom, and the author of the bestselling romantic suspense novels *Stranded*, *Shattered*, and *Submerged*, winner of the 2013 Holt Medallion for First Novel and the Colorado Romance Writers 2013 Award of Excellence. She and her husband have two daughters and reside in the D.C. Metro area. She can be found online at *danipettrey.com*.

Center Point Large Print
600 Brooks Road / PO Box 1
Thorndike ME 04986-0001 USA

(207) 568-3717

US & Canada:
1 800 929-9108
www.centerpointlargeprint.com